"Mon Dieu, I believe you love me."

Jennifer was dumbfounded. What with all that had just passed between them, she thought he had lost his sanity, yet she had an unutterable urge to thrust herself into his arms, tell him yes, tell him that she loved him very much, but the words wouldn't come and the way into his arms at that moment appeared an unnavigable path. Adrien was lying there, stretched out, naked, adopting that cynical little half-smile that so infuriated her. She waited a half minute longer for more sensible conversation from him. None came.

"Believe what you will," she answered. "I'm going back to my room. I'm in no mood for sexual gymnastics."

ABOUT THE AUTHOR

Jackie Weger has been committed to a career
as a writer since winning a contest in a trade
magazine over ten years ago. Born in Mobile,
Alabama, Ms. Weger has done extensive
traveling and now resides in Texas.

Books by Jackie Weger

HARLEQUIN AMERICAN ROMANCES
5-A STRONG AND TENDER THREAD
48-COUNT THE ROSES

These books may be available at your local bookseller.

For a free catalog listing all titles currently available,
send your name and address to:

Harlequin Reader Service
P.O. Box 52040, Phoenix, AZ 85072-2040
Canadian address: Stratford, Ontario N5A 6W2

Count
the Roses

JACKIE WEGER

Harlequin Books

TORONTO • NEW YORK • LONDON
AMSTERDAM • PARIS • SYDNEY • HAMBURG
STOCKHOLM • ATHENS • TOKYO • MILAN

Le cœur a ses raisons que la raison ne connaît point.
The heart has its reasons which reason knows nothing of.
—Blaise Pascal

———————————◆◆◆———————————

In memory of Misty, the daughter of a daughter

———————————◆◆◆———————————

Published March 1984

ISBN 0-373-16048-8

Printed in Canada

Chapter One

He wanted a wife, progeny—a link to the future wrapped in the solid foundations of the past.

This was on his mind, bitterly so, as Adrien Merril stood behind the French windows absently watching sheets of gray water slam across Bayou Lafourche. The spring rains were late, and farmers, ranchers, and fishermen had heaved collective sighs of relief when storm clouds had gathered. For many, Adrien Merril among them, rain meant the difference between small wealth and poverty; it meant bank loans met, shoes bought, food in larders, tithes paid, boats scraped, and the coming season's seed contracted for—unless the government stepped in and put a ceiling on sugar, rice, and beef-on-the-hoof, and limits on the shrimp harvests. Then, regardless of how nature lent her hand, regardless of how many acres of lush green cane grew in plowed and precise fields, there would be no profits. And all along the bayou Cajuns would grumble in their plucky way because there would be no extras, yet spirits would be subdued, not broken. Adrien raised cane, cattle, and rice; thus he was as relieved as his neighbors to see the rain, but he hated it when it pushed him indoors like this.

Though the wind dropped down out of a black sky and keened around the house, ruffling new leaves on ancient oak, magnolia, and cypress that grew in the lawn, the house itself was an oasis of serenity. Only the soft golden peals of an antique clock delicately dividing the hours into halves intruded on his thoughts. To Adrien this serenity reflected his loneliness.

And the clock, chiming its way into the future, reminded him that this spring and last he had not been paired to a mate. The sense of loss that surged through him was attuned to nature, like sap rising, rising, rising, until it permeated every branch, every twig. It was a primordial sensation. He anticipated it, felt it, tried to ignore it and could not.

His eyes swept the drenched landscape. It was a land he knew well—a land that could provide or take away, full of marsh that hid danger and dry mounds that gave a man sure footing, if only he knew where to look. He remembered himself as a little boy, following his father's footsteps, exactly, safely, hunting in the swamp for muskrat, wild turkey, deer. And always the success of the hunt, coming home wet and muddy, his legs tired, his back aching from carrying a man's share of game and too proud to complain. There was his mother, smiling, lifting the weight from his shoulders, then setting large mugs of steaming milk-filled coffee before him and his father on the worn rosewood table. Then she would lean against the great double sink and listen to his eagerly recounted tale of the hunt. Adrien had envisioned this scene often over the past several years, with one slight change—he was now the father and it was *his* son who eagerly recounted the hunt, and *his* wife smiling and leaning against the sink in the warm old-fashioned kitchen.

He, like his father before him, had been born in this very house at the edge of the deep Louisiana swamps, where cypress trees, gnarled and bent, leaned into quicksand and spreading limbs cast a verdant gray over black turgid water. Lafourche was a land of legend and practicality, and Cajuns, so enmeshed in its history, seldom knew where legend ended and practicality began. Nor did they endeavor to separate the two. They were the direct descendants of Acadians savagely torn from their families and their land by the English in 1755, and it took them ten long, hard, deprived years to reach the French settlement in New Orleans from Nova Scotia. That Longfellow had enriched their history and trials with his poem *Evangeline* did them no harm, and to this day there remained a handful who claimed direct bloodline to the exquisite and proud heroine of the poem.

The Acadians carved a life for themselves in the swamp and on its rich silt-fed borders. There were deer, wild turkey, ducks, and fish on which to feed, and foxes, mink, and alligators to skin for trading or ready cash. In the good rich earth they grew rice, cane, and corn, and on it they built gaily painted houses in which to raise their families. They loved gossip, music, and laughter and they did not want to change.

But the land was not always kind, and the swamp, never. Acadians died of swamp fever, snakebite, malaria, and disease that no name had been put to. And sometimes the careless, or a young animal who strayed from its more experienced mother, became an occasional meal of a clever alligator lurking under the mantle of silken, slippery mud.

Adrien sighed inaudibly as a duck swam into his view. She waddled over the ridge of earth thrown up by waters that flowed in the bayou, inspected her clutch of eggs hidden in tall grass, settled her soft down underbody upon them, then tucked her head under her wing to wait out the storm. Instinct told her that the barat was not a threat to her nest, that it wouldn't dump so much rain that the creek would rise above its banks, sending her eggs tumbling into its muddy brown waters. A hundred years ago men had built a dike at the mouth of the bayou where it joined the Meche Sebe, and floods no longer swept away the thick mounds of earth bordering Lafourche.

Adrien reflected on the duck, her fertility, and the offspring she would produce. The primordial sap that rose within his body gave over to a stab of longing. He shook his head with amazed wonder that he could envy one of God's simple creatures.

The arm of the bayou that flowed past the house was choked by hyacinth, no longer navigable by pirogues, and so shallow, it could be negotiated by a man in hip-high boots. He had often been that man. Proud of his heritage, Adrien was tanned the dusky bronze of the lowlander. His Acadian features were angular and bore lines of sexuality that were subtly evident in his stance, in his straight back, and in the swing of his hips when he moved. A man who was sometimes arrogant, often intricate, and wholly erudite, there was about him an unexpected aura of masculine mystery—a toughness, an emotional intellect, an invincibility, bred into him by his ancestors and the harsh landscape. An inch shorter than six feet, he gave the impression that he towered over those about him. He had a stalwart-looking face: a solid jaw cut square across the bottom with a cheek that was favored with a dimple when he smiled. He hated the dimple and made a diabolical effort to contain his smile to a mere tilt at the corner of his mouth, which often caused genuine glee to be mistaken for cynical amusement. This cynical tilt lent his full lips an aspect of sardonic irony that women loved and felt compelled to attempt to penetrate. An almost straight nose, hooking a bit to the left, jutted between smoky-brown eyes bracketed with weathered lines. The eyes were shrewdly alert and chameleonlike, deepening in colour when he was angry, or amused and seldom missing much.

Today, against the damp cool air he wore an L. L. Bean tattersall shirt whose collar and cuffs looked at home with a gray ragg sweater and tailored herringbone slacks with soft leather inserts at the pockets. On his feet were hand-sewn oxford shoes.

The antique clock named the hour and drew Adrien away from the window. He took a sip from the demi-tasse he held in his hand and muttered a low oath. The coffee was cold. That was the problem with these damn cups, he mused. By the time the liquid was cooled, it was too blasted cold to drink. He strode to the side table and poured a second cup, added a dollop of brandy, and cursed again when the liquid overflowed the tiny cup.

"Berty!" he called, bellowing out the name, shattering the silence of the house while keeping his eyes on the entrance of the drawing room until his cousin and sometimes housekeeper appeared.

In the kitchen, arranging food on the very rosewood table that figured so in Adrien's visions, Roberta Merril Brown paused at hearing her name and wiped her hands on the starched white apron covering her gray linen dress. She had a serious, thoughtful face and faded brown eyes that seemed intent on something in the distance, in the future perhaps, as though she looked beyond her troubled existence to hope or death. At fifty-six she was frail, though not diminished in force, sad but not unhappy, curious, though her curiosity had ceased to exist, replaced by acceptance.

As she emerged from the kitchen she unfolded starched white cuffs to cover her thin wrists. She loved this big old house, she reflected, and wished Adrien would fill it with laughing children. At this thought a fearful ache of guilt clutched at her, a powerful and painful force that was as deeply imbedded in her muscles as her illness. It was her fault that Adrien's wife, Eleanor, had run off, her fault that the new life growing in Eleanor's womb had been discarded like a speck of unclean flesh.

Berty wished for the thousandth time that she had never left the hospital at Carville. Then that day two years ago she wouldn't have been in her cottage, wouldn't have been anywhere near Lafourche. The memory of the agonizing morning locked in her mind like a frame of film standing still, never to move forward or backward....

It was one of those mornings when the heat clung and humidity mingled with the sweat on the upper lip. Ralph, the dried-up old prune of a handyman, as gnarled and bony as a cypress stump, knocked on her cottage door with a message from Adrien. Would Berty stay with Eleanor the few days he would be away at a cattle auction, her cousin wanted to know. Eleanor couldn't or wouldn't go. In the first weeks of pregnancy smells made her nauseated, and the reeking earthy aromas in an auction barn were among the most offensive.

Happy to answer Adrien's summons, happy to feel herself returning to the mainstream of bayou life, Berty hurried up to the big house and found Eleanor propped up in the vast palisander bed that had been in the family for more than a century. Her mass of silky blond hair, loosened from its braids, cascaded over the goose-down pillows. Eleanor was pouting, in an uncertain mood.

"Berty! Thank God you're here. I thought Adrien was going to go off to Dallas and leave me all alone," she exclaimed petulantly.

"He would never do that, not now," Berty said soothingly, straightening the light coverlets about Adrien's bride. Eleanor picked at the edge of the lace-trimmed sheet.

"He would...he would...and there's absolutely nothing for me to do here. This house is like a prison. There's nothing around it but swamp."

"Why, that's not true," Berty replied cheeringly. "We have lots of neighbors, and they'd be delighted to have you—"

"In those broken-down old houses? Only painted on the front? Just to talk about babies or crops or the size of the tomatoes in their gardens? Ugh! How boring."

Berty was taken aback by the vehemence in Eleanor's tone. It was the first inkling she had that all was not as it should be with the newlyweds. "You just feel that way now because so much is changing inside your body. These people want to be your friends. And the houses just look tumbledown on the outside. It's the weather. Inside, they're as spotless as the head of a pin. Here, sit up," she coaxed. "Let me brush your hair, then I'll braid it and put it up the way you like it."

"That might help," Eleanor agreed, reveling in the attention. "I'm miserable, and it's so hot. I don't see how you can wear those starched collars and long sleeves day in and day out, especially on a day like today." Eleanor turned her great violet eyes curiously on Berty for a moment. "Why do you wear that—that uniform all the time? Is it another Cajun custom I haven't heard about?"

Berty tried to avoid answering. Eleanor poured on the charm so that Berty could see why Adrien was so fascinated by her. "There shouldn't be any secrets between us, Berty. After all, you're Adrien's only living blood kin," Eleanor cajoled, "and I'm his wife. We're friends, aren't we?"

"I hope so," Berty said, drawing the brush through the long golden hair. Hesitantly she told Eleanor that she had patches of numbed skin on her arms, on her back, and near her collarbone, that the doctors had diagnosed Hansen's disease.

"Hansen's disease? Berty, that sounds positively dull. I've never heard of it."

"Oh, yes, you have," Berty said laughing. Dull! Heavens. She would have to tell her doctor, she thought. He would get a laugh out of that one. "The Bible calls it leprosy."

Gasping air, horrified, Eleanor cringed away from Berty.

"Oh, God! Get away from me! Don't touch me!"

"Eleanor, please. It's—I'm not contagious and I was diagnosed early. It's arrested. I'm not going to lose a hand, or my nose. Goodness, you're behaving like this was the middle ages."

Eleanor moved to the foot of the bed, clinging to a carved post, her face pale, her eyes wide with fear. A hand flew to her stomach. "Is it genetic?"

"Why, no. Let me explain it to you—"

"No! I want you out of here. I can't believe it! I can't believe Adrien would even let you in this house. around me. He wants this baby," she said sourly, revealing for the first time in her manner that she was only pregnant to accommodate her husband, that she didn't share in his joy "Out! Get out!" she screamed. "Oh, my God! Leprosy!"

Berty backed out of the room as Eleanor, wild with fury, began snatching at coverlets, her gown, her hair—anything Berty had touched. It was always the same when anyone found out, she reflected sadly. People looked at her with a mixture of contempt, pity, and fear. It pierced her to the quick. She would never forget that feeling. Her own husband had reacted the same as Eleanor, recoiling in horror, abandoning her when she was at Carville. Now she kept her secret locked in—safe, away from strangers. And if any of their neighbors knew, none spoke of it. Berty missed being loved, missed being touched. Adrien understood. He was fearless, thank God. But when he returned from Dallas, he found the house empty. Eleanor had gone, taking nothing. And though fearless, he had gone mad at Eleanor's disappearance.

Now he was watching for Berty when she entered the drawing room, thumping his fingers impatiently on the side table so that the delicate porcelain vibrated, giving off silvery little clinks of music.

"Berty. What took you so long? I was just about to come looking for you. Bring me a decent-size cup," he said, then his glance left her and traveled back to the side table, and something, some inner control, snapped. "Get rid of these damn things, will you?" He flung his hand, indicating the demitasses and the porcelain coffee warmer.

What new madness was this? "But—but you said to leave everything as it was—"

"I know. Can't a man change his mind? Anybody who'd walk in here right now would think I only entertained midgets. Dispose of them."

"Oh? Are you having company?" Few had crossed the threshold since Eleanor had left. Was a miracle in the making? Adrien was coming alive once again. He gave her that stubborn cynical glare behind which he hid so many of his emotions and said nothing more. Berty shrugged, replaced the cups, and exchanged the coffee warmer for a silver thermos filled to its brim. "Ralph will be up to the house in a few minutes," she told him. "Dinner is almost ready."

"Start without me," he ordered. When he was alone in the drawing room once again, Adrien filled the man-size cup with coffee and brandy, then turned to the life-size portrait that hung on the wall opposite ceiling-high shelves filled with rare and costly books. Lifting the cup in a self-mocking toast, he muttered "Eleanor" and drank the laced coffee in several long swallows.

For a moment he stared resolutely at the portrait, devouring the blond beauty that looked out. He felt nothing beyond the warmth of the brandy as it trickled into his belly. His eyebrow arched as he waited. Nothing. No feeling. No emotion. But this was inconceivable! Her portrait had always been able to stir in him the indescribable passion that had racked his body at her loss. He waited for the hate to come, the tearing that lodged in his throat and made him unable to swallow or talk. He advanced closer to the painting, as though to tempt fate, challenging the memory of her.

Still, he felt nothing. Then, abruptly, as though throwing off invisible chains, he dashed out of the room into the wide hall and up the stairs, taking them two at a time.

In his bedroom he began yanking drawers from their tracks, and, retracing his steps into the upper hall, dumping their contents to the floor below. He went into the bath, scooped up bottles and jars, and those too he dumped over the banister. A flacon of Joy hit the landing, shattering, spilling its jasmine-scented fragrance into the air.

At the clatter Berty emerged, running from the kitchen, saw the mound of clothes, sniffed the air, and glanced up. "My word, Adrien, what are you doing?"

"Spring cleaning," he murmured, laughing grimly with no hint of merriment. "I suppose nothing in this life is as we want it, eh, Berty? Or as we wish it. It's only what we make it." He began to laugh again, then pulled himself together with an actual physical effort. His face was stern, his eyes resolute and almost hard. Glancing down, he read the look of puzzlement and disbelief on Berty's face. He smiled, his mouth sardonic. "Did you think that cleaning is just the province of women? These are the supercharged eighties. Where's your sense of equality? Burn all of that," he said, pointing to the soft mountain strewed at her feet. "Burn every last piece."

"Burn?" She was shocked, dismayed. "In this storm?" She gestured toward all the lovely clothes, a feeble protest. "These are good clothes, some are new. It would be a sin—"

"Sin?" Adrien gripped the banister, his voice coming to her low and barely audible. "The sin was Eleanor's, not yours, though I know you think it was, and not mine. Why should I do penance? Why should *we*? Tell Ralph I said to burn them, every single piece. You understand?"

Berty nodded, at once fascinated and terrified at this strange twist of madness. She found her voice. "All right, but Eleanor—"

"That's another thing," he interrupted. "Don't ever speak her name aloud in this house again." The look on his face was ominous, almost threatening.

Berty stared in doleful silence as Adrien pivoted and returned to his room. Unconsciously her wrist encircled by its starched white cuff swished against her dress as her fingers patted her bony chest, searching for the amulet, the gris-gris, she wore around her neck against the loup-garou. A simple woman, she was caught between two worlds—that of her practical self and that of the superstitions of Acadian folklore. Her fingers closed over the small bulge and just as quickly she snatched her hand away, chastising herself with shaky laughter. What evil spirit would come near her? A woman with leprosy! But just to be on the safe side, she offered a prayer to God for the *letiche*, the ghost of Adrien's baby who died without being baptized.

Though steeped in folklore from childhood, Adrien

Merril was a man of the practical world entirely, and no superstitions held him in check as he stood in the middle of his large airy room, surveying his behavior in his mind's eye. His hands trembled as though he had just performed some emotional trespass. This should have been done months ago, he thought, feeling queerly elated. He had exorcised a devil-witch that had haunted him far too long. The purging, coupled with a peculiar sensation of freedom, left him taut with nervous energy.

He checked every drawer in the huge ten-foot-high armoire that had been built by Francois Seignouret more than a hundred years ago in New Orleans, to be certain not a shred of Eleanor remained. He glanced at the monumental rosewood bed, remembered Eleanor lying in it, a thick golden braid over her creamy shoulder. The silk-lined canopy, constructed to carry mosquito netting that was so needed when Prudent Mallard had first designed it, was now held back with loops of silk rope. It was designed for love and used for lust...his own and Eleanor's. After stepping away from the bed, he threw open the window and inhaled the rain-washed air.

The storm was abating, the rain softer, dripping steadily into Spanish moss that clung to trees like graceful streamers of tatted lace. The moss was a parasite and it housed others—nests of tree ticks that scurried to close up infinitesimal rips in their dens, where even a single drop of water could be considered a flood. On the underside of leaves, larvae, snug in silken cocoons, fared better. They waited only for the coming day and bright, hot sun to emerge as butterflies to take their first stupendous flights of freedom.

A peacock screeched and flew up into the twisted branches of a cypress. A hen was nearby, and the male bird railed at the rain for interrupting his strutting mating dance. Watching the cock's antics, Adrien laughed and stretched, as though he too were emerging from a cocoon. The indignant cock balanced himself on a limb above the hen. Suddenly, without warning, a paroxysm of repulsion overtook Adrien and the laughter that had welled up so freely died in his throat.

Had he behaved like the peacock? Strutting and railing like a fool over Eleanor? he wondered. The answer, one he didn't like, settled uncomfortably in his conscious mind. More than foolish, he must have been blind not to acknowledge his mistake, naive not to see through Eleanor. Berty's illness had been the excuse Eleanor needed and grasped to rid herself of a husband she didn't love and a child she didn't want.

With a sudden flash of clarity he understood. For the Eleanor of Paris, London, New York, and Palm Beach, Adrien had been that something different, that exotic man—a new toy. And like a child after Christmas, the newness had worn off, leaving only boredom. What a fool he had been. And two whole years wasted!

No, he decided inwardly. Not wasted. Perhaps Eleanor had unknowingly done him a generous favor. Numbed and angry by her desertion, grown mad by letters from her attorney, he had thrown himself into work on the ranch. His cane crops the past year had reached all-time high yields, and the cattle breeding program was a success far sooner than he had dared to anticipate. Had Eleanor stayed, he might not have had such singlemindedness, such relentless purpose. Eleanor had been the mistake of a lifetime.

It was a mistake he would not repeat.

Still, a man needed to take a wife, provide heirs to make his mark on the land, define his heritage.

The rain stopped, and clouds, no longer black, parted, displaying a multicolored rainbow arching over the Louisiana bayou. The arrogant peacock flew down from his perch and once again began to strut, his tail fanned in fanciful iridescent array. The dull, colorless hen followed.

The telephone on the bedside table shrilled into life, and as Adrien reached for it, he made a mental note to tell Ralph to give the strutting gentleman an extra ration of corn.

"Allo? Adrien?" the gravelly voice belonged to Jean Baptiste Dubois, a short broad man with dark brooding eyes, a long French nose, and fists the size of a muskrat trap. He was graceful and very quiet in all his movements so that if he kept his mouth shut, there wasn't a finer hunting companion in all of Louisiana. Being awkward and shy about strangers, and though he had loved his father, Jean had been unashamedly delighted to be called from college to run their family ranch upon the old man's death. Jean was married to one of the outstanding beauties in the parish. For this Adrien could offer no explanation. It seemed to him that Barbara had just appeared one day, petite and delicate and adoring Jean. The next thing Adrien knew he was standing in front of the baptismal font as godfather to Jean Jr. dubbed Frenchie, who was all pink and round with fat little legs that kicked with an energy that would do justice to an athlete pumping iron.

"What about this rain, eh?" Jean growled pleasantly in Adrien's ear. "The cane is going to be six feet high in two weeks and line our pockets with a little green gold for a change, no?"

Adrien laughed at Jean's enthusiasm. "Maybe, if we can get our tractors through the mud so the saw grass doesn't take over."

"Ah, I wish I had your worries," Jean said with mild affection. "What do you care if your crops fail—you have that big old hotel in New Orleans to keep you. The rest of us Lafourchaise have to work."

"I have to plow every dime of profit back into that monster just to keep it from tumbling into the Mississippi," Adrien retorted. "But if you think it's such a good deal, I'll trade it to you for those ten acres of bottom land you—"

"No! No! No! Just this once I'll pass," Jean spat. "But cattle is why I called. The regional cattle association forwarded me a letter from a man named Ballesta. Seems he's interested in crossing his Brahmas with Limousin. He wants somebody who's doing that sort of breeding to come down and look over his operation to see if it will work for him. Says he wants to buy a small herd of heifers if it will. He's in Colombia."

"South Carolina?" Adrien queried, alert and far more interested than he let on.

"South America. It's why I can't go. Barbara thinks I'm too sexy for all those senoritas."

"Barbara's blind."

"I'll forget you said that because of Frenchie," Jean warned. "Anyway, you ought to go. This Ballesta is paying expenses, too. Besides, you've been at this longer than I have. I wouldn't have a herd to sell if he walked in my front door with the cash right now, or even a year from now, but you do. Anyhow, you need to get off the bayou for a while, see—"

"You're out of line," Adrien snapped.

"What's a line between friends," Jean shot back. "You'll go, no?"

"I'll think about it."

"Hmm, well, don't think too long. This Ballesta fellow wants a breeder real soon, like next week."

Jean Baptiste Dubois cradled the telephone softly. He and Adrien had grown up together, went to school together, fought and hunted together. He knew Adrien well. If Adrien had a weakness, it was his combativeness, which had increased since Eleanor had decamped. Sometimes Adrien merely tested people to see how a person would react. Other times he probed to discover hidden fears or weaknesses. One of these days, Jean thought, Adrien was going to drive that probe into somebody who'd turn it right around and stick him good. That ought to get him back on solid ground, he mused, hoping he'd be around to see it. Adrien had been on the near side of quicksand since Eleanor left. Jean had stopped believing in the loup-garou when he was nine years old. At his first meeting with Eleanor, he began to believe again. He thought Eleanor a collector. She collected anecdotes about Lafourche with which to regale her city friends, and she collected Adrien just to show them that she could do it. Adrien had a "don't fence me in" attitude, and Jean often wondered had Eleanor not left when she did, if their marriage would have lasted. Probably would've, he decided, if she'd had the kid. Adrien was sometimes so traditional, he had more starch than Father DuMont's priestly white collar.

Chapter Two

Jennifer DeWitt's heels clicked in staccato rhythm on the cobblestones as she rounded a corner of the Guilbeaux Hotel and made her way to its front doors. Overhanging limbs from massive oaks lining the boulevard shaded the hotel's outdoor café that was tucked charmingly behind a calligraphy of wrought iron fence that separated it from a busy thoroughfare. A pale green translucence filtering through leafage scattered a mottled pattern on crisply starched tabletops, protecting guests from the searing early morning sun. The shade did little to protect them from the stifling New Orleans humidity. One group clustered about a linen-draped table—regular guests drinking their café au lait leisurely, ignoring the humid air with native resignation. Jennifer smiled and waved as she passed in their view.

Several responded in kind and casually followed her progress across the terrace. They noted that she wasn't beautiful in the exacting sense of that word, yet there was something striking about her. It was partly a certain cachet about her piquant features that compelled one to look twice, perhaps even a third time, to imprint them on memory. Or it might have been the captivating manner in the way she moved, which caused the Fiorucci yellow silk to rustle softly against her rounded curves. Then there was her abundant brown hair, sparkling with red highlights, which was wound into a chignon; smooth and perfectly formed, it caught the eye as it nestled against the slender column of her neck.

As Jennifer passed from view the coffee drinkers went back to chatting, and the doorman, dressed in subdued black with a snowy white shirt, greeted her, touching his fingers to his cap. "Morning, Miss De-Witt," he said smoothly as she glided by.

"Good morning, Harry," she replied. "Is it always this hot in March?"

"No, ma'am, and it'll cool off once we get some rain. Can't understand what's holding it up," he said, rolling his eyes skyward, as though an inspection of the sun-drenched heavens would give him a clue. "It's been dumping buckets over the bayous for more than a week now. Reckon it'll catch up to us soon."

The air-conditioned comfort of the spacious lobby enveloped Jennifer while the plush carpeting muted the sound of her heels, as now, with a practiced eye, she swept the lobby area, the mezzanine, and the entrance to the restaurants and lounge. There were only the normal morning bustle of employees gearing up for the day and a line of guests waiting to check in or out. She sighed contentedly as she waited for the elevator to take her to the first floor, where her office was located. Since the explosion of Mardi Gras more than a month earlier, she had entered the hotel each day with a sense of bedlam tripping around her ankles. Nothing in the ten months that she had worked at the Guilbeaux had prepared her for the frenzy of carnival, although its intensity had reminded her of New Year's Eve brouhahas in her native New York.

She felt a pang of homesickness, then the image of Frank Crompton fluttered through her mind. If only he could see her now, that two-timer! She would delight in rubbing his nose in her success—her rapid advancement from trainee to department head amidst a glamorous background, while he continued to do little more than shuffle papers at the radio station where he worked for her father.

Jennifer pictured the unexpected events that day last May that had catapulted her from a secure and planned future in New York to independence in New Orleans....

There had been a sense of joyous release in the soft spring air. It swirled around the American University campus, littered with proud parents and just-graduated students. She and Frank were among those graduates while the sun beamed down on Washington, D.C., as though it meant to do its part in celebration of the day. For all its ceremonial pomposity, Jennifer thought the day was a milestone that pegged an ending to an era of learning. As she hurried across the campus she was more anxious than most to get on with her life, for after high school she had let two whole years slip by while she worked for her mother.

Her mind traveled to the future. Ahead of her was a life all planned, just the way she wanted it. Waiting for her in New York was a job at the United Nations, and then there was the excitement of planning her wedding and finding an apartment. Something small and cozy and dreamy for herself and Frank. Not expensive, of course. Frank had a beautiful voice and would be working for her father, who was program director for the most popular radio station in Manhattan. Mrs. Frank Crompton. Jennifer Crompton. A marvelous-sounding name, she decided. There was no question about it: She was one lucky girl!

She ran up the steps to her dorm and burst in on her

roommate, Beverly, busily packing her last few belongings.

"Whew, I'm glad that's over with," Jennifer exclaimed breathlessly, sweeping off her cap and gown in a single fluid motion. She was standing in the tiny room, clothed only in a pink silk teddy, fanning herself with her mortarboard. "You'd think the aristocratic American University would forgo the barbaric and uncivilized ceremony of commencement, especially in this weather." She swiped at a barely perceptible line of perspiration on her upper lip before folding and stuffing the discarded robe into a plastic bag, along with the cap, after having removed the tassel. She put on a silk dressing gown to cover the teddy.

"You worked up your own sweat, running across campus like that, like you usually do," Beverly admonished fondly. "You're always chasing after life. Relax now, let it catch up with you for a change. And graduations are not barbaric, they're a culmination, an ending, and a beginning. If we didn't have them, most of the kids wouldn't know where play left off and work began."

"Oh, pooh! Beverly the Philosopher," Jennifer teased. "Personally, I'd just as soon have had my diploma mailed to me—"

"What? Deprive your parents of the only visible ritual that shows their money was well spent? Shame on you."

Jennifer caught Beverly's eye and grinned. "Just think. Four years ago we were raw malleable pieces of wet clay, and now we're objets d'art—intelligent objets d'art, of course—and it's time for us to brave the savage lions in society."

Beverly paused as she folded her own gown, bagged it, and tossed it on top of Jennifer's. "For your information, I'm braving the savages of New York Medical in Valhalla."

Jennifer squealed with delight and hugged her friend. "Beverly! That's wonderful. When did you find out you'd been accepted?"

"Just a few minutes ago. My parents brought the letter with them," she answered, extricating herself from Jennifer's embrace.

"I'm happy for you, Bev, but—say, what about that interview for the job in New Orleans? You know"— she mimicked a dozen earlier conversations—"the sultry city, a potpourri of cultures—French, English, Spanish, Portuguese, and as Catholic as Boston?"

"New Orleans will just have to manage without me," Beverly said, grinning. Off the desk at the foot of her bed she lifted a pale vellum envelope and dropped it into the gray trash can. "So much for New Orleans."

There was just then a commotion beyond the door— squeals and shouts and doors slamming. Jennifer looked into the hall. Frank stood on the top step while scantily clad girls made for the nearest room or bath.

"Frank! What are you doing here? You were supposed to meet me at the car, where Mother and Daddy are waiting—"

"I know. I have to talk to you, Jennifer—now! Come downstairs." His handsome face wore a determined scowl.

"What is it? Why such a serious look?" she asked when they were settled in the living room, where several bored parents were milling, waiting for their daughters. Frank sat across from her in the old maroon chair that had a spring loose. He shifted his weight and cleared his throat as if he were preparing to give some great and worthy speech. Jennifer touched his hand. He jerked away. She felt a curious sinking sensation in her stomach. Something was dreadfully wrong. "Has something happened?" she asked, alarmed.

"Yes, sort of," he answered slowly. "Look, Jennifer, I don't quite know how to say this, but I'm not going to dinner with you and your parents tonight—"

She sighed with relief. "Heaven's. Is that all? You had me frightened to death. I thought the world was coming to an end or something."

"Jennifer, shut up!" he said abruptly. "Listen, what I'm trying to tell you is that I'm not marrying you."

For an instant Jennifer stared at him, her mouth agape, as though he had just told her some bizarre, unbelievable story; the earth was spinning out of orbit, the moon had fallen, or the arctic ice cap had melted and the world was drowning. She gulped air, felt herself sweeping through a darkness to a deeper darkness, yet she saw that she could focus clearly and Frank Crompton was central in her view. "Wh-what do you mean? We love each other. We're going to be married. Soon!"

He shook his head. "No. I'm marrying Julia Prescott."

Julia. Sweet, cuddly little Julia Prescott. A ninny! she thought.

"I wanted to tell you sooner, but there was the interview with your father in New York."

Jennifer felt hollow, like her insides had been ripped out and scattered as so much offal. Had her heart stopped beating? Her hand flew to where it should be and found it pounding. Humiliation began to flood her body. "Julia? Frank, why Julia?"

He looked straight at her. "She needs me, Jennifer. You don't. You don't know it, but you just want marriage to break away from your mother. And you're too independent. I know that sounds contradictory, but it's the way you are. You go in ten different directions at once, and, well, I don't want to have to try to keep up with you. Besides that, you're two years older than I am."

Jennifer was stunned, yet her anger overrode her humiliation. Her voice rose to a pitch that caused others in the room to glance her way. "We talked about that. You said it didn't matter."

"Well, it does," he said loftily, standing up. "Look, I hope this doesn't mean I won't get the job with your father."

"That's it. That's it! You used me just to get a job at the station."

"I didn't. Oh, maybe I did. But I didn't think it would go this far."

She stood up, leaning into his face, her fists clenched. "You went to bed with me and you didn't think it would go this far?" Suddenly she realized the room was silent except for slight, embarrassed rustlings as people stared, shifted, then turned away. She looked about her wildly, felt the humiliation sweep a red tide across her face as tears began to run down her cheeks.

"I'm sorry," Frank muttered.

"You're more than sorry—you're reprehensible!" she shouted through her tears. She felt utterly wretched. The warm, comforting world she had dreamed of was gone, in an instant. The reservoir of happiness she had planned was empty. Frank turned to go. Jennifer jerked on his shirt, pulling him back.

"You're forgetting something, aren't you?" She took his ring from her finger and threw it at him. It bounced off his chest and rolled across the floor. A dozen pairs of eyes watched it until it came to a stop at the toe of a pair of brown leather pumps.

Jennifer felt herself the center of attention. She turned to face the cluster of parents who were now watching them openly.

"We're drama majors," she announced, forcing a cold smile. "What you just witnessed was our graduation performance." With that she walked out of the room, her chin up, her back straight, her shoulders so squared, the delicate bones in her spine showed against the thin fabric of her dressing gown. It would be weeks before she could think about this scene with equanimity, but when that time came, she thought it was a good exit—a perfect exit, one that would have done justice to a tragedienne in a Eugene O'Neill play.

When she returned to her dorm room, it was empty. Beverly had gone. Jennifer stood in the middle of the tiny room, pivoting slowly, trying to draw some comfort from the familiar surroundings in which she had lived for the past four years. But it was now stripped of everything loved and used and familiar—bare. The independent streak that so worried Frank Crompton asserted itself. Jennifer made the split-second decision that would launch her into a new and unfamiliar world. She reached into the trash can and retrieved the vellum envelope Beverly had discarded just moments before.

Jennifer grew up the only child of Hank and Nell DeWitt in a household that was often hectic, sometimes broke, but always full of warmth and love. Nell's ancestors had come to America as pioneers, Irish farmers working their way from Ellis Island to the Finger Lakes of western New York State. Four generations later they were farmers in the central plains of a stark and cold Kansas. Their Irish, boisterous nature caused the sameness of the plains to displease them. During the Depression they worked their way back east, gravitating to the cluttered tribal rites of New York theater. It was into this world that Nell had been born. She gave up the stage after Jennifer was born to open her own drama studio.

Through Jennifer's veins ran the legacy of a people dedicated to the earth, the forest, withal primitive; an earthiness that provoked a sophistication, the veneer of the theater only lightly touching her. To Nell's dismay the pull of Jennifer's heritage, of the land, was like a spoor leading her away from the glamour, the clutter, and from Nell herself.

Hank DeWitt was the first in his family to be born on American soil. As Lithuanians, his parents had been displaced after World War I. They wandered over Europe like gypsies until talk of war began again. Fearful and wanting a home, they immigrated to the United States, found a tiny apartment in Brooklyn, determined never to move again. Hank grew up on American hot dogs, the Brooklyn Dodgers, and fascination with the power of the spoken word on radio. He made communications his career. He dropped all the cyz's in his surname, juggled those letters left, combined them into DeWitt, and was satisfied. It sounded Flemish rather than Lithuanian, but at least it was pronounceable. He was respected, determined, intelligent, and excessively conservative. He loved his wife and adored his daughter, though without the possessiveness that appeared in Nell. She had tried subtly to guide Jennifer into the theater, but Hank would have none of it.

"She goes to college this year! That's final, Nell. You've had her two years in that studio of yours, and all she wants to do is keep books. You're being selfish."

"I'm not," Nell had retorted indignantly, her bracelets flying up and down her arm in emphasis. "Jennifer loves being in the studio. Do you know that since she began filling out all those hideous government papers we've never had a grant refused?"

"See? Selfish. Jennifer organizes that little box of chaos you call an office, and you use it as a claim to her. You have to let go, Nell. She'll go to my alma mater in Washington, and if she wants to come into your studio after she graduates, I won't say a word against it."

"I wish I'd never heard of Lithuania," Nell had complained, blaming his nationality as she usually did whenever she lost an argument to him.

Hank had laughed as *he* usually did. "Then perhaps I would've been born a Frenchman."

Nell had arched a perfectly plucked eyebrow. "And been far more interesting, I suspect."

During the years Jennifer was at college, Nell brooded, partly to aggravate Hank and partly because she was unwilling to accept that Jennifer was grown up. She filled every available space with Jennifer's photographs so that no matter where one looked, one encountered Jennifer's intriguing countenance. She had a wide forehead with an entrancing widow's peak, and arched expressive eyebrows—those from Nell's side of the family. From Hank came her straight nose, set between high cheekbones, which gave her face its shape, and layers of sooty lashes that rimmed oval brown eyes flecked with golden barbs that seemed to promise wild delights—which worried Nell no end. Jennifer's lips were soft and full with a dark provocative beauty mark at their edge. Her chin was strong with that fragile balance one often sees in heart-shaped faces, and her skin had a radiance that reminded Nell of the finest K'unlun jade.

To Nell's utter dismay, after college, Jennifer had not come home to stay. She had been in New Orleans for almost a year now, and for this Nell blamed her husband and Frank Crompton. On rare occasions Hank came home for lunch, and today he found Nell reading a letter from Jennifer.

"Well, what does she have to say?" he asked between mouthfuls of slumgullion, a stew of meat, vegetables, and potatoes.

"That she's busy, busy, busy," Nell answered glumly. "She seems to like New Orleans just fine."

"Good, I'm glad to hear it."

"I suppose that oily Frank Crompton is still working for you?" she asked with dramatic distaste.

"You ask that every day, and the answer today is the same as yesterday...yes, he is, because he's a hard worker. He's doing commercial voice-overs."

"I wish you'd get him a job elsewhere, then Jennifer might come home."

"Where would you suggest?" Hank asked, humoring her.

"Siberia."

"At the moment," he said dryly, "I don't happen to have any colleagues in the Russian radio network."

"If it hadn't been for you," Nell complained, harking back to an old argument, "Jennifer could have been a famous model or an actress, but no!" Nell had entered Jennifer in every baby contest that came along, had taken her to agencies to promote Jennifer for commercials in the then new television industry. Hank had put a stop to that. He recognized in his wife an unhealthy possessiveness that made her want to clutch and save everything that was dear to her. For Jennifer's sake he kindly, but firmly restrained Nell.

He wiped his mouth with a napkin, got up and walked around the table, and took Nell's face in his hands. He softly kissed her lovely lips. "Jennifer is twenty-five years old and all grown up now," he murmured. "If you had your way, she'd be tucked into your apron pocket for the rest of her life."

"Oh, Hank, it's just that New Orleans is so far away. It's nothing but swamp, mosquitoes—"

"and full of history, color, language, arts, and the site of the next world's fair," Hank finished. "Let Jennifer go, Nell, and take all those theatrical woes downstairs and teach them to your students. If they practiced being *you*, they'd all be Academy Award-winners."

Jennifer had arrived in New Orleans determined to make it on her own. She interviewed at the elite Guilbeaux Hotel and was hired as a management trainee. Her first two months on the job were spent learning how every department in the hotel functioned. She worked behind the front desk in reservations, spent a week in sales, and had hostess duty in the dining room. She spent a single disastrous day in the telephone room at its ancient switchboard under the eagle eye of Myrtle, the telephone supervisor, and two more weeks in housekeeping, during which she worked in the massive storeroom, learning how to inventory and issue everything from linens to liquors.

One of the first things she perceived was that every room in the hotel had a name or a number, like streets in a small hamlet. The lounge was the Pirate's Cove, paneled in dark wood with antique ship's lanterns throwing off streams of ivory light, and was a watering hole for several dozen local businessmen. The Guilbeaux was off the beaten path for tourists, and that, along with the excellent hors d'oeuvres provided by Petri Cato, the executive chef, kept them coming back. By this time Jennifer knew most of the regular guests by name, and the hotel became her home away from home.

After her tour in the Cove, she was assigned to Ellie Broussard in the small catering office, where she threw herself into the work with a vengeance. She learned room setups, how to cost out menus, and how to plan meetings, dinners and wedding receptions.

Her salary was much lower than she expected, but the perks that came with the job made up for it. She got all her meals free, her laundry and drycleaning done by the hotel valet service, and her dues paid into the Hotel/Motel Association. She went to meetings once a month and got to know her peers working at other hotels in New Orleans.

Jennifer had to work all the holidays: Fourth of July, Thanksgiving, Christmas, New Year's, and Mardi Gras, as well as All Saints' Day, which was a moving and revered holiday of local custom, whereby relatives cleaned headstones of the departed, covered graves with flowers, and lighted candles. Many families set up chairs at grave sites and received their neighbors in regal and solemn fashion, the ritual itself being far holier than the honoring of the departed. She worked ten- and twelve-hour days with every other weekend off, and this affected her personal life. The hotel used up all her energy, and she was too exhausted to date.

The Guilbeaux's manager, Ethan Britz, was impressed with her ability to learn fast and accurately, and the skill with which she handled the guests. He promoted her to catering manager, and assigned her a small staff and a desk in Ellie's office. The hotel functioned as a small city within itself, and Mr. Britz was its mayor.

Jennifer learned that a guest was always right to his face and cursed solidly behind his back. There was gossip. If a maid discovered something titillating about a guest on the eighth floor, within ten minutes busboys in the dining room would be discussing it. Idle talk and news traveled by some invisible network; no one was safe from it, and the hotel staff thrived on it. Yet Ethan Britz forbade it.

New Orleans did not have the electric vitality of New York and Washington, but there was a certain something about the city—a pulse, an appetite, a self-restrained sensuality that lurked just beneath its surface. Jennifer was totally caught up in its excitement.

In her free time she walked all over New Orleans, learning her way around. She visited the wax museum on Conti Street, the French Market for vegetables, fruits, and spices, and wandered through the Vieux

Carré, sampling pièces de résistance of local cuisine, which included red snapper, oysters, shrimp, crabs, crawfish, frog's legs, and chicken—or *poulet*—cooked in a hundred ways, each one better than the last. She took a ride down the Mississippi on the steamboat *President* and a tour into the swamps where Jean Laffite, a Creole patriot to Louisianians—a pirate to the rest of the nation—had operated. She spent time in Jackson Square and discovered the best underground restaurants, and when she tired, she sat at the foot of the Moonwalk with the Mississippi lapping at her feet, dallying away free time watching ships and barges make their way along the river while she sipped on Creole café au lait and ate mouth-watering beignets—square, puffy French doughnuts—bought from the Café du Monde. She rode quaint electric trolleys to and from work most days, but sometimes walked.

New Orleans had cold, damp winters, hot, humid summers, and spectacular magnolia-scented springs. Jennifer loved it. She thought of Frank less and less and surprised herself one day when she couldn't bring his face to mind. The humiliation she had felt at his betrayal faded, but her determination to avoid serious and intimate relationships never waned.

Chapter Three

"Oh, Jennifer, am I glad you're here early," Ellie Broussard exclaimed breathlessly as Jennifer entered the office. An impeccably groomed forty-five-year-old widow, Ellie was always slightly flustered, slightly breathless, and slightly in awe that she actually held a position at the glamorous Guilbeaux. She had been the food and beverage director for twelve years. Glad to have some help in her department, she had been kind and helpful from the moment Jennifer had been assigned to catering. A sympathetic look on her face said she had some unpleasant news to convey.

"Mr. Britz wants you to get the Carnival Room ready for Adrien Merril. You're to arrange meals for six, for one day, possibly two, beginning with breakfast tomorrow. I know it's short notice"—Ellie paused to take a long draw on her cigarette—"and Wilcox is hovering in on this one. Merril is one of Mr. Britz's favorite guests, and Wilcox is practically holding his hand. You know what that means." She slashed the air with her cigarette, cutting through its stream of smoke. *"En guard!"*

"Oh, foot!" Jennifer muttered under her breath. What a way to start the day. Mr. Britz's fidgety attention to details almost always caused confusion, no matter how exactingly she planned a meeting or a meal, and now tò have his secretary, Wilcox, breathing down her neck ... Wilcox hated her, and it had all begun the day Jennifer had arrived for her interview....

The executive offices were located on the mezzanine, up a short curved staircase from the lobby. Eva Wilcox, Executive Secretary, was sitting at her desk, surveying the entire lobby area like a haughty queen overseeing her kingdom. Unsmiling, she watched the newcomer ascend the stairs, appraising Jennifer shrewdly as she glided across the expanse of Burgundy carpet. Wilcox knew at once who Jennifer was, and she lumped her with all the rest—the young aggressors, the college graduates—that wanted to—no, insisted on—starting at the top, unlike she, herself, who had had to work her way up. It was true, Wilcox mused acidly. The younger generation didn't know the first thing about hardship or hard work. It wouldn't take her two seconds to put this snobby college kid in her place. She smiled coldly as Jennifer approached her desk.

Jennifer bore the harsh scrutiny with a feeling of strange unease. She had dressed carefully in a smart off-white silk suit and a pale yellow blouse, and had worn sensible medium-heeled Naturalizers, so her clothes couldn't possibly be what the woman seemed to be objecting to. It was just preinterview jitters, she told herself, shrugging off the feeling, as she stopped in front of the desk.

"I'm Jennifer DeWitt. I have an appointment with Mr. Britz," she said, giving the secretary her most winning smile while proffering her hand across the typewriter. Wilcox's eyes dropped to Jennifer's outstretched hand, then shifted back to her face.

"DeWitt ... oh, yes ... the graduate from American University." She made graduate sound like a dirty word. Jennifer let her hand fall to her side, embarrassed, and knew at once that she would never be able to like this woman.

"Sit over there," Wilcox directed, pointing with a pencil to a narrow side table. "Fill out this application."

"Is that necessary before the interview?" Jennifer questioned. "I did send my résumé."

Wilcox smiled unctuously "We're just one big family here, no favorites. *Everyone* fills out an application. You're no better than a dishwasher, dear."

Fuming inwardly, Jennifer took the application and filled it out. Still, Wilcox kept her waiting another thirty minutes before telling Mr. Britz that she had arrived. By then it was fifteen minutes past the appointment, so that it appeared to Mr. Britz that Jennifer had not been prompt. After the interview, Mr. Britz returned her into Mrs. Wilcox's care with the instruction to take Jennifer to accounting to sign a payroll slip.

"So, you talked your way into the job," Wilcox said when Mr. Britz was out of earshot.

For the second time that morning Jennifer bit back the remark sitting on the tip of her tongue. *Be pleasant.* she ordered herself. *This is your first day on the job... best foot forward.* She forced a smile. "Yes, and I'm happy to be aboard and a member of the family," she said, quoting the very words Mr. Britz had used not five minutes earlier.

"Oh, don't get too happy, dear. You won't last long," Wilcox predicted maliciously in honeyed tones, eyeing Jennifer from head to foot. "We know your type around here, Miss DeWitt. You party all night, flirt with the guests, and expect to get by on your looks. So, don't waste your time. You're not allowed to date guests. Get caught and get fired—that's how it works here at the Guilbeaux."

"Mr. Britz explained the rules," Jennifer replied coolly, knowing that for some enigmatic reason, in Wil-

cox, she had made an enemy. Since then she had ignored the noxious secretary as much as her job allowed, suffering little more than a few barbs from
Wilcox's razor-sharp tongue. No one other than Mr.
Britz seemed to care for his secretary, so Jennifer had
brushed off her remarks like she would any pesky in-
sect.

Wilcox's hostility had one unexpected sidelight. It
inspired Jennifer to learn faster, work harder, and
double-check details until she excelled in her work. Mr.
Britz was pleased with her and said so, and his approval, more than anything Jennifer had said, seemed to
silence Wilcox. But Jennifer didn't doubt that like a
fox, Wilcox was waiting for her to make a mistake,
then she would pounce.

Now, running her finger down the list of functions
written in the over-size banquet book—their Bible—
Jennifer determined she would get around Wilcox on
this Merril thing, too—somehow.

"There's already a meeting scheduled in the Carnival Room tomorrow," she said to Ellie. "What about
the Esplanade or the Harlequin Room instead?"

"I don't think so. You'll have to unschedule it, move
it, or change the name plates on the doors—again."

Jennifer sighed inwardly. "Okay, musical meeting
rooms it is." She slid behind her desk, picked up a pencil, and pulled a pad toward her. "What do they want to
eat?"

"I don't know, Wilcox didn't say, but there's another thing. The dumbwaiter's on the blink again, so
you'll have to charm Vinnie into serving the meals. Mr.
Merril insists on that old rascal."

Jennifer uttered an unladylike expletive. "It'll take a
bulldozer to prod Vinnie out of the dining room. I can't
imagine *anyone* actually asking for that old goat."

"Vinnie adores Mr. Merril. All the same, it wouldn't

hurt to see if you can build a fire under maintenance."

"I will," Jennifer said, making a note. "I don't recognize Merril's name. Is he a regular?"

"He used to be, but I haven't seen him in a couple of years. He told Mr. Britz when he checked in last night that he'd spent a few days in South America, trying to sell some cattle. Just play it cool on this one," Ellie cautioned.

"Oh, sure...cool," Jennifer remarked sarcastically. "What about the food he wants served? Am I supposed to be clairvoyant? Do you think this Merril will have enough sense to get in touch with me before the day is out?" The thought that she might have to get the menu information from Wilcox caused her voice to be more cutting than she had intended.

"Talking about me?"

The soft masculine brogue that snapped out the query mimicked exactly Jennifer's sarcastic pitch. Both she and Ellie gasped as their attention was drawn to the man standing in the doorway. A warm rush of embarrassment crept up Jennifer's neck and fired her cheeks. She had been caught in a faux pas, and the man who was now leaning against the doorframe, staring at her, his arms crossed, had returned the insult. The edge of a smug smile tugged at one corner of his mouth. If there had been a hole in the floor, Jennifer would have gladly stepped into it.

In the space of a heartbeat she knew that here was no ordinary man. He leaned into the wall with indolent grace and the confidence of a man who feels comfortable everywhere he goes. His hair was dark, his skin the color of toasted almonds, and he wore a tan paisley shirt tucked into finely tailored brown cords. There was a squareness about him that was impossible to ignore, as his face was all angles and shadows, held together by a determined chin. He had wide shoulders, slightly rolled, yet indisputably squared—even the line of his torso was square, streamlined, with no break between his hips and chest. There was a vague hint of arrogance in the way he just stood there, looking at her. *He's too sure of himself,* Jennifer thought. *I just might bring him down a notch or two or three—puncture that masculine vanity and wipe that silly little smile off his face.*

"I don't know if I'm talking about you or not," she said. Ellie sucked in air, furtively trying to warn Jennifer to back off. Jennifer glanced at Ellie but went on. "Didn't anyone ever tell you it wasn't polite to sneak up on people?"

With a low moan Ellie hid her face behind a file folder.

To his private mortification Adrien grinned and felt the dimple in his cheek deepen. He didn't answer, as he was tongue-tied by an odd emotion he had never before felt. He had never seen a woman so strangely beautiful—not on the Bayou, not in New Orleans, not even in his dreams. Her eyes were flashing gold animated, and she had wonderfully round breasts thrusting against the buttons on the yellow silk. He tried to keep his eyes off them and could not. A prickle of sensation ran along his spine, jolting him into action. Lord! She must think him a speechless idiot. He moved away from the door and pointedly addressed Ellie, who reluctantly came out from behind the file folder.

"I'll want the usual, Ellie," he ordered, as though it had only been yesterday that he was last in the hotel, instead of a year or more. "Fried soft-shell crabs and omelets for breakfast, shrimp gumbo for lunch, and steak and oysters for supper. Tell Petri, no grits on the breakfast," he emphasized. "Arrange a salad bar for both lunch and supper. We'll order our drinks from the Cove."

Determined to demonstrate how indifferent she was

to the man's intentional snub, the instant he turned away from her, Jennifer dropped her eyes and gave her attention to the morning mail.

But Ellie, for all her breathlessness, was having no part of this. She waved the file folder in Jennifer's direction. "I'd be happy to help you, Mr. Merril, but that's Jennifer's job now." Jennifer shot her colleague a scathing glance, but Ellie ignored her, lighted a cigarette, and, pretending innocent aplomb, applied herself to the task of adding up the morning breakfast receipts.

Turning back to Jennifer and skewering her with a mocking glance, Adrien said, "Is that so?" Then he mimed her gaffe. "And does Jennifer have enough sense to arrange menus for me?"

A splinter of agitation pierced her reserve. *All right,* she thought defiantly. *If that's the way you want it...* She returned his glare. "I have plenty of sense, and regardless of what you might think, I didn't mean to be deliberately rude. Please," she said, stressing the word, "sit down." She pointed with one rose-tipped finger, indicating the heavy straight-backed chair in front of her desk. "It'll just take a few minutes to write up your order and set the times you want service."

With easy strength Adrien lifted the heavy chair and swung it around the desk within inches of Jennifer's. He sat down and leaned provocatively close, trailing one powerful forearm across the back of her chair. "Now, where shall we start?" he asked smoothly, one black eyebrow arching slightly.

For an instant Jennifer was too startled to respond. The scent of him assaulted her nostrils like a strong and ungovernable gust of wind that beats at doors and rattles windows. There was an early morning smell about him, of breakfast bacon, soap, and Yves Saint Laurent. He was invading her space, that indefinable aura that each calls his own, and when she shifted away from him, his hand shot off the back of her chair, pressing firmly against her spine

It was like sitting next to a huge piece of granite, one that she could not budge, nor get around, except stone never smelled as seductive as this, she thought.

Jennifer was rattled.

The feeling heightened her resolve to be thoroughly businesslike. When he leaned in even closer, almost enveloping her in the circle of his arm, she swallowed hard and began to spit out questions with the rat-tat-tat of a machine gun. He answered briskly, giving his responses, with a derisive impatience that matched her own while she scribbled furiously. It took ten minutes before the menus and table setups were adjusted to his satisfaction.

Tilting his chair back, Adrien folded his hands in his lap and relaxed, his manner suggesting that Jennifer, not he, was the intruder behind the desk. Although his fingers were no longer applying pressure against her spine, there was still the sensation of warmth, impossible to disregard. He stared openly at her profile as she penciled in his last few remarks on the forms in front of her.

Jennifer was aware of his blatant inspection, and her indignation was building. A caustic remark was forming on her lips, but a cautionary, minatory thought reminded her that the man was a favorite of Mr. Britz's, and one who basked in Wilcox's dubious care. If she put this man in his place now, she'd regret it later. Luckily, Wilcox hadn't accompanied Merril to her office. If the executive secretary had overheard her thoughtless remark, there'd be hell to pay. Mr. Britz was a regular wrath-of-fury when he discovered an employee being disrespectful to a guest. But, damn it! Merril had already gone over her once. Wasn't that enough?

It wasn't. The sun shone through the window, casting coppery highlights on Jennifer's hair, and several wisps teased the golden hollow of her cheek. Adrien was holding in check the urge to reach out and brush them away from her face and behind the sweet circle of her ear. While he was trying to guess her age his eyes settled on the beauty mark at the edge of her mouth. He thought, *There's something unusual about this woman. I wish I could put my finger on it.* He had no time to begin a new relationship. There were things far more important that claimed his attention. Then he found himself letting the chair's front legs down firmly to the floor and leaning close to Jennifer, brushing her ear with his breath. "I wonder what Mr. Britz would say if he knew members of his management staff gossiped about guests behind their back?"

Had he read her mind? she thought. That was the last straw! Jennifer slammed the pencil down and stood up. "Mr. Merril," she murmured with stately autocracy, "considering your behavior over the past ten minutes, I wouldn't put it past you to carry some off-the-wall tale—exaggerated, I might add—to Mr. Britz."

"That's good," he responded lazily, unfolding his long squarely built body to stand beside her, "because I will if you don't have dinner with me tonight." The invitation was so unexpected, it took Jennifer by surprise. She was bereft of words. "You're taking too long to say yes," he taunted. "I may have to insist on lunch, too."

Jennifer found her voice. "No! I can't. I have to help Ellie in the dining room during lunch."

"Dinner it is, then," he said, seizing the advantage. "Where may I pick you up—here?"

"No—no. Wait a minute." Good Lord, how had this happened? She'd been baited, trapped, and ambushed. "Can't we talk this over?" It was against hotel policy to date guests. Although many employees broke this rule, Jennifer never had.

"The only thing I'm willing to talk over is the time and place you want me to pick you up."

"Really, I can't," Jennifer said, trying out a conciliatory approach. "We aren't allowed—"

"We'll be the souls of discretion," he interrupted, guessing her reluctance. "We won't come near the hotel." Then he just stood there, like an immovable chunk of stone. Jennifer glanced over toward Ellie, who was paying no attention, or pretended she wasn't. No help there. She turned back to Adrien Merril and reluctantly gave him her home address.

"Seven thirty," he said, feeling a small surge of triumph.

Jennifer watched him saunter down the corridor, whistling softly to himself. After he disappeared around the corner, she spun around and reproached Ellie.

"Didn't you see what he was doing? You weren't much help. That was a low thing to do—siccing him on me like that, and after all the times I've helped you out—"

"You're the catering manager."

Jennifer sat down and put her chin in her hands. "Petri could use me for hamburgers," she complained, mentioning the Guilbeaux's executive chef. "I feel like I've just been chewed up by the original wolf."

"You probably have," Ellie said succinctly, then she smiled coyly. "Don't you think Adrien Merril just flat out exudes sex? If I were twenty years younger and Wilcox weren't on his coattails like a mother hen, I would've taken his order, and without all that smart talk you dished out." She sniffed disapprovingly. "Anyway, I warned you to play it cool on this one."

"You sound as though you actually like this man,"

Jennifer accused. "He was rude, insolent, and entirely too forward—"

"So? That's how I like my men," Ellie drawled. "Besides, as rogues go, he's all right. It's just in this part of the country, you have to watch out for those Cajuns, they're kind of tricky." She cast a sideways glance at her younger co-worker. "I don't see why you should be so glum. You should be ecstatic. After all, how many men ever make it to this office? All we ever get are harried mothers of the bride, secretaries making last-minute arrangements for their bosses, and belligerent *chairpersons*." She wagged a finger at Jennifer. "Tell me this: When was the last time you were asked out to dinner? You didn't even have a date on your birthday. You could apply for membership in the Old Maid League."

The reference to her personal life ruffled Jennifer. She struck a haughty pose. "I don't need a man around to make my life complete, and I had a very nice birthday...thank you. It so happens it was the first one I ever really had to myself, and I enjoyed it, so don't go spouting old wives' tales."

Ellie snorted. "Oh? What do you use to warm your tootsies with on a cold winter night? You young women astound me, always rebelling against nature. If men and women weren't supposed to co-mingle, why do you suppose God created them?"

"If you mean why did *She* create men, it was probably an oversight."

Ellie blushed. "That's blasphemy."

"I've just been blackmailed into having dinner with one of Mr. Britz's pets. That's the blasphemy." Jennifer shrugged eloquently and rallied. "We can't sit here talking about your Adrien Merril all day. We've got work to do. I'll take these menus to the kitchen.

After he bites my head off, Petri will probably be delighted to cook for old Britz's favorite patron.''

"Tut-tut, *mon amie*," Ellie remonstrated as she brought another cigarette to her lips. "If you'd stop rushing headlong into everything, you wouldn't end up in so much hot water."

Ellie was right, Jennifer admitted as she took the back stairs that led into the kitchen. Think first, act later; that was going to be her motto from here on out. On the other hand, she mused, if she didn't speak up for herself, who would?

Throughout the remainder of the day she kept a wary eye out for Adrien Merril. Later, when she passed through the lobby on her way to the dining room, she cast a look at the mezzanine. Wilcox was hunched over her desk, typing. Merril didn't show up in the restaurant during lunch, or in the Carnival Room where Jennifer set up the U-shaped meeting table at one end and a round dining table for eight at the opposite end. But Wilcox, with the instinct of the hunter, bird-dogged her, inspecting every tiny detail. She wouldn't be satisfied that the arrangements were correct until, exasperated, Jennifer showed her the plans initialed with deft strokes by Adrien Merril.

Wilcox hung around in the Carnival Room, fidgeting with the chairs and restraightening the already perfectly draped tables. Jennifer escaped, offering up a silent prayer that the meeting and meals would go without a hitch.

For all his bold aplomb, Merril had given the impression that this meeting was important to him and that he would accept nothing put in the way of its success. With this in mind, Jennifer had flagged all of his instructions with the red VIP tags so that the kitchen staff, and especially Vinnie, wouldn't drag their feet.

Then, to her dismay, she discovered that the tagging had not been necessary. Merril had already approached Petri and Vinnie by the time she had hand-carried the food orders to them.

He was ordering her staff around as if he owned them. It was one more reason for her to feel indignant.

Chapter Four

The sun was a brilliant ball of red, sinking far into the west, when Jennifer left the hotel, her work complete. The events of the day crowded her mind, and so intent was she on her musings that she passed the trolley stop, her subconscious pointing her feet in the direction of home. Her thoughts were turned so inward that she even failed to notice the fingers of red and gold that shot from the sun, illuminating baskets of geraniums that marked her path, warming their colors to a deeper, richer red than nature had ever provided. She was wavering in her decision about having dinner with a guest. If it got back to Britz or Wilcox, it could mean her job. Merril had got her between a rock and a hard place, damn it! She bracketed that thought and held it.

Jennifer had found an apartment in a secluded cul-de-sac in the corner el of an old and once-elegant home that was hidden behind tall wrought iron fencing and a dozen graceful magnolias. Its weathered form had long since been stripped of paint by subtropical damp, and her private entrance, a pair of floor-to-ceiling French doors, looked out onto a wisteria-laden porch. The apartment boasted a small bedroom with a brass bed, a dresser with a faded mirror, and an air conditioner that managed enough cool air for comfortable sleep—just.

The dressing room-cum-bath was almost as big as the bedroom, and its central occupant was an enormous porcelain tub with ugly claw feet. Paul Bunyan could've bathed in it, and when Jennifer filled it to the rim with water, she floated. The only other room in the apartment was a vast living-dining-kitchen combination with fourteen-foot ceilings. It came furnished with a ragged but serviceable Duncan Phyfe sofa and, against the back wall, a one-tub sink, a tiny electric stove, and the oldest living General Electric refrigerator, which wore its motor on top like a white silk hat. It growled, spewed, fumed, and walked across the wooden floors, managing somehow to produce ten perfect ice cubes each day. With a pennies to nonexistent budget, Jennifer purchased from Sears a redwood picnic set for dining—thirty-nine dollars, delivered. She padded the benches and covered them with lightweight yellow canvas, and she filled one end of the six-foot table with potted plants, cut flowers, and a pair of antique candelabra that she found in the flea market in the Vieux Carré. In the windows facing the street, which received filtered sun, she went native with baskets and baskets of flowering geraniums.

Nell DeWitt, fearing her daughter had fallen into some pagan, artless culture, had shipped Jennifer a secondhand Oriental rug, a Childe Hassam watercolor reproduction, and from Brentano's a book on Oriental erotic art with a note that said she knew she should've talked to Jennifer before now about sex, but that this book contained all the things Jennifer SHOULD NOT DO. It was the closest Nell had come to admitting Jennifer was now a woman and on her own. Jennifer smiled, displayed the book on the coffee table in front of the sofa, unrolled the carpet in front of that, and hung the watercolor in the huge old-fashioned dressing room. The total effect was light, airy, colorful, and welcoming.

The apartment was Jennifer's private sanctuary. Her only two visitors were her landlady, Miss Pennyforth, and the landlady's immoral old yellow tomcat, Fred. Miss Pennyforth presented herself once a month to collect the rent. Fred came every day.

Jennifer's thoughts, fantasies, and desires were her own to do with as she wished. In her months in New Orleans she came to understand that her mother's extreme possessiveness had blunted this kind of freedom. This awakening blossomed, and Jennifer hoarded it with all the ferocity of a lioness protecting her newborn cubs.

She realized what many people never learn—that freedom in itself was a form of entrapment. An entire nation was controlled by traffic signals—red for stop, green for go. She summed it up in one simple thought: Society gave off red and green signals.

Men were attracted to Jennifer, but she encouraged none. She made no close women friends, preferring her privacy, and she felt no need to share her thoughts, her ideas, her dreams. Yet she hungered for that special bonding human beings crave but choose all sorts of charades to conceal.

Jennifer was becoming expert at charades.

The brief encounter with Adrien Merril earlier in the day was on her mind as she performed the ritual that had become a habit when she arrived home. She aired the apartment, propping open the doors with old spring-handled flatirons, allowing the wisteria-scented breeze to float through, bringing with it the outdoor smell of leaves and earth that somehow had a calming effect after a hectic day at the hotel. It also allowed Fred to amble in and take his accustomed place at the end of the sofa.

Jennifer surmised that Merril was a man to whom order and control were as necessary as breathing. He was a man certain of his own superiority. He was a challenge. And Jennifer, with her surge of self-assurance and freedom, felt equal to that challenge. Historically it was the struggle between the sexes, and in this Jennifer had little depth of experience. It was a struggle that used as its weapons sex and sexuality; envy and hate; sarcasm and laughter; tears, compassion, and conviction.

Jennifer didn't know it, but she was going to war.

Thirty minutes after she arrived home and was stepping from a cooling Tatiana-scented bath, there was a rapid knock on the dressing room door. Immediately Jennifer thought, Miss Pennyforth—the rent was due. "Just a minute," she called, grabbing a towel and throwing it around herself. She opened the door and took a startled step backward.

"You!" Merril loomed in the doorway. "What are you doing here so early?" She had planned to be waiting for him on the swing on the porch. She didn't like her private sanctuary being invaded like this.

"Just making sure you weren't changing your mind," he said. The truth was, he couldn't wait. His hand pressed on the door while Jennifer maneuvered to get behind it.

"You just gave me the idea," she said angrily. "Move back."

He held his foothold in the door. Jennifer was reminded how immovable he had been that morning. "Do you always leave your house wide open when you're bathing?" The inflection in his voice suggested she didn't have the sense God gave a flea.

"No. Yes, damn it, when it's hot."

"You answer doors nearly naked, too." His eyes,

darkened in delight, traveled pointedly to the soft rise
of her breasts above the towel.

"Obviously, I do," she said with hostility. "And I
can tell you *just* hate it." She slammed the door in his
face.

She had never met a man so full of abrasive gall. If
she had to put up with this all night, she'd be sick—
with indigestion. That is, if she lasted long enough to
get something to eat.

Jennifer dropped the towel to the floor and stood on
it as she began to dress. She sprayed the air with Tatiana, moved into the seductive cloud, let the mist settle
on her body, then massaged it into her skin. Next came
silk stockings with garters, a pair of lacy tap panties,
and a strapless creation of gossamer apricot. Its fitted
bodice gave emphasis to her small waist, and the calf-
length skirt with a handkerchief-point hemline clung
exactly right against her full curved hips.

She shaped her chignon with nimble fingers, and it
was only after she jabbed her scalp unintentionally with
old-fashioned combs that she made an effort at self-
control. The man who was waiting for her on the other
side of the door, and probably still standing there, she
thought, was just as brash tonight as he had been in her
office. Yet there was something about him that intrigued her. She wished she could identify it as she began to apply her makeup.

Her lips were in a grim line when she began to out-
line them with a bronze pencil. The discovery brought
her up short. She wiped away the ragged line and began
again, this time carefully filling in their fullness with
glazed apricot lip gloss, the cosmetic only a shade
deeper than her dress. It took several quick strokes to
highlight her cheeks with cinnabar red, then, almost as
an afterthought, using a sable brush, Jennifer dusted
her shoulders with Eighteen Carat. The effect was dra-

matic. She hesitated to don the matching snug-fitting bolero, deciding to carry it over her arm against the chill of the March evening.

When Jennifer stepped out of the dressing room, she found Merril collapsed comfortably in the nonsagging end of the sofa. He swiveled around to look at her, stood up, then swept her with an all-encompassing glance.

"My, my," he said softly, almost purring. "Who'd you have in there with you—a fairy godmother?"

His reaction couldn't have pleased Jennifer more. "Several, as a matter of fact," she said, and padded into the bedroom for shoes. They added two inches to her five-foot-six-inch frame—hardly enough height to be able to look down her nose at the man, but enough to bring her up to his chin and then some. She put some mad money into a sequined evening bag, as it was in the realm of possibility that she'd need every penny of it to get home.

Jennifer emerged from the bedroom. "I'm ready."

Adrien had switched on a lamp against silvery evening shadows and was browsing through the book of Oriental art. He seemed to have to drag his eyes away to acknowledge her. He stood up slowly.

"Say, exactly what kind of a book is this?" He loved books, even owned some rare volumes, and some of them dealt with sex. What surprised him was to find so graphic a depiction, even if it was art, in Jennifer's apartment.

The thought passed hurriedly through Jennifer's mind that Merril sounded judicious, as though he were a member of the moral majority. "It's a book on Oriental erotic art. But you can see that for yourself. My mother sent it to me."

"Your mother?" His words were soft, but they transmitted his astonishment. His reaction completely unmasked his cynical facade. He looked approachable, human, puzzled. Suddenly, there was an uncommon thread of excitement lurking within Jennifer. She broke into laughter, then walked across the room and took the book from his hands.

"Yes, my mother. It was her way of telling me about the birds and the bees. She included a note warning me that I should not do anything described between its covers." She laid the book aside. "Actually, it's a classic and not designed for prurient interests. Did you find it intriguing?"

"Somewhat," he muttered dryly, ending the discussion. "Give me your key, and I'll lock up." Jennifer passed him the old-fashioned latchkey. He growled an imprecation that a safety pin would do as well or better.

Seconds later she was impressed to find that he had kept a taxi waiting all this time at the top of the cul-de-sac. In it they sat close, arms and thighs touching. Jennifer shivered. The fragrance he wore was easily recognizable—Kouros. Its erotic, seductive scent lulled her, causing a prickle of delicious anticipation to circle her scalp.

After a few minutes of silence that Jennifer could no longer stand, she asked, "Tell me, Mr. Merril, are you in a good mood or a bad mood?"

The sound of her lilting voice made Adrien's heart jump, but his voice registered only amusement. "Good. And call me Adrien. Why do you ask?"

"Because I can't tell, and I thought perhaps you were regretting having asked me out,"—using very effective coercion, too, she admitted silently.

He laughed, a pleasant throaty sound. "No, no regrets. What are you, anyway? A pessimist?"

It was Jennifer's turn to laugh. "A realist—I think."

There was more silence. Jennifer was thinking *Well, where do we go from here?* The ice was broken, yet an uneasiness of manner lodged between them. Each was waiting for the other to volunteer that something personal—that tidbit of information that gave newly made acquaintances a clue on which to build a foundation of friendship—or something more. It did not have to be the spoken word. An acceptance written in body language could be read as easily as bold penmanship on thick paper. Instinctively, Jennifer waited for the indicator, so that when the sign in the middle of the path was met, she would know whether to turn back or to take the wider avenue of exploration.

The taxi skirted Jackson Square, filled with sketch artists, touristy hubbub, gaiety, and pigeons. It came to a halt at the top of a badly lit narrow alley. Adrien stepped out and paid the cab driver. Jennifer followed, then hesitated when he headed into the alley. What did she know about this man? Only that Ellie had said he was a favorite of Mr. Britz's—and that wasn't exactly a recommendation of character.

Adrien noticed her hesitation. "I'm not dragging you into some den of thieves or worse. The dinner club is just there, at the end," he said, pointing to a pair of massive intricately carved doors under a weak yellow light. Jennifer let loose a small sigh.

While she watched where her feet were going Adrien was observing her. There was a freedom in her step, an independent bearing in the way she carried herself, her head slightly forward, as if she were ready to take on the world and twirl it about her head. *Perhaps she's about to take me on,* he thought. The smell of her was intoxicating. He remembered the feel of her beneath the yellow silk she had worn that morning. He stepped closer and took her elbow in an old-fashioned way, just so he could touch her.

As they entered the restaurant through a recessed archway, a white-jacketed maître d' hurried up to them and welcomed Adrien effusively. Jennifer arched an eyebrow but held back a retort about the big tipper and man-about-town image that provoked such behavior in maître d's the world over. "You must come here often," she said instead.

"Not really, only when I'm in New Orleans," he answered politely.

Another conversation dead end. *Three strikes and you're out,* Jennifer told herself.

The club had an atmosphere of rich understated elegance, New Orlean's elite—no tourists. A jazz combo played a soft melody, drawing couples to a small parquet dance floor. Jennifer caught the swirl of a purple hem as it flashed in a pivot under a primrose glow cast by sconces lining the walls. The maître d' led them to a velvet-covered banquette, snapping up the reserved sign as she and Adrien glided into their seats. Once again his thigh was aligned with hers, and this time she became aware of the raw sensual energy he emanated. She crossed her knees to move her leg away from his.

Adrien bent closer, draping an arm along the banquette behind her, touching her bare shoulder lightly with his fingertips. "You always seem to be shifting ten feet away from me. I don't bark or bite...." He paused and whispered sotto voce in her ear, "You think maybe I'm going to swallow you whole? Do I look dangerous?"

Jennifer laughed. Finally, an opening. "No, I don't think that's it. But a few inches is hardly ten feet, and I don't really know what you will or won't do—do I?" *Show me.* She offered up the challenge with a smile that was deliberately provocative. The mood in the restaurant fed her senses. The music rippled sensuously, murmured conversation and muted cutlery were an undertone, and the man next to her was attractive. Also, he had kept his word. They were away from the prying eyes and ears of the Guilbeaux. Relaxing, Jennifer let her guard down. Her gaze met Adrien's, and she felt that inexorable chemistry vibrate between them.

"Give me half a chance—" he began as the sommelier appeared at his elbow. "Ah, Jacques," he greeted the waiter like an old friend. "We won't be dipping into your marvelous wine cellar until our dinner is served. For now, bring the lady a Du Plessis, and for myself, Glenmorangie on the rocks." The sommelier bowed and backed away as though he were leaving the company of royalty. He never spoke a word.

"So. How do you come to be working at the Guilbeaux?" Adrien asked, turning his attention back to Jennifer.

"A friend of mine had an appointment for an interview with Mr. Britz. At the last minute she couldn't make it, so I applied instead."

"I think," he said quietly, "that I shall be forever in debt to this friend."

Jennifer smiled, saw the color of his eyes deepen as he looked at her, and found herself thinking *I like the way his hair curls around his ears.* The sardonic quality of his mouth seemed to have an appeal of its own.

Their drinks were served. "What's this?" she asked, intrigued. A fluffy cream concoction in a long-stemmed glass sent up the aroma of pecans. It tasted of nuts and mint.

"If you were anywhere else but here," he said, waving a hand depreciatingly, indicating their luxurious surroundings, "you'd call it a mudhopper. It's a mixture of praline liqueur, white crème de menthe, and cream. Sometimes it's whipped up with vanilla ice cream, though. Like it?"

"It's good." Their eyes met again over the rim of her glass as she sipped. The chemistry was working overtime, sending tiny sparks of electric current shoot-

ıng through Jennifer. She wondered how he was taking
it. Then she knew. His eyes left her face, traveled
boldly to her bare throat, across her shoulders, until his
gaze rested briefly on the shape of her breasts thrusting
against the apricot fabric. There was no mistaking the
smoldering, intensive look. Jennifer felt a rush of longing. It had been months since a man had looked at her
like that. She corrected herself: since she had *wanted* a
man to look at her like that. *Careful. He's a hotel guest,
remember?* she thought. *You know nothing about him—
whether he's married or not, what sort of a person he is,
what he does for a living. So—ask, instead of sitting here
like a bump on a log.*

But Adrien took the initiative abruptly. "How old are
you?"

"Twenty-five. And you?"

"Thirty-four."

"You look younger."

"So do you."

Oh, God, Jennifer thought. *I wish we could get ten
words going—somewhere!*

"Are you one of those career women?"

She caught the inflection on *those.* "Are you a chau-
vinist?"

He shook his head, frowning. "You seem to have an
answer for everything. Actually, I don't know what
chauvinism is."

You know, all right. But I'll take the bait. Impulsively,
she quipped, "It's a disease. Most men have it in some
form or another. It manifests itself in typically absurd
behavior. You can find it in men who want to dominate
women, men who fear womanhood... men who fear
women—period. And then," she added mischievously,
"there are those men who force women to go out with
them—using blackmail."

Adrien regarded her with a look of astonishment.

"Do you really believe that I'd run tattling to Britz? Why in God's name would I do that?"

"As I said before, how do I know what you'd do? I hardly know you. In fact, I've never even heard your name until this morning, and then it was only to learn you're Ethan Britz's pet."

"His pet!" Adrien exploded with laughter, drawing quick glances from diners at nearby tables. "I'm nobody's pet, unless you want to take me in as a stray?"

"I'll pass," Jennifer said dryly, but she was smiling. "I'm already feeding one decrepit old stray. Two is out of the question."

"This stray—he's the four-legged variety, I hope." Adrien was remembering the book on her coffee table.

"I don't see that it's any of your business, but yes, and he's far more mannerly than the two-legged one I'm sitting next to right this minute." Their legs and thighs were touching. Adrien had been subtly applying pressure and he moved an inch or so away.

"Touché," he said softly as the waiter approached to take their order. At a nod from her, Adrien ordered for them both. While he discussed the menu she observed him from under lowered lashes. He was wearing a creamy beige shirt of tightly woven silk that stretched across his wide shoulders and fit his square torso snugly. He was casual in that he wasn't wearing a tie, even for these opulent surroundings, yet there were gold links in his French cuffs. The open neck of his shirt revealed a matt of dark curling hair. She noted his profile, the slightly off-centered nose, and that somehow, their thighs were touching again.

The sommelier was right behind the waiter and took Adrien's order for *Sauvignon blanc*. Then he bowed away with an imperious nod, still not having spoken. Jennifer raised her lashes to find Adrien smiling at her with unchecked amusement.

"What's the verdict? Will I do?" A seductive note had crept into his voice.

She smiled, flushing slightly. "I didn't mean for you to catch me staring, but since you did, I'll answer. I think you'd do fine as a politician, a ditch digger, and possibly...as a fullback for the New Orlean's Saints. I'd like to know what you really do. What's your meeting at the hotel about? The one I set up?"

Adrien hesitated. Few employees of the Guilbeaux knew he was the sole owner, and the less who knew, the better he liked it. The place was rum-full of bootlickers, and he couldn't stand to have people cowtowing to him. It was too interruptive. He did all of his business through Britz and the executive office. Later perhaps, he might mention casually that he owned the hotel. "I hope to sell a herd of cattle to a rancher in South America. I've asked a few men I know who have dealt with foreign sales and know the ropes—shipping procedures, costs, quarantine, things like that—to meet with me. It'd be a lot easier and cheaper to ship just semen, but the rancher isn't set up for that kind of an operation," he said, warming to his subject.

Jennifer nearly choked. "Semen?"

"Yes, what we do—"

"Mr. Merril, could we dance?" she asked, almost soundlessly, quickly.

Adrien had been seeing the Ballesta operation in his mind. Jennifer's interruption jolted him back to the restaurant. He focused on her and laughed. He understood her discomfiture immediately. "We can," he said, getting up and holding out his hand to her. The combo put out a haunting rhythm, the trumpet player blowing soft, sensual notes of laid-back jazz. Jennifer's pulse quickened and throbbed to the beat of the music.

Adrien was a skilled dancer, and once their feet seemed to move of their own accord, he held her, leaving a few modest inches between them—enough that he could look at her in the dim light. "Now, if you don't mind," he murmured, "tell me where you've been living, where you grew up, who loves you"—his hand tightened at her waist—"just since you came to earth."

Puzzled, Jennifer laughed softly. "Earth?"

"Yes," he said, watching her face. "Aren't you a dryad guarding some magical forest?"

Jennifer felt a marauding thrill. He liked her. Her brain was sending out signals, a warning, but she was intrigued, curious about a man who made her feel far more like a woman than she ever had, yet he had barely touched her—until now. Their knees touched, their thighs; her breasts swelled inside the apricot gauze, brushing his chest. "Oh, I'm from an island we earthlings call Manhattan," she said, swaying against him. He held her there and he wasn't granite at all, she discovered. He was warm solid flesh, rippling with sensations. She wondered if she was imagining it all.

He bent his lips to her ear. "Who loves you?" he queried again softly.

"Besides my parents, you mean?" she said against the solid cords of his neck. She wished they could stop dancing and stand still, so she could lock her knees. Her legs felt weak.

"Especially besides your parents." His lips were now at her temple. Jennifer's body was vibrantly alive with erotic sensations as his contours melded with hers. While the music swirled around them his hand moved up to caress her velvety bare skin above the low-cut bodice. The nerves along her spine tingled, sending an evocative message racing through her veins. Somewhere from deep inside she dredged up the words to answer him. "Lots of people," she murmured.

With her eyes closed, her head nestling at his chin,

Jennifer's lips rested against the open collar that exposed the taut cords in Adrien's neck. She wanted more; she wanted to feel his skin against her lips. She moved her head to inside his collar and pressed a soft and lingering kiss near his collarbone. Beneath her lips the vein in his neck pulsed.

His fingers stopped stroking her back suddenly and slid to her shoulders. He pushed her away, but not to such a distance that other couples on the dance floor noticed, or were impeded, but so their bodies did not touch.

Jennifer looked into Adrien's face, shocked to see his eyes were no longer smoldering. They were ice-brittle. In the low light his features were shadowy, yet there was no escaping the sharp angular chin, the broad cheeks, his face, entirely devoid of expression. His body had been full of passion. She wasn't guessing. She had *felt* it! Confusion rippled across her face.

"Let's get back to our table," he said.

In their absence the wine and salads had been served. Adrien submerged himself in the task of pouring wine, passing the salt. He didn't look at her. Jennifer knew she was being rebuffed, and she got angry.

"Look, I don't know what went wrong out there." She nodded toward the bandstand. "Things might have gotten just a little out of hand, what with the music—"

"You haven't done anything to go to confession about," he snapped.

"Me? Mr. Merril, in case your mind has instant erase, I'll remind you that we were a duet."

He looked directly at her. *Mon Dieu,* he thought, *but she is magnificent!* Her eyes were flashing gold; even angry and confused, her voice was modulated and soft. "I asked you to call me Adrien, yet you persist in Mr. Merril. Why is that?"

"What difference does it make? You'll just be Mr. Merril again tomorrow at the hotel." She shrugged into her bolero and picked up her purse. "I'm leaving. Will you walk me to the door? It might save you some embarrassment."

His fingers curved over her wrist. "Keep your seat. Just forget it. Maybe I made a mistake."

"Oh? Is that a declaration that's supposed to be shot around the world on a rocket?"

Adrien sighed. "Just tell me one thing: Are you here just to protect your job? Or do you like me?"

"If you're inferring—"

"I'm *asking.*"

"Exactly what are you asking?" Jennifer said quietly.

"I want to know if you kissed me out there on the dance floor because you thought you had to, to keep your job."

Jennifer thought about it. "The answer is no. And I could've figured out a way not to have dinner with you, too."

"That answers my question—fully. Now, let's eat."

"Sorry, but I'm not hungry." There was a quiet finality about her words. She rose slightly, preparing to leave.

Adrien knew he had blundered. "Wait!" He uttered the words with a kind of careless desperation. "I haven't had a real date in more than two years. I've forgotten how to act." Jennifer hesitated, then laid her purse aside. Of all the hundreds, thousands, millions, of words to choose, he had picked exactly the right ones. And if his words stopped Jennifer, they shocked Adrien himself. Somehow they just slipped past his hidden inner core and shot out. He shook his head as if to clear it of the incredible.

The next few minutes were filled with awkward

pauses; jerky little sentences, and false starts and stops like hunters trying to find the right footpath in a forest cut with a hundred trails. Warily, Jennifer maintained one of those silences that people always feel they have to fill up with chatter. Adrien succumbed. He did not mention Eleanor or his ownership of the Guilbeaux Hotel, explaining away his lack of social life because he had been so involved in work on the ranch and cattle breeding program to the extent that he had had no time for outside interests. By the time impressive bowls of lobster bisque were set before them, prepared as only a New Orlean's chef could, conversation was smoother. The ease with which Adrien found himself talking to Jennifer astonished him.

After their sumptuous dinner they sipped on Drambuie, an ancient and delicately flavored liqueur of Scotch distilled in honey. Adrien's voice was like a palliative, and as they left the restaurant Jennifer knew with that earthy instinct Nell so hoped would never surface that there was something about this man that was linked indelibly with her future. She was impatient. She wanted that future link *now*, in the present, where it was possible to grasp.

"Adrien," she said with deliberate softness, using his given name for the first time and liking the way it sounded on her tongue. "If my motive for having dinner with you tonight is still in doubt, you could always ask me out again and see what my answer would be."

"It's something to think about," he murmured, giving her a half smile but no invitation. At the back of his mind was the promise he had made to himself. He wasn't about to act the fool over a woman a second time.

Jennifer looked at him out of the coolest corner of her eye. Her antennae were swirling. She had given Merril the perfect opening to ask her out again, and he had brushed it off like a minor inconvenience. "Well, don't think too hard," she told him sarcastically.

"No strain at all," he retorted, appraising her as he might a newborn calf with championship lines. "Let's walk," he insisted when they emerged into the street from the alley. He took her hand, guiding her along the narrow walk teeming with pedestrians. The crowds were normal, but nothing compared to the masses during Mardi Gras or like they would be again in a few weeks time for the New Orleans jazz and heritage festival.

Jennifer fumed, hardly noticing as they passed the market sheds nestled against the river, darkened now, many of the stalls covered with sheets and canvas to protect mounds of fruits, vegetables, and an array of used merchandise. For more than a century the buildings had served as a sorting and selling place for flowers, fruits, spices, tobacco, and food. The scents of chicory, anise, and clove were locked into the wooden rafters, sharing air with the damp, musky smell of the Mississippi as it flowed past toward the Gulf of Mexico.

"You lied to me," she announced, appalled at her forwardness as the words tumbled out. They were deep inside the French Quarter now, where the very air reverberated with jazz pouring from open doors and sidewalk cafés. Tourists, fascinated by sidewalk barkers, shouldered one another in an effort to press closer to entrances held open by doormen and bouncers offering an enticing preview of strip shows or female impersonators. In past visits to the Quarter, Jennifer would have been just as eager as tourists for that titillating, teasing view, but now Adrien occupied her whole mind. He stopped short, jerking her around to face him.

"I don't take kindly to being called a liar," he said harshly, "so explain."

"You do wish you hadn't asked me to dinner."

He sighed. "I regret a lot of things in my life, but tonight is not one of them." His eyes appeared black and intense as he looked at her. "I think I sense the problem here. You expected me to fall all over you, push myself on you—the first-date ritual. What's the matter? Are you disappointed that you haven't had the opportunity to give me that coy little slap on the wrist?" He sounded more and more cynical. "Something tells me you've never been out with a gentleman."

"Oh? Am I out with one now?" She jerked her arm free, pivoting to look for a taxi. There was none in sight. This area of the Quarter was closed off to vehicular traffic at night. Seemingly undaunted by her caustic remark, Adrien slipped his arm inside hers, locking it to his side.

"The end of a perfect evening," he twitted. "C'mon, I'll find us a cab and get you home. My day will start early tomorrow and so will yours. We need to be in bed." Jennifer cut him a scathing look. "Sorry if I said a nasty word—separate beds, obviously. I wouldn't want to ruin the perfect impression you have of me by suggesting something as droll as us sleeping together."

"You're so thoughtful," Jennifer said scornfully, noticing the cynical curl to his lip.

Adrien seemed immune to her digs. He laughed. "Something tells me we're headed for a love-hate relationship."

Love-hate, Jennifer thought. What in the world did he mean by that? Two blocks past Bourbon Street he hailed a cab, and as they settled against the seat he made no effort to touch her. It had been a curious evening—all ups and downs like a pogo stick—but what now? Would he demand a good-night kiss? Would he insist on coming in for coffee? Make himself comfortable on her sofa? Loosen his tie? He wasn't wearing a tie. Jennifer let that thought slide.

As the taxi drew up to the cul-de-sac Adrien asked the cab driver to wait. So much for coffee, Jennifer thought. That only left... Adrien unlocked her door, handed her the key, guided her firmly inside, then pulled the door closed between them. Jennifer felt a stab of keen disappointment. Her emotions had run the gamut today, being jumbled like a ball of string unraveled by a playful kitten. In spite of everything, she had wanted to be kissed, expected to be kissed, anticipated it even. Damn!

"Lock the door," Adrien commanded, waiting on the porch until he heard the latch turn. He took a few steps, stopped, then backtracked and rapped softly on the door. "Jennifer? Are you there?"

"Yes," she said, pressing her ear to the door, listening, her breath hung up somewhere between her heart and her throat.

"You're wrong, you know, about pegging yourself a realist. You're a romantic—a very perverse romantic."

She heard him chuckling as his footsteps died away. There was an insistent notion in the back of her mind that something remarkable had just happened. The thought plagued her until she drifted into sleep.

Chapter Five

The following morning Jennifer awoke far earlier than usual to find dark clouds scudding eastward across the sky. Harry's prediction that the rains would be leaving the bayou country for New Orleans was on target.

Rushing through dressing, she threw on an ivory silk blouse, tied the jabot haphazardly, added a plain-tailored but well-fitting taupe suit, and spent less than a minute with her cosmetics, highlighting her cheeks with blush and her lips with dusky rose. With the ritual of habit her fingers nimbly formed her chignon—smooth, elegant, and the perfect complement to her heart-shaped face. Jennifer was early to work. Adrien drew her to the hotel like a magnet.

The first drops of rain were spattering on the sidewalk as she entered the lobby and hurried through without even sweeping it with her habitual speculative glance. In the office they shared, Ellie was putting on the starched white smock she wore when she had to work as cashier in the coffee shop.

"Jennifer! Good grief," she exclaimed, glancing at the wall clock, "you're more than an hour early. Something go wrong?"

"No, nothing, it was just one of those mornings—I couldn't sleep. Might as well be at work as lying around the apartment. Besides, I wanted to make sure the Merril function went off without a hitch." She slipped off her suit jacket, hung it on the back of a chair, and sat down, flipping through the files on her desk.

Ellie watched her with interest for a moment. "The Merril file is the one right on top... it has that red VIP label."

"Oh, so it is. Thanks. I just overlooked it." Jennifer glanced up and smiled. Ellie gave her a wide grin and snorted.

"So. How was your date last night?"

Jennifer dropped her eyes, assuming exceptional interest in the file. "Nothing spectacular."

Ellie sensed the snub. "I see. You're telling me that our Mr. Merril didn't bowl you over? Our Mr. Merril, whom you referred to yesterday as the original wolf? I suppose last night you were Little Red Ridinghood and put the beast in his place?"

"Adrien Merril was a perfect gentleman and not the least bit distracting, so stop all your little innuendos," replied Jennifer huffily.

Smiling wickedly, Ellie walked over to Jennifer and leaned her hands on the desk. "Not distracting, eh? Then, why couldn't you sleep? Why are you here an hour early? And—why is your blouse on inside out? Or is this just something else you overlooked?" she drawled, cackling like a triumphant old hen.

Looking down, Jennifer saw the tiny, telltale inner seams at her shoulders and again at the cuffs on her wrists. "Damn!" she muttered.

Still laughing, Ellie went on. "After you've got yourself put together, and after you've checked on Mr. Britz's pet, we have a staff meeting this morning at nine. The memo is on your desk. Better have your projections on line and know to the penny how much your department has spent and made. The word is around that we'll be having a gritty financial set-to; our elegant new comptroller is going to tell us all how not to spend money."

"Are things that bad? Isn't the hotel making money?"

Ellie shrugged, dropping her cigarettes into the smock's over-size pocket. "I don't know. We should be, but maybe inflation is cutting into profits, who knows?"

"Well, inflation is eating into my pocket," Jennifer said. "So I hope Britz and finance don't come off with any excuses about our raises." Jennifer was thinking about her weekly take-home pay of two hundred and twelve dollars. She had refused all offers of cash from her parents in her bid for independence, and her budget was stretched to the limit like a worn-out rubber band.

Ellie stopped in the office entrance, looking back over her shoulder. "That's what I like most about you, Jennifer . . . you're always so optimistic. It's therapeutic, and so very, very naive in this business."

Jennifer grinned. "Stupid, you mean?"

"It's amazing how fast you catch on." Ellie snorted and added a derisive hiss. "You'll end up owning this place one day." With a wave of her cigarette she was gone.

The staff meeting was being held on the mezzanine in the board room that adjoined the executive offices. When Jennifer arrived, she was surprised to find that she was almost the last to get there. Only Britz, and Milton Richards, the hotel comptroller over finance, were absent. A dozen or more department heads were milling around the sixteen-foot meeting table, and an undertone of grumbling and discontent filled the air.

Jennifer joined the chief engineer, Al Albert, at the coffee trolley. He was a quiet man, not easily ruffled, not easily impressed. Al ran his repair and maintenance department with the finesse of a well-oiled machine. He had a bald head, craggy features, and bushy gray eyebrows that compensated for lack of hair above his brow, and as usual he was chewing on the stubb of a dead cigar. His tan overalls were precisely pressed and pushed against the buttons pulled taut across his belly. Jennifer touched him lightly on his arm. "Al, thanks for getting to the dumbwaiter so quickly. It really pulled me out of a bind. If we'd had to compete with house-keeping for the service elevator this morning, I'd never have gotten an important breakfast meeting off the ground."

Al grunted. "We spliced a few chain links, but the damn thing is worn out, so don't overload it," he said gruffly, yet pleased with the thank-you. Jennifer always took time to let him know she appreciated the work he did for her department. Everyone else just took him for granted, screaming their heads off if he couldn't affect instant repairs. "What's going on here this morning? You know?"

She shrugged. "You probably know as much as I do. It's about money, or lack of it—"

"Jennifer! Where've you been keeping yourself? I haven't seen you for a month." The nasal voice, and the spidery, vein-prominent hand on Jennifer's waist belonged to Myrtle Best, chief telephone operator. She was a small birdlike woman, topped with spikey white hair, her face a map of wrinkles that led to a scrawny neck and disappeared into the Peter Pan collar of her blouse. When Myrtle smiled, as she was doing now, the wrinkles changed course like a hundred miniature creeks exploding from mother river with no place to lose themselves except beneath the round white collar.

"Behind my desk and out of the telephone room,"

Jennifer teased. "Or don't you remember...you chased me out."

"Whew! Don't remind me, girl." Myrtle turned to Al. "Jennifer could get into *The Guiness Book* with the most disconnects in two hours flat. It was the only time I've ever wished the hotel would burn down around me." She smiled fondly at Jennifer, and the creeks along her jawline took off. "I like you, I just don't want you anywhere near my switchboard. Let's have coffee."

Al moved in the direction of his archenemy, Mrs. Stacy, the executive housekeeper, who hounded him to keep the wheels on her linen carts in working order. Better a well-known foe than the unknown, he thought uncomfortably. Myrtle tugged Jennifer around the coffee service.

"Want to hear the latest?" she asked, lowering her voice to a whisper.

"Is this straight from the telephone wires, or just gossip you've heard?" Jennifer teased.

Myrtle made a face that caused her wrinkles to back up and change direction. "I don't listen in on phone conversations," she said loftily. "Well...hardly ever. Eva Wilcox and our new man at the gate are a number."

"What new man?"

"Richards. Richards, the financial wizard," Myrtle expounded.

Jennifer was skeptical. "He's not new, he's been here six months, and besides, what would he see in Wilcox? She's frozen."

"Hah! Ever hear of hidden fires?" Myrtle asked, sotto voce.

"I thought he was married." Jennifer sipped her coffee, paying only polite attention now to Myrtle. She couldn't give credence to such a wild rumor. Wilcox was too prim in her uppish way to have an affair with anybody. She only loved herself.

"Aren't they all?" Myrtle sputtered. "Speaking of the devils, here they come. We'd better find a seat."

Britz and Wilcox filed in, followed by Milton Richards. Wilcox took a chair to the left of Britz so she could take notes. Richards pulled up a chair and, with the approval of Britz, shared the head of the table. The comptroller had that look about him that every successful accountant strives for: *See how well I manage my money? I can do that for you.* He wore Brioni suits from Italy, Princess Mara ties, Gucci lace-ups, tailored shirts from London's Savile Row, and he had a habit of shooting his French cuffs so that you managed to glimpse their discreet monogram. Jennifer thought him attractive, but suave. She had spoken to him once or twice only, her business with finance taking her no farther into that office than the first two desks: Accounts Receivable and Accounts Payable. She seldom had reason to wander any deeper into the maze of glassed-in cages behind which Milton Richards held court. Mr. Britz tapped on a water glass for attention, and the room fell silent.

"I'll get right to the point, folks. We are in a financial crisis. The profits in the Guilbeaux over the past year have fallen drastically." There was a ground swell of murmuring and grumbling around the table. Britz held up his hand for quiet, his brows knitting together in a frown. "I know you've all been doing your best, but the cost of food, linen, wages, the devaluation of the dollar, and the general overall sad economic picture have pushed us to the wall. Milton, here, whom you all know, has put together a plan to keep us afloat...not only that," Britz said with a condescending smile on his thin lips, "it's a plan that will put us above the crest, so to speak. His plan has my approval and that of the owners." This last statement Jennifer took to be a warning that upper management would tolerate no fractious back room maneuvers that might throw a monkey wrench into the plan. Britz sat down, leaned back, folded his hands over his double-breasted paunch, and nodded to the comptroller.

Richards unfolded himself with the grace and smoothness of a male model preparing to walk down the runway. He shot his cuffs, unbuttoned his jacket, parked one hand on a hip that was enclosed in a thin alligator belt, and with the other picked up a pencil, staring at it for a moment before he lifted his eyes and casually moved his gaze around the room. A marvelous technique for grabbing and holding attention, Jennifer mused. Her mother taught that very same dramatic pose to her students. The man was an actor, but she couldn't fault him for that.

"The first thing," he said in a low sonorous voice, "is that we are going to watch our cash flow very carefully. This means all petty cash vouchers will go to the executive office for approval first, then to me in finance—"

Al Alberts leaned forward, interrupting. "You mean petty cash for over a hundred dollars, don't you?"

"No, chief, I mean *all* expenditures... all requests for cash...." His eyes narrowed and looked intently at those in the room. "And I expect there to be damn few of those. You must anticipate your needs for your departments, and send all orders for purchases to our purchaser. That is why he's in the storeroom.... He'll buy what you need at far greater savings than you can, by buying in bulk. That goes for linens, soaps, what have you." He looked directly at Mrs. Stacy, who squirmed, trying to make herself invisible. Richards looked down at a folder on the table, flipped a page, read for ten seconds, then looked up—at Jennifer. She felt a weak-

ness wash over her, a tiny trembling of fear. Why was
he zeroing in on her? she wondered. Catering was in
order, she saw to that, and she seldom used a petty cash
voucher. Everything she bought or rented for her department was billed directly to the hotel and paid by
accounting. Jennifer caught sight of Wilcox out of the
corner of her eye. The executive secretary was smirk-
ing. *Oh, ho, so you're behind this,* Jennifer thought.
That put the steel into her backbone. She met Richard's gaze with her own.

"Miss DeWitt, there is an expenditure in your department for Allbritton's Florist...two thousand dollars just in February alone. Could you explain this,
please?"

"Yes...yes. When customers desire flowers or deco-
rations for functions, we order them from the florist,
then add the cost to their function bill. The flowers in
February were for two wedding receptions and the
East-West New Orleans Bridge Tournament banquet."

"I see...and do you use Allbritton's exclusively?"

"Yes. It was established practice before I started
here, and they've always come through, even on short
notice."

"Hmm, and what does Allbritton's pay us for this
piece of exclusive business?"

"Why...nothing. Are they supposed to?"

"I should think we'd be getting up to a twenty percent discount on each order. Taking exclusive orders
for flowers makes you their agent. Also, this procedure
means that we are paying out *our* cash while waiting for
the customer to pay us. Please discuss the situation
with Allbritton's. If they want the Guilbeaux's exclusive business, they should be willing to compensate us,
and in the future ask them to bill their customers directly. This hotel will no longer be responsible for
flower orders. Now...."

Jennifer no longer listened as Richard's voice droned on and on, tearing at each department. In a way she was glad that he had gotten to her early in the meeting. At least it was over and she knew what was expected of her, though she dreaded calling Betty, who took all the hotel's orders at Allbritton's.

As the meeting wore into the late morning, nearing noon, Jennifer became nervous. She wanted to get out of there and check on the Merril luncheon, in addition she had appointments with two prospective customers in the afternoon. The minutes seemed to crawl by with the image of Adrien's face and the feeling he aroused in her seeping into her consciousness. She had not seen him this morning, only heard his voice as he addressed the group he had brought together, and Vinnie was managing nicely without his usual garrulousness. Just the same, the lunch break was the perfect time for her to enter the meeting room unobtrusively, get a glimpse of Adrien, perhaps even have the opportunity to speak to him—on a professional basis, of course. It wouldn't do to hint of *anything* personal. *Oh, why*, she thought, *didn't I just behave myself last night, instead of being too huffy, taking everything he said the wrong way?*

She was jerked out of her musing by Milton Richards's voice. "Yes, Miss DeWitt? Was there something you wanted to say?"

She glanced around the room to find that only she, Richards, and Wilcox remained. My God! she thought. The meeting had broken up and she had been a million miles away. She covered herself quickly.

"Uh, well…perhaps I do have a question or two, but I think I'll hold them until I do a bit more research in my department." She smiled at him, including Wilcox in an offhand way. But Wilcox had eyes only for the comptroller. Perhaps there was fire behind the smoke in Myrtle's gossip after all.

"I like your attitude," Richards answered, and Jennifer was struck again by how smooth the man was; too smooth, too suave, too picture perfect. She was too fault prone herself to freely take to someone who espoused such perfection, but she didn't actively dislike the man. He was, she surmised, just doing his job. Richards continued, saying "I only hope the rest of our department heads are as cooperative."

Wilcox stepped in between Jennifer and Richards, bringing the exchange effectively to an end. The look she conveyed on Jennifer could only be matched by that of a pregnant cobra.

Jennifer said thank you, made polite excuses, and left, promising herself to keep out of the comptroller's way. Wilcox had him marked for her exclusive territory. The poor man, Jennifer thought with a shade of sympathy.

Ten minutes later she found Vinnie in the service room that housed the employee elevator and dumbwaiter. He was verbally coaxing the straining dumbwaiter up from the kitchen. "Don't know how long this dang thing is going to hold up," he said glumly upon seeing Jennifer. He shoved open the door and looked down the shaft. The chain-link cables were vibrating, but moving. He sighed. "Finally..."

"How's everything going, Vinnie? Any complaints?"

"Not so far, but I'm thinking I ought to just use the elevator tonight for their dinner, or maybe you could get them to move down to the dining room? There's only six of 'em."

"No way. Mr. Merril expressly asked for the Carnival Room and privacy, but I agree. Go with the elevator tonight. I'll just go have a word with Mr. Merril. Call me in my office if there's even the slightest whiff of trouble."

"Will do," he agreed, turning back to the dumbwaiter, his ancient shoulders bony against the fabric of his waiter's jacket.

Vinnie's a walking historical monument, Jennifer thought as she made her way down the carpeted corridor to the meeting rooms. She wondered vaguely how long before Richards's plan included pensioning the old-timers off—it was bound to come. It was a sad thought.

In the Carnival Room the small group of men were shuffling around, stretching, moving to get blood circulating again. After her own meeting, Jennifer knew just how they felt. The room was filled with smoke, ashtrays overflowing. She stopped just inside the door, caught Adrien's eye, and smiled. He returned it with an impersonal one of his own, so brief, it barely revealed the tips of his strong white teeth, then his attention went back to the man he had been conversing with. Jennifer moved about the room, cleaning ashtrays, removing used cups, straightening table linen, noticing to her dismay that the starched white surfaces had been used as note pads. Columns of figures crisscrossed the slick cloth. Damn! Mrs. Stacy would call her, complaining about that, she knew. She moved as close to Adrien as she dared. For all the attention he gave her, she might as well not have existed. When Vinnie marched in with the luncheon trolley, she had no excuse to linger. She looked back over her shoulder as she left to find Adrien watching her. Was it her imagination that he seemed a little disappointed? Maybe she should have approached him, spoken to him.

In her office a delegation of three women were waiting to see her. Ellie made the introductions.

"These ladies are Mrs. Smithe, Miss Combel, and Mrs. Garrett. They want to plan a luncheon. Ladies," she said, turning to Jennifer, "this is Miss DeWitt, our catering manager. She can make all your arrangements." With that Ellie stubbed out her cigarette and left for the coffee shop.

"Miss DeWitt," Mrs. Smithe began, "we're school-teachers and we want to provide a luncheon—a private luncheon, because we wish to serve liquor." Mrs. Smithe blushed below her blue-gray hair. "It's for the secretary at our school. She's leaving us to get married." Mrs. Smithe blushed again while the other two women sat silently but nodded their heads in agreement.

Jennifer gathered the details—fifteen guests including the honoree, with the function on a Saturday—then she began suggesting menus. The women kept shaking their heads no at each offering. Everything was too expensive. Finally, she offered; "What about roast beef, string beans with almonds, baked stuffed tomatoes, hot bread and champagne cocktails?"

Mrs. Smithe looked dismayed. "But...well...don't you have anything we can afford that sounds just a little more exciting?"

Jennifer thought a minute. "Well, what about *rôti de boeuf, haricots avec amandes, tomates farcies au four,* and *pain chaud?*" she asked in her best textbook French.

"Oh, yes," they all three chirped. "That sounds perfect."

Jennifer smiled and wrote on the form in front of her: roast beef, string beans with almonds, baked stuffed tomatoes, and hot bread. Then she wrote out a copy in French for Mrs. Smithe. The ladies left, chatting happily among themselves.

Jennifer forced herself to work in her office for two more hours. She brought the banquet book up to date, costed out some menus for a civic group that planned a meeting the following week, and reluctantly made the call to Betty at Allbritton's Florist. To her surprise Betty was sympathetic and also business wise.

"Ahhh, Jennifer, don't take it so to heart. Frankly, we've been expecting this. We've been wondering when Britz would wise up. Listen, tell your friend Richards we give a fifteen percent kickback for exclusives and not a dime more."

"A kickback. Is that what you call it? Isn't that illegal?"

"Naw. Grow up. You're in the big league now."

"Fancy that," Jennifer said, laughing with relief, and hung up.

The remainder of the day flew by. She met with the two appointments that had been scheduled and gave them a tour of the hotel. "We've been on this very site since 1840.... There are four hundred twenty rooms in three wings with penthouse suites on the eighth floor that overlook the French Market, the Mississippi River, and historical St. Charles Street.... We offer butler-maid service from seven in the morning until eight at night—just pick up the telephone, no extra charge.... This is our grand ballroom. It can handle six hundred for cocktails or three hundred fifty for a sit-down meal. It has its own built-in stage. The chandeliers are Italian, and before the hotel was wired for electricity it took nine hundred candles to light the room...." Jennifer knew the tour by rote, and, to keep it from being boring, introduced the potential conventioneers to Petri, the executive chef, and to Henri, the sous chef, who flirted charmingly and demonstrated his ice-carving skills. And before their attention began to lag, she led them into the Pirate's Cove for cocktails, where they met with James Buford, Sales Director, who completed the sales pitch. If they decided to bring their meeting to the Guilbeaux, Jennifer would meet with them once again to plan menus, etc.

She had a late afternoon lunch in the coffee shop, hardly noticing what she ate. Every spare moment her mind was crowded with thoughts of Adrien Merril. If only last night hadn't turned into a sparring match. He piqued her interest, and there didn't seem to be anything she could do about it. All day long she kept telling herself she didn't want to get involved, and when by six o'clock Adrien had made no effort to contact her, she decided the attraction was one-sided. She went into the service kitchen to inspect the dinner preparation for Adrien's supper. Petri glowered at her for being so forward to question his ability.

"You may not know it, but I've been cooking since before you were born. I think I can still manage a few dozen oysters Rockefeller, and broil a steak or two," he sputtered with indignation. Jennifer smiled weakly and retreated as he began tossing raw meat onto an open grill.

For once there was nothing for her to do, no last-minute details to handle, no emergency to unravel. She went back to her office, put on her jacket, tucked her purse under her arm, and locked the door. Ellie had gone home at five. Jennifer paused at the elevator.

It wouldn't hurt, would it, to just walk past the Carnival Room? After all, she was the catering manager. Everything might be going well as of ten minutes ago, but one could never tell. Vinnie was old. He might need some help. Yes, she'd better check one last time. She walked around to the south wing, stood outside the door, and listened, trying to drum up the courage to breeze into the room effortlessly as she would if it were any other function that she had booked. All she wanted was a glimpse of Adrien Merril, the opportunity to offer him a smile and remind him that she existed.

At the end of the hall the elevator hummed and came to a stop. Wilcox emerged. Jennifer's stomach fluttered. With the whirl of activity today she had forgotten that Wilcox was bird-dogging her at Britz's insistence—or was it? she thought. Wilcox was coming toward her with a kind of grim determination. She braced herself for the encounter.

"I'm so glad I caught you," the secretary erupted in such a syrupy voice that Jennifer was instantly wary. "Is there any problem with Mr. Merril's meeting and food service?" she said in a hopeful tone of voice. She looked Jennifer up and down and sniffed loftily.

"Just fine and going smoothly. No complaints."

"Mr. Britz thinks the world of Mr. Merril, you know."

"Yes, you mentioned that before." They stood staring at one another for a moment in an uneasy silence. Jennifer wished Wilcox would leave. She put her hand on the doorknob. "I was just going in to check with Mr. Merril one last time before I go home."

"Oh, that won't be necessary. I have a message for him from Mr. Britz. If there are any problems, I'll see to them."

Jennifer was dismissed. She hesitated. Wilcox was usurping her job. Stay cool, she ordered herself. Let it go. "In that case..." Jennifer managed a smile and turned to leave.

"Oh, Jennifer," Wilcox called her back softly. "There's been a little talk, you know." She touched Jennifer lightly on her arm. "This is another of your designer suits, isn't it? A few people are wondering where all your money comes from.... You haven't been visiting the guests' rooms, have you?" Wilcox gave a conspiratorial little laugh designed to grind the insult in deeper.

For a heartbeat Jennifer didn't comprehend the dig, and she had expected Wilcox to blurt out something about herself and Adrien.

"You do dress far above your salary...." Wilcox added, then let her voice trail off.

The innuendo was unmistakable. Mr. Britz demanded that the women who worked at the Guilbeaux maintain a pristine reputation, but Jennifer knew, as did everyone else, that the bell captain was often prevailed upon to provide an attractive woman for entertainment to certain guests. As long as these attractive women were not on his staff, Mr. Britz pretended the situation did not exist. Jennifer scarcely noticed the gleam of triumph that flickered in Wilcox's eyes as her anger boiled up.

"Eva Wilcox, that is an uncalled-for slur. This suit, and most of my clothes, for that matter, happen to be left over from my college days." She snatched her arm out from under Wilcox's slender fingers. "I won't tolerate you attaching any slanderous remarks to my name—you're the only one who's doing any talking. I'll tell you something... if you want to play rough, two can have a go at your little game. Come to think of it... there *has* been some talk—about you and our illustrious chief accountant. He's a married man. Suppose *that* got back to Britz? Who do you think he'd let go? You, or the miracle worker who's supposed to put us back on the financial road to success?"

Wilcox paled. "I'll get you for this," she whispered as Jennifer turned and stalked off down the hall. Sensing the secretary's malevolent gaze on her back, Jennifer hurried out of sight, taking the stairs instead of waiting for the elevator.

All the alarms were going off in Jennifer's head. A bad mistake, she reflected as she made her way to the front of the hotel and waited for Harry to whistle her up a taxi. The rain was only a fine drizzle now, and it matched her mood. Could people feel drizzly? Gray? she asked herself. Settled in the back of the cab, Jennifer chastised herself for letting Wilcox push her to the edge like that. The funny part about the entire exchange was that the "working" girls who hung around the Cove were polite, well mannered, and, Jennifer had to agree, exquisitely dressed. What was it about sex that made everyone want to label it? The self-righteous, moralistic attitude that Wilcox espoused while sleeping around with the finance director on the sly angered Jennifer as much as Wilcox's innuendo.

At home, her anger was slow to dissipate. She ate a cottage cheese salad, made herself a cup of tea, took a bath, pushed Wilcox out of her mind, and let a vision of Adrien take its place. She remembered the way his hair curled around his ears and lay on his strong neck, the shape of his fingers, the feel of him against her on the dance floor. She sat by the telephone, willing it to ring. She wove a dozen romantic fantasies about Adrien, then remembered that he hadn't mentioned a woman—not a mother, a sister, an aunt, or a wife. She began to feel depressed.

Jennifer left her vigil by the telephone to open the door to Miss Pennyforth. For a single heart-stopping instant she imagined Adrien Merril on the other side of the door. Common sense told her otherwise. Only her landlady ever came to the inside entrance that led to the rest of the house.

"Rent due," Miss Pennyforth chimed, shuffling into the apartment. She was as shabbily elegant as her house. She wore light blue gabardine dresses in the summer and black in the winter, with detachable white collars trimmed in hand-tatted lace. On one end of her stout body she wore her gray hair in tight precise curls, and on the other, brown cotton stockings rolled down to her ankles. Jennifer had never seen her in any other footwear than heelless carpet slippers. She shuffled farther into the apartment while Jennifer counted out the two-hundred-and-ten-dollar rent.

"I can't ever get over how you made this old barn of a room look so cozy, Jennifer. It never looked this good when Papa was alive...."

"Of course, everything just wore out on us. We lost all our money in the stock market crash, you know." Jennifer sounded the ritual comment in her head in unison with Miss Pennyforth's apologetic air. Miss Pennyforth was consistent if nothing else. Jennifer smiled as she handed over the rent.

"Here you go, Miss Pennyforth. Sorry I'm a day late."

"That's okay. I never worry about you paying." She folded the money and tucked it into one of her voluminous pockets. Jennifer sighed as the money disappeared. Rent week always left her with two dollars out of her paycheck.

"Uh... Jennifer, I hate to do this, but what with utilities going up again and all, I'm going to have to raise your rent. Not much," she said quickly upon seeing the look of dismay on Jennifer's face. "Maybe if you used a fan instead of that air conditioner—"

"Miss Pennyforth, I couldn't live without that air conditioner."

"I know, I know. You northerners do complain about our weather so. But you would get used to it. If—"

"How much more, Miss Pennyforth?" Jennifer asked, dreading the answer. The old woman lived in a world all her own, the traditions of the South her bedrock. Northerners to her were all carpetbaggers, but she had taken Jennifer as a tenant because Jennifer worked at the Guilbeaux, where she and her father had gone for brunch after church every Sunday before the old man died. Miss Pennyforth had not set foot in the Guilbeaux in twenty years.

"Well... I was thinking—fifteen dollars?"

Jennifer sighed. "I can manage that. Did you want it this month?"

"Do you have it? If it wouldn't put you on hard times—"

Jennifer excused herself, went into her bedroom, and out of her drawer drew out the small cache she always put aside to see her through rent week. She was beginning to become disenchanted with independence. Freedom was expensive. Now, if a man like Adrien Merril wanted to take care of her... Jennifer's head snapped erect. What in the world was she thinking of? She could take care of herself. An increase in rent was just a little setback. She'd just have to learn to be more conservative with her cash, that's all. Besides, hadn't her mother always said when a man holds the purse, a woman's freedom is only as long as the purse strings? Nell, though, Jennifer realized, had developed other, just as effective means to curtail freedom, a possessiveness that only stretched as far as the umbilical cord. Jennifer felt she had cut that and she wasn't about to trade it for another kind, no matter how well camouflaged. She returned to the living room and gave Miss Pennyforth the additional fifteen dollars.

"Thank you, Jennifer. I'm sorry—"

"It's okay. I understand. Really."

"You're a sweet girl. Not like some I've had here, I can tell you." She shuffled toward the door. "Oh, I don't see Fred around here tonight. The way that cat has adopted you. I declare! Did you bring him any food scraps? That cat eats better than I do with you feeding him."

"No, I forgot. We had a busy day. I'll bring him some tomorrow," Jennifer promised, anxious now to be rid of her landlady. She ushered Miss Pennyforth to the door. "Good night—"

"Till next month, then, unless you'd like to have tea with me one evening?"

"That would be nice, Miss Pennyforth, I'll look forward to it. Good night again." Jennifer closed the door. Miss Pennyforth was lonely. *I'm lonely*, Jennifer thought. *No, I'm not. I'm just confused.* It was the effect Adrien Merril had on her. What was wrong with her, anyway, acting this way? The man had forgotten she was alive. She had given him the perfect opening to ask her out again and he hadn't. And why should he? They were about as compatible as the Calico Cat and the Gingham Dog.

She paced the floor for another hour, never farther away from the phone than a yard. It sat on the end of the picnic table, a lump of plastic, unfeeling and silent, never coming to life. Jennifer went to bed, her feelings in a turmoil. She spent a restless night in a maze of "if only" dreams.

Chapter Six

Saturday dawned bright and clear with no hint of yesterday's rain. It was one of those sparkling spring mornings when the sun shone, the sky was cloudless, and the birds twittered away happily as they built nests for the coming generation. The glorification of nature! Jennifer thought as she walked to work. Every known creature was blissfully mated properly in nature's scheme of things—except her. She was probably nothing more than a statistic in some nameless government report: *The number of women opting for careers instead of marriage in the United States is etc. etc. . . .* She passed a young couple out for an early morning stroll. They were holding hands. Everywhere she looked, animals, birds, and people were caught up in spring fever. It was a disease of the spirit, she thought dejectedly. With all the medical miracles, why couldn't they invent an innoculation against it, she thought, to protect women like herself from being attracted to men like Adrien Merril?

It was her weekend to work. If it hadn't been, she would've asked Ellie to trade with her. With Merril in mind she had dressed this morning, choosing a chic silk broadcloth frock, patterned in turquoise and white stripes, that cinched her waist with a thin cotton belt. She wore tiny pearl earrings, and the comb that locked her chignon in place had a colorful turquoise flower.

Jennifer presented to herself all sorts of illogical reasons for Adrien's seeming reluctance to date, except the most unpalatable—that he was married. She was determined to see him today, talk to him, even if it meant interrupting his meeting with some excuse or other. He had to ask her out again. He just had to—if he wasn't a married man, she thought. She'd have the answer to that today. Positively!

When she arrived at the Guilbeaux, Vinnie was manning his post at the entrance to the coffee shop. He would remain there until eleven thirty, then he would shift to the formal dining room when it opened for lunch. But he shouldn't be at his usual post this morning. He was supposed to be serving Adrien Merril's group in the Carnival Room. A quiver of uneasy apprehension pressed down on Jennifer as she crossed the lobby as fast as her dignity permitted.

"Vinnie! What are you doing here? Why aren't you in the Carnival Room?" She stood aside so that several guests could enter the café and waited impatiently while Vinnie led them to tables and offered menus.

"Mr. Merril canceled his meeting for today," he told her.

"Oh, dear," Jennifer muttered in a strangled whisper. "When did this happen? How do you know?"

Vinnie shrugged, posturing a classic Gallic gesture. "Petri told me when I came in. Mrs. Wilcox gave him the message."

Wilcox! Surely the executive secretary wouldn't have countermanded catering instructions out of spite. No, not that, Jennifer thought. It wouldn't have been wise on her part to anger a guest who was so well liked by Britz. Jennifer glanced toward the mezzanine. Wilcox wasn't at her desk. Ellie was off today, so no help there. What had happened? she wanted to know. An unnatural calm swept over Jennifer, belying the panic that was beginning to swell beneath the surface. She hurried behind the front desk and checked her mail slot. Nothing. No message. No mail of any kind. She went around to reservations and flipped through the metal box that held all the guests folios. No Adrien Merril. That meant his ledger had already been sent to accounting for billing. He had checked out! Without saying good-bye. Without saying thank you. Without asking to see her again. She had another thought. A thin straw. Perhaps he had checked out but was having breakfast in one of the back booths in the coffee shop. She passed through on her way to the kitchen, glancing this way and that. No Adrien. In the kitchen Petri was laying out strips of bacon on a sheet pan, readying them for frying.

"Petri. Good morning."

He lifted an eyebrow. "I'm too busy with this prep work to make you any French toast." He was still smarting over her visit to the kitchen last night.

"That's okay. I'm not hungry. Say . . . Petri, have you had any breakfast orders this morning without grits—I mean specifically without grits?"

The chef looked at her like she had gone over the edge. "About a dozen. You want a bowl?" Jennifer hadn't heard him. She went out the door into the kitchen and headed up to her office.

There she sat unhappily at her desk, her chin in her hands. "We were ships passing in the night. No, not even ships," she whispered. "Just a small, insignificant bit of life's flotsam thrown together for a few hours."

The disappointment she felt was intense, like a physical blow.

Late afternoon sun bathed Lafourche in glittering gold. As it dipped beyond the western horizon shadows lengthened, spilling leafy patterns through the many paned French windows. Adrien watched the shadows dance across the Persian nain-and-silk carpet, its red-and-gray pattern in sharp relief where the sun's rays struck it.

He held a glass of whiskey and out of habit—a habit he couldn't seem to break—he looked to the wall where the portrait of Eleanor had hung. It still surprised him to see the four Cecil Everly lithographs there, even though he had supervised their hanging himself. He turned away from the prints, giving his attention to the personnel file lying open on the carved table between the sofas. "Jennifer DeWitt" was typed across the top. He formed her name on his lips and felt little gremlins with pitchforks poking around somewhere in his belly. A vision of her leaped to his mind. It was as clear as if he were seeing her image on a motion picture screen—his personal screen, for his private viewing.

Her heart-shaped face, unblemished, with huge almond-shaped eyes, was attached to a slender neck—a neck with inviting hollows...hollows he wanted to bury his lips in. He closed his eyes, willing the vision to disappear, for Jennifer DeWitt wasn't his kind. The pitchforks began to jab at him unmercifully. Choosing a wife, the right kind of wife, was rather an exacting job. He was older now, more experienced in the ways of women. And experience would lessen the chances of him making a wrong choice a second time.

Certainly, Jennifer DeWitt was all wrong.

She was a city girl—New York, Washington, high-rise apartments—much the same as Eleanor had been. It was a comparison he disliked making.

He was a Cajun. His family had lived on the bayou for two centuries. Six generations of those Merrils had lived in this very house. It was built by his ancestors of spliced, mortised, and interlocked timbers between which a filler of mud and moss was covered with white-washed plaster. As opposite from an elegant New York apartment as one could get.

She was used to high fashion, excitement, the theater.

He went to cattle auctions, stock shows.

She was independent; a part of that generation of women who saw marriage—if they regarded it at all—as an extension of their career, not a career in itself.

He was a man who liked to be in charge of things—all things: ranch, wife, children.

Despite these things, and a profile that reminded him of Eleanor, Adrien discovered he was fascinated with Jennifer. He liked the way she walked, the bite in her voice. He remembered her dancing in his arms, and his thoughts lingered on her mouth, the shape of her lips, the tiny provocative mole. He woke up thinking about her—he went to bed thinking about her. A peculiar sense of longing began to invade his body and it fostered arousals when he least expected it.

She was bright and warm and lovely, and he knew he had to see her again. Still, she wasn't his kind. But Adrien craved Jennifer DeWitt, and he was not a man to fret over trifles.

He refreshed his drink, picked up the folder, and went into his study. It was here in this room that he brooded about things, rolled them around in his mind and looked at them from every angle, sorting bits and pieces until they made sense in his orderly brain. The room itself was chaotic. It was as if the order in his brain did not extend to the surfaces about him, yet there was a pattern to the chaos that Adrien understood, created even. The room was his private space, the one place he could insulate himself from the rest of the world. It was a haven, as soothing as a dry island found deep in the swamp without all the dangers. Charts lined one wall, depicting cows photographed, numbered, and inseminated, as well as their offspring, rates of growth, and feed conversion, and next to that a three-foot-long graph recorded costs of feed, semen, housing, and medications. Well-thumbed ranch and cattle magazines filled corners and were stacked on the cowhide sofa. Framed and unframed photographs of his family littered the rest of the walls. Some were hung neatly, while others were thumbtacked into available space, their corners curling with age. Once all these photographs had been in the drawing room, but Eleanor had insisted they be removed. "It's gauche to have one's family pictures scattered about a room like this," she had told him with a seemingly superior sense of fashion. So he had taken them all down and put them in his study. Actually, he liked having them in here better. There was the last picture ever taken of his father, standing over a rogue alligator that he had killed, one strong muscular hand holding open the jaws to reveal jagged rows of menacing teeth. There was a faded photograph of his parents on their wedding day— April 1935. His mother had been slender then and slender when she died, crippled with arthritis, nearly blind. She had loved him hard and chastised him gently: "Ah, Adrien, look at those big muddy footprints following you on my polished floor. Loup-garou will find you easily tonight, no?" Or when he had come home from school, clothes ripped, face bruised from scrapping with his schoolmates, "Tsk, tsk...to think your papa and I despaired of ever having you—perhaps I'm still in despair, no? Fighting, fighting, is that all little boys know?" Then, eyes twinkling, "You didn't bite off anybody's ear, did you? That's against the law...." And then, when she lay dying, reaching up to touch his face that was then only a blur to her, a swollen finger tracing his bent nose, "You must learn to stay away from those angry bulls, no?" A gentle smile. "You are a lot like your father, the bulls, too. Strong, yet you hide your gentleness behind your manhood. Find a wife, Adrien. A woman will show you a new path, a different strength. Promise me?"

"I promise, Maman," he had said.

"And take care of my roses. If the vine begins to die, you must take cuttings— Oh, but tell Ralph, he knows. Now," she had whispered, "get the priest. I go to join your father." She had felt the tears on his cheeks. "Ah, don't be sad. Would you deny me that happiness?"

His eyes moved from the picture of his mother and those memories to settle on a faded sepia tintype of old Uncle Jean-Marc, whose arm was draped around John L. Sullivan, the most popular pugilist who ever lived. The picture had been taken in front of the Olympic Athletic Club on Royal Street in New Orleans. It was dated September 1892. Uncle Jean-Marc had been dead for three quarters of a century, and the Olympic Club had long ago been destroyed by fire. It was to Uncle Jean-Marc, a high roller, a gambler of his day, that Adrien owed the thanks for the inheritance of the Guilbeaux. The old ruffian had won the hotel in a hand of French *poque* in a marathon game that had become legend. Too bad, Adrien mused, Uncle Jean-Marc hadn't willed a bucket of gold with which to keep the white elephant prim and polished and in operating condition. Of late he had more than once thought of selling the hotel or just shutting it down. But then he remembered its two hundred eighty employees, many too old and set in their ways to find work elsewhere. And who would hire them, anyway? They were part of the hotel's lasting charm. To shut down the hotel would be the same as shutting off their lives. And now there was Jennifer working among them. He would bring in some auditors with good business sense, let them go over the hotel with a fine-tooth comb, find every way possible to increase revenue, to keep the doors open.

"Adrien? Supper's almost ready." Berty stood in the doorway, peering into the dim room at Adrien sitting behind his desk in the shadows. The study faced the east, and no late evening sun rippled through windows to add its soft golden light. He switched on a lamp, illuminating the disorder on his desk. Out of it he picked up a letter and used it to wave Berty into the study.

"Good. I'm hungry. But can it wait a minute? Sit down." He waited while she found a spot on the sofa and settled gingerly on its edge. "We're going to have company. I've received an answer from that rancher I visited several weeks ago. He and his family will be here next week."

Berty gasped. "But—but—"

"No buts," Adrien stated firmly. "They're coming, and you're staying." Berty had another disease—misocainea—an abnormal aversion to anything new, any change in her life. It often struck victims of Hansen's disease who themselves were frightened and who suffered illogical, insensitive, and ignorant reactions from their own families and friends. Since her confrontation with Eleanor, Berty had seemed to withdraw more and more into her own world.

"I could go back to the hospital while they're here, no?" she ventured, *where I'm safe, where I'm not humiliated.*

"No! You don't need the hospital and you don't need to fear that everyone or anyone I bring here will react like Eleanor. You were just an excuse for her to leave me...not the reason."

For a moment Berty was speechless. Something had happened, something to ease Adrien's mind about El-

eanor. She could tell in the way he mentioned her so
casually. There was still the bitterness, an irony in the
sound of his voice, but none of the angry madness that
he had so often displayed in the past. Adrien took her
silence for acquiescence.

"That's settled. And if Ballesta likes what he sees
here, then I'm certain to sell him a small herd, which
will put us in the black for once. Then all I'd have to
worry about is that damn hotel." He looked fully at
Berty as an idea whipped into his mind. "Why don't
you consider going back to work at the Guilbeaux, sort
of keep an eye on things for me?"

"No . . . no. I couldn't." Panic began to well up inside
her. "All those people—and I don't have the strength.
Suppose they found out?"

"Found out what? That we're related? That was one
of Papa's rules. It wouldn't matter to me. I'm not
against nepotism. As for anything else, who's to know
unless you go around whispering—"

"It's no joke. You're making it into a joke."

Adrien sighed. "No. It's just that I hate to see you
wasting your life away here—"

"But I'm happy. I fish, crab, take care of you," Berty
protested.

"Aha! And who was it that told me when I was . . .
oh, about seventeen or so, that she had a lust for life? I
remembered that word for weeks afterward. It sounded
so evocative. I imagined you doing all sorts of things,
you know."

Berty blushed, and the flush brought an attractive
glow to her pale face. "That was before—" she stam-
mered, *years before I got sick, before my husband deserted
me, before Eleanor left you.*

A gentle laughter rippled through Adrien's square
bulk. "Yes, before . . . You think about it, though. Anyway, when the Ballesta family arrives, you won't have

to do everything here alone. I'm bringing in some people from the hotel."

"Who?" Berty could barely get the word past her lips. Her hand flew to the amulet around her neck.

"The catering manager for one. You don't know her, but she's very efficient; and the sous chef, Henri Augustin. You remember him?"

Berty could only nod. Her mouth had suddenly gone dry. She remembered Henri. He was big, but with that gracefulness one finds so surprising in large people, and flirtatious. She remembered Henri's eyes—vivid blue. They lit up when she walked into the busy hotel kitchen. Then she had been a married woman whose husband worked offshore on an oil rig in the Gulf. Her instinct, an inner feeling she refused to put a name to, made her keep a circumspect distance from the cook. But he pursued her anyway, an amiable spirit... Then came the disaster, her world crashing down upon her...the tiredness, the numbness in her hands and feet.... She went to a doctor...test after test was made...and everything happened fast after that.... She went to Carville and began to live—exist—in this vacuum. Henri was a part of that other life, when she had been happy, carefree, and loved. It was only after Adrien's mother, Marie, had died that she mustered the courage to leave the hospital, her cottage there, and return to Lafourche. And now what was she to do? Was there any of that courage left? A movement caught her eye, and her gaze left inward thoughts and focused on Adrien. He was putting a folder in the middle drawer, locking it, and talking to Ralph, who appeared in the doorway. He looked back to Berty.

"Well?"

"What? What?" she asked, wondering what she had missed.

"Can we eat now?"

"Yes." She followed behind him slowly as they left the study while her past pitched itself into the present, bringing with it emotions Berty had sought for years to smother.

Chapter Seven

Time dragged by for Jennifer. Work at the hotel went on steadily. Cost cutting was at its zenith, and every expenditure, no matter how small, was scrutinized by Milton Richards, who seemed to have his finger at the core of every department. Management staff began to grumble that Mr. Britz was merely a puppet manager. Eva Wilcox was found in Richards's private office as often as she was at her desk on the mezzanine, and that continued to fuel gossip that she and the account executive were an item. Jennifer could care less. The more attention Wilcox paid to Richards, the less she gave to Jennifer. One troublesome fact, though, was that performance reviews with their attending salary increases would not be given until November instead of the promised June, and wage increases—if any—would come only in December.

In the midst of all this activity, gossip, rumor, announcements, and work Jennifer was facing her own personal crisis that was mounting to epic proportions. She was trying to forget Adrien Merril, but thoughts of him, instead of weakening, became more constant. For days she remembered the way he looked—his face, the crooked nose, his piercing dark eyes, his wide shoulders, the tiny tufts of hair on his fingers—which wasn't enough. She conjured up pictures of him naked, in bed, making love to her, and she saw his hands moving over her body. She recalled exactly the smell of him at their first meeting. Breakfast bacon, Kouros, and the barely perceptible carbolic scent of Lifebuoy soap. She took to frying bacon every morning, saturating the apartment with its particular odor. She bought a dozen bars of Lifebuoy, using it to wash her face, her hands, her underwear. She pestered the woman behind the men's cologne counter at J.D. Holmes until she had a half dozen samples of Kouros. These she sprinkled on her pillows, which she hugged to her body when she went to bed.

She told herself that she was crazy; that somehow she had just become infatuated; that things like this didn't happen to real people; that things like this only happened in the movies... and then she would imagine that she heard the sound of his voice, his laughter. Once she recognized the scent of Kouros on the street and, turning, followed a square-shouldered man for two blocks down Dauphine Street while her heart thudded in her chest and the feelings in her stomach intensified. She became tense, moody, and irritable.

To prove to herself that nothing was out of the ordinary, she accepted a date with a colleague who worked at the Hilton. They had dinner and went dancing in the French Quarter, and she found herself comparing the man to Adrien. When he tried to kiss her good night, she railed at him for trying to take advantage of her. Confused, he left, backing down the sidewalk, shaking his head, wondering what he had done wrong.

Jennifer thought of quitting the Guilbeaux and going back to New York. She talked herself into this, called her parents, and afterward, talked herself out of it. But mostly she talked to herself about Adrien Merril.

She couldn't sleep. The nights seemed an endless string of dark loneliness. And when finally, exhausted, sleep did overtake her, she hated to get up and go to work. At last when she would drag herself out of bed, she hurried to the hotel, for it was there she hoped to see him. She imagined that he would step out from behind one of the tall marble columns, or that she would run into him in the coffee shop or in the Cove, or that she would glance up and see him standing on the mezzanine. When these hopes came to naught, she kept to her office, certain that she would look up and find him standing there.

Adrien Merril became an obsession, and now she bathed all over with Lifebuoy soap, bought a flacon of Kouros, and put the white porcelain container next to her bed. She cooked bacon twice a day and fed it to Fred.

At work very little penetrated her brain. To get her attention people spoke to her twice, three times. And if someone or something did manage to get past the vision of Adrien, it was there only a short time until some thought, some imagined happening, would push it out. She was insane. She needed a doctor. She had a disease. The cure was Adrien Merril.

One tiny lucid part of Jennifer's brain had not been overwhelmed by the Merril fixation, and it pleaded for a return to sanity, to common sense, for her to go back to the life she had led before the man had stepped into her office. As Jennifer slid into a back booth in the coffee shop she was feeling especially dismal. She promised herself that this weekend, her glorious weekend off, she would throw out the bacon, pour the Kouros down the drain, give the Lifebuoy to Miss Pennyforth, and rid her mind once and forever of Adrien Merril. That gave her two days to get used to the idea—today and Friday.

"Hey," Ellie commented, bringing over a pot of coffee and filling two cups, "you look like you just buried your best friend, then dug him up to see if he was really dead. Did you walk to work again this morning? Must be something in the air making you this way.''

"I look that bad, truly?"

"Oh, you look marvelous, but that's just the resilience of youth." Ellie administered the barb with a half smile as she sat down and lit up a cigarette. "Want to tell me what's bothering you?"

"Nothing, really," Jennifer replied, employing remarkable understatement. She glanced out the double doors leading to the terrace.

The sun was washing the tables with an early morning pink. "It's nice out," she said wistfully. "You know, Ellie, that's the only bad thing about this job. We stay cooped up from dawn to dusk most of the time."

"I hate to tell you this," Ellie warned in a low voice, "but there may be something else bad about this job for you this morning."

Jennifer's nerves drew taut. She had let something slip past her; forgotten to set up a meeting, mixed up food orders, made an error in billing. Something. She waited for Ellie to continue.

"Mr. Britz wants you in his office right away this morning. I saw the memo on your desk. He's been fluttering around here since six, and you know how out of the ordinary *that* is," Ellie finished, a low note of warning in her voice.

Jennifer fumbled for a pretense of hauteur. "I don't know what he could possibly want to see me about. Things have been running smooth—"

"Only because Lady Luck has been riding on your shoulder." Ellie snorted dryly, not the least bit fooled by Jennifer's show of confidence. "You've been out of it for a month."

"I know," Jennifer admitted. "But I'm okay now.

I'm just tired. Really. I need this weekend to relax," among other things, she told herself. She let loose a shaky sigh. "I suppose there's no time like the present. I'll go see what Britz wants now."

On the mezzanine Wilcox greeted her with a forced smile. "Go right in, Jennifer. Mr. Britz is expecting you—and has been for some time now," she added, managing to make the words sound like a whip cracking in the wind.

Jennifer passed Wilcox with a curt nod, giving the secretary the same deference she would a coiled, ready-to-strike snake. She knocked on Britz's door, announced her presence, and walked into the inner office.

The manager's office was a bastion of male elegance, with thick beige carpeting and carved Italian furniture that gave off a sense of authority. Mr. Britz sat behind the huge oak desk as though by some magic alchemy the character of the room would increase his stature. He was reviewing occupancy projections, and as he bent over the printouts the sun streaming in from the window behind him bounced off his bald head. He glanced up at Jennifer, his brows drawn into a thick frown. She began to feel pensive.

"Ah, Miss DeWitt," he said formally, indicating with a wave of his hand that she should sit in the overstuffed and uncomfortable brown leather chair in front of his desk. Uh-oh, she thought. She must be in hot water! Britz had snickered about that chair dozens of times. Its front legs were two inches shorter than the back so that anyone sitting in it continuously felt like getting up and, Ethan Britz hoped, out of his office. He offered it to intractable guests who couldn't understand why they had the urge to make their complaints and then leave so quickly. Britz also offered it to employees he expected to discipline. She lowered herself to its very edge, her back straight, her chin up, and a slightly defensive frown on her heart-shaped face.

Mr. Britz cleared his throat, his hands moving to straighten the already neat stack of papers on his desk and then moving unconsciously to a dust mote that danced in a sun ray. "I have a rather unusual assignment for you," he said finally.

"What—?" Jennifer began, startled, then clamped her mouth shut. Obviously, this was not going to be a discipline session. The tension along her spine eased.

"One of our guests who was here several weeks ago is having a small intimate dinner party for some clients and a few friends. He's requested, specifically, that you handle it; see to the food, flowers, the usual task of a hostess."

Part of her job was closely aligned to that of a social secretary, especially here at the Guilbeaux, but that was not extraordinary. Jennifer was puzzled. "I don't understand. Why are arrangements being made through you? Why not contact my office directly?"

"The event is to be held in his home on Bayou Lafourche," Britz continued as though Jennifer hadn't spoken. Lafourche. She almost swooned. "You'll recall Mr. Merril, I'm sure, a most important patron." Jennifer could only nod her head stupidly. "Arrangements have been made for your transportation." He handed her a large manila envelope that she accepted automatically. "There's a guest list, instructions, and so forth. Henri will be joining you later, and he'll bring the foods you designate that might not be available locally on such short notice." Britz took a deep breath. He wasn't used to giving such long explanations. Mostly he just barked orders and left the details to Wilcox and, more recently, Milton Richards.

Jennifer was too dumbfounded to speak a word, even if she had been able to get it past the lump frozen in her throat. Her thoughts raced. Could she refuse? Probably not and keep her job. Did she want to? Definitely not!

"This is a plum of an assignment for you—Jennifer." He used her name stiffly, an indication that she had entered the world of the elite. "You will also have to get his house in order, but that should be no problem for you...we've trained you well, I think." His pudgy fingers were thrust at her again. "Here's a petty cash voucher for two hundred dollars generously provided by Mr. Merril for any personal expenses you might incur on his behalf. Give it to Eva to record on your way out." His hands were busy again with the nonclutter on his desk. "Uh, I was asked to impress upon you that this will be a formal affair and to bring clothes suitable for such an occasion. I'll expect you back at your desk on Wednesday." She was dismissed.

"But—but today is only Thursday."

Britz shrugged his tailored shoulders. "All the information is in the file you have." He stared at her pointedly. Dismissed again.

Jennifer wasn't aware that she had been holding her breath until she was in the outer office. It whooshed out.

"Anything wrong?" Wilcox asked with an inflection of hope.

Smiling, Jennifer looked directly at the older woman. "Quite the contrary. Everything is fine...just fine." She gave Wilcox the voucher.

The secretary's eyebrows shot up when she looked at it. "I'll just run this over to Milton and pick up the cash for you," she volunteered with uncharacteristic sweetness. Jennifer opened her mouth to protest but caught herself just in time. Wilcox probably used any and every excuse possible to meet as often as she could with Richards. It wasn't too hard to figure out what would happen if she refused the woman's offer. The secretary would be her enemy for life and well into the hereafter as well, she knew. Jennifer agreed with all the grace of a combatant waving a white flag.

"Thank you. I'll wait here."

Fifteen minutes later Jennifer was in her office, the contents of the envelope spread out on her desk with the reality of what was about to happen causing delicious tinglings to zip up and down her spine. Was there a cloud nine spinning across the heavens? She felt she had an express ticket. If Adrien Merril needed a hostess, he didn't have a wife. How lovely.

Her instructions were precise: A cab would pick her up at her apartment at four that afternoon, and take her to an air terminal for a short flight to Lafourche in a private plane. There was a guest list: Ballesta, family of three; a couple named Baker; another named Dubois. So including herself and Adrien, there would be nine for dinner the coming Sunday. A breeze to handle, to prepare for, she thought. The Ballesta family was staying for a few days to look over the cattle operation on Adrien's ranch. They were arriving at three Sunday afternoon. It was possible that by five o'clock this afternoon she would be in Adrien's house, in his company. Jennifer did some mental aritmetic. Seventy hours between five this afternoon and three o'clock Sunday. A lot can happen in seventy hours, she thought. Her anticipation grew, and with it a kind of dread. What should she say, how should she act? What would he say? Suppose he didn't like her? Suppose he hadn't even thought about her? Suppose—

"I seem to be carrying on the bulk of this conversation," Ellie said, touching her on the shoulder.

"Oh, Ellie. I didn't hear you come in."

"That's nothing new. Your hearing's been impaired for weeks. Now your sight's going. I've been standing here for two minutes. So what was it? What happened? I'm beside myself with curiosity."

"Happened?"

"In the executive office, for heaven's sake! What did old Britz want?"

"Get this," Jennifer replied, making a supreme effort to cloak her words with annoyance. "Adrien Merril has hired me right out from under Mr. Britz to play hostess at a dinner he's giving Sunday night—at his home on Bayou Lafourche."

Ellie didn't speak for a moment, taking an inordinate amount of time to remove her smock and hang it on the coat tree. Then she struck a match, touched it to her cigarette, inhaled, and looked at Jennifer through the ribbon of smoke as she exhaled. "He didn't really hire you out from under Britz," she announced.

"What do you mean, he didn't?" Jennifer held up the envelope. "It's all right here—see for yourself."

"I mean," Ellie said breathlessly, "you work for Adrien Merril...we all do. He owns the hotel—lock, stock, barrel, and deficit."

Jennifer was incredulous. "You're joking."

"I resort to sarcasm, I tell racy stories, but joke about my bread and butter? Never! I'm a widow, remember? Anyway, Wilcox told me yesterday. She had to work late and came down to dine. I had a cup of coffee with her. You know how she is—she'd tattle on a rip in a lace slip. She wants you to know what she knows so you know she knew it first—if you know what I mean," Ellie finished.

No wonder he was so...so standoffish, Jennifer thought. It put a different complexion on things. The first rule of business etiquette was, never get involved with your boss. A rule of propriety that put Adrien Merril off limits. *Who are you trying to fool?* asked a little voice that was beginning to plague her.

"That doesn't change anything," she said determinedly. "I'm going."

"But this is your weekend off. I thought you needed some rest. Not twenty minutes ago you were saying—"

"I know what I said, but Adrien's estate, or ranch, or house—whatever, is on some bayou. That means fresh air, and it's away from the city. I'll get plenty of rest, have a mini vacation. Besides, I want to go."

Ellie swept her co-worker with an all-encompassing glance, and observed Jennifer's excitement: delicate features that were animated; brown eyes that were shot with gold, glittering; and inward radiance. And Mr. Merril was *Adrien* no less. "Well, well, well, and I believed you when you said the original wolf hadn't made an impression on you."

Jennifer wavered. "He didn't. You're imagining things." She shoved the envelope haphazardly into her handbag with trembling fingers.

"Oh, yeah?" Ellie snorted. "I'm an elephant's aunt. And you, *mon amie,*" she said succinctly, "are lost."

"Phooey! Stop behaving like I'm rushing off to some mysterious assignation. It's only a job, same as I do here, and I can handle myself."

"Sure you can," Ellie said, wagging her cigarette at Jennifer. "Just remember that what you young folk call the new morality us older folk call sin."

"Look who's talking." Jennifer laughed. "Isn't there a certain Monsieur Grimeaux?"

"A venial sin, then," Ellie amended stiffly. "Nonetheless, you be careful."

"Of what, for heaven's sake?"

"You were the one that branded the man a wolf, not me."

"First impressions aren't always accurate. I made a mistake. Don't worry about me, I'll be fine, and I've got to get going. There's a lot I have to do before four o'clock. See you Wednesday."

In the kitchen Jennifer gave Henri the list of foods and spices he was to bring to Lafourche and discovered he had known about the event for the past week. "Henri, if you knew about this, why didn't you mention it?"

He shrugged his great shoulders. "Mrs. Wilcox said—"

"Oh, never mind," Jennifer retorted with disgust. She had a feeling, faint but growing stronger, that Wilcox had orchestrated a maneuver to hold back information that cut drastically into her prep time. Wilcox probably hoped she would make some ghastly error and have to suffer the wrath of Britz and then Adrien Merril, since he was now known to be the force behind the hotel.

As she emerged from the hotel onto its cobblestoned terrace, Jennifer vowed that there would be no problem with this affair. It was just a matter of keeping her mind on her work and not on the owner of the Guilbeaux.

Back at her apartment, when she began to pack, she realized that although she had nice clothes, there was nothing on the order of sweeping or formal. The apricot silk was elegant, cocktailish, just right for the Vieux Carré, but not— She wished she knew what Adrien's home was like. Bayou Lafourche had a romantic ring to it. She needed something romantic then—very romantic. She convinced herself that even though this was strictly a business function, it would be prudent for her to look her best—if only for Adrien's guests. Against her better judgment and pressed for time, she spent a frenzied hour visiting department stores in downtown New Orleans, finding nothing to her liking. Frustrated, she began searching side streets, hoping to find a small out-of-the-way boutique. Instead, she discovered a sample house, one that sold exclusive model designs to the public after clients had ordered the originals.

There were racks of silks, satins, and laces, all size three. Jennifer moaned audibly as she searched for a six. Finally, with the help of a sympathetic sales clerk, she found exactly what she wanted—a silk-lined gossamer gown of creamy beige, with mother-of-pearl buttons from its mandarine-style collar to hem. The fitted sleeves and the collar were trimmed with vignettes of Chantilly lace. The gown kept to her curves from breasts to hips, then flared gently with a gathered pleat at the back of the knee, giving it just the right amount of élan. She paid for the dress with the petty cash, saying a silent prayer that it came under the heading of unforseen personal expense. A necessary extravagance, she argued. On the way out of the shop she stopped at the perfume counter, spending fifty dollars out of her rainy-day cache for a flacon of Balmain's newest scent, Ivoire. When she stepped into the street, she had exactly seventy-five cents left in her purse. It cost her sixty to ride the trolley home.

At precisely four o'clock a taxi pulled to a halt at the top of the cul-de-sac. Jennifer panicked. What if she were expected to pay the cabdriver and be reimbursed later? While her luggage was hauled to the trunk she frantically rummaged through all of her suit jackets, purses, and blazers until she came up with six dollars and thirty cents. She expelled a sigh of intense relief, but she needn't have worried.

When the driver stopped on the tarp next to a building set apart from the huge commercial air terminal and Jennifer offered to pay him, he explained that he had already been paid, and very handsomely, too.

For the trip to Lafourche she had donned slim-fitting gray gabardine slacks with a matching bush jacket. A western kerchief knotted loosely around her neck and comfortable Wedgies on her feet offered the casual viewer a quick dash of red. A disreputable, but still serviceable small-brimmed hat shaded her eyes from the bright sun and rode the top of her chignon with unconcerned éclat. It was practical attire, but on Jennifer it looked like high fashion.

As the cabdriver unloaded her suitcases Jennifer stood in the late afternoon sun, feeling its warmth pierce her straw hat. She knew it: In this heat she should have worn a blouse underneath the jacket. Then, at least, she could have removed it to cool down. She felt a line of perspiration begin to trickle down between her shoulder blades. The breeze coming her way off the runways increased her discomfort—it was hot and smelled of tar. A man came out of the small building and approached her.

"Miss DeWitt?"

"Yes."

He nodded. "We've been expecting you. I'm Jake Durant." He picked up her luggage and hefted them under muscular arms. "Let's get you out of this hot sun," he declared, and Jennifer followed him to a small silver plane parked on a wide apron at the side of the building. He plopped her luggage down, helped her climb onto a small foothold, then onto the wing and into the tiny cabin. She heard her luggage being tossed into a baggage hold of some sort behind the wing, then the man who called himself Jake entered the plane.

When the motors began to whine, she buckled herself into one of the comfortable leather seats. Almost immediately, to her satisfaction, she felt a blast of refrigerated air. The plane vibrated, Jennifer braced herself for takeoff, then the cabin door opened. Adrien stepped into the narrow aisle. Having planned this entrance in a secret effort to discern her reaction, he was at an advantage. He had known exactly the moment they would meet again.

His unexpected presence on the plane was stuff of Jennifer's dreams. She had hoped and prayed fervently to come upon him somewhere—anywhere—and now that it had happened she was caught unawares. She managed a startled, soundless oh that shaped her mouth, forming an entrancing moue. Adrien benefited from her expression; it told him what he wanted to know. A roguish twinkle glinted in his eyes as he went forward to the cockpit and settled himself in the pilot's seat.

Jennifer was a nervous wreck. She couldn't catch her breath. All the thoughts, visions, imagined happenings she'd invoked the past month leaped into her brain, a solid block of kaleidoscopic images that bounced off every nerve ending in her body. She tried to block them out, restore some order, but it was as fruitless as attempting to bail out the *Titanic* with a teaspoon. She watched Jake slap Adrien on his back, get up, nod to her, and leave the plane.

Oh, dear, now what? she wondered. She had her answer immediately as the small aircraft began to taxi for takeoff. They were airborne in a very few minutes, but Jennifer barely noticed. She was already flying. Her eyes were riveted to the back of Adrien's head.

Once they were level, he turned, motioning for her to join him, pointing to the copilot's seat. Propelled by the hunger she had for him, Jennifer followed his suggestion without hesitation. The area was small and close, and it was impossible not to brush against his arm as she maneuvered into the seat, impossible not to get a whiff of his male scent. Her fingers trembled with the over-the-shoulder safety harness. Adrien, watching out the corner of his eye, saw her difficulty. He put his hand on hers.

"Let it go," he said. The motors were humming smoothly and conversation was just possible.

"What are you doing here?" Jennifer asked. *How stupid! Can't you think of anything exciting to say?*

"Had to do some shopping and pick up my catering manager," he returned, tossing her an amused grin. What was he so happy about, anyway? Yet the last half of the sentence gave her a warm glow.

"Why did you cancel the second day of your meetings last month?" *Why didn't you call me? Write? Say good-bye?*

"We got everything done in the first day. Didn't you get my note? I left it on Eva Wilcox's desk. It's not as difficult to ship cattle as I had thought—just expensive. Why? Have you missed me?"

Jennifer told him no. His eyebrow shot up, but he didn't pursue the issue. Right then she couldn't have handled an exchange, anyway. She was thinking of the note—the note for her that he had left with Wilcox and that Wilcox had not delivered. All the miserable days she had spent might not have been had she gotten that message, no matter how inconsequential, how innocent it may have been. Damn Eva Wilcox and her air of superiority, she thought. She would confront the secretary the minute she returned to the Guilbeaux.

As Adrien guided the plane into a westerly turn the sun irradiated the cockpit with blinding incandescence. He pulled on aviator glasses that gave him a rakish look. "There's an extra pair in the pocket over there," he said, indicating a zippered flap next to her elbow. She put them on, but they were too big and kept sliding down her nose. To compensate she pulled the brim of her hat down over her eyes.

"Want to fly this thing?" he asked suddenly.

"Sure. Do you think I can?"

"Nothing to it," he answered, demonstrating the controls once. "Have a go at it."

She did well for a few minutes, absorbed in and enthralled with flying the aircraft. She, who couldn't drive anything with wheels except a bicycle, was soaring through the sky like an eagle. The exhilaration made her laugh excitedly. Adrien was watching her. She noticed, saw her reflection in his glasses, and felt instinctively the depth of his gaze. The bubble of exhilaration burst, confounding her with desire. The controls forgotten, the plane dipped alarmingly.

"Mon Dieu!" Adrien growled, grabbing the steering gear in front of him. "You want to kill us both?"

Jennifer collected herself, smiling sheepishly. "Sorry," she quipped, "but it serves you right."

Though his attention was on the aircraft, at her words his mouth tilted in a small knowing smile. Jennifer wished she could see his eyes. Something had passed between them. Time. A link. A wanting. Naked desire. Up until her meeting with Adrien Merril, Jennifer's life had been governed by fixed principles of good sense and practicality. She knew who she was. She knew what she wanted. The hunger she felt for the man next to her gripped her like a steel vise and the realization held her hostage.

For the next twenty minutes he concentrated on flying while she was busy with her own thoughts, and neither attempted conversation until Adrien began his descent.

"That's the bayou," he said, pronouncing it by-ya, and for the first time Jennifer caught the sound of a slight accent, not French exactly, but not English either. She looked down at the waterway, a black ribbon at first, until they drew closer, then it looked green, blue, and purple by degrees. The line of trees along its shoreline was broken here and there with groups of houses, each of them painted a bright green, blue, or pink only on their fronts; backs and sides were a weather-washed gray. When Jennifer commented on this, he laughed.

"What guest ever sees the side of a house or comes in the back door? It's a waste of good paint."

"Oh." She wanted to ask him about his home, but didn't dare.

He concentrated on following the main waterway for a moment, then left it, flying low over what seemed to Jennifer to be a highway paved in lavender.

"Heavens! What in the world is that?"

"Hyacinth," he said, following her pointed finger. "In bloom. This arm of the bayou has been choked to death by them." All at once the trees appeared at eye level, so close, Jennifer ducked involuntarily.

In the next instant, Adrien was setting the plane down with hardly a bump on a packed-earth runway. He taxied up to a hangar, little more than a metal shed that was shaded by moss-hung oaks, and cut the engines.

"Safe and sound," he said teasingly as Jennifer straightened up in her seat.

"I didn't think I was in any danger," she replied, slightly embarrassed at her self-protective gesture, and feeling certain that he had purposefully skimmed the trees, showing off. "You will admit, though, that you did come close to clipping those trees?"

"It's the only way in or out, if you're coming by air," he explained.

"I'm glad you told me. I'll go home by bus."

The cabin door opened, and an explosion of voice reverberated in the tiny plane. Adrien led her to the door, in which a young muscular, darkly handsome man stood, chattering away to them in a French dialect so foreign to Jennifer, she understood little of what was said.

Adrien silenced the young man with a word and in-

troduced Jennifer to Etienne Beauchamp, one of the
cowboys and all-around hands on the ranch.

"Speak English, Etienne. Miss DeWitt knows French,
but not Cajun." Etienne whipped off his hat and said
allo in that musical accent, displaying the rare shyness
that, given opportunity, blooms into lasting friendship.
He offered Jennifer a work-calloused hand, helping her
down from the small aircraft. She was directed to a blue
pickup parked in the shade of spreading tree limbs
draped with lacy, gently swaying moss. Her luggage and
packages were unloaded, then Adrien and Etienne
worked to push the plane into a quanset-type shelter.

Standing in the shade, the gray-green moss forming
a ceiling over her head like a thousand delicate flags
waving welcome, Jennifer swished at a mosquito. A peculiar feeling surged up in her as if she were coming
home after some long, long trip. The emotion was so
strange, catching her by surprise, that she glanced
about her, trying to fathom its source. The earth under
her feet had a soft springy feel, the air a damp woodsy
smell, and there was all around her a sense of freshness
of vitality. The sounds were new to her: the buzz of
hundreds of insects, birds cooing to their mates, the
squawking of a crow, the distant rat-tat of a wood-
pecker busily drilling holes in a cedar split by lightning.
She couldn't put a finger on what had triggered the odd
sensation, yet she felt its presence as though the earth
itself were a part of some ancient ritual that she should
know—felt herself as a figure in a living diorama as
though she were the reservoir for all the life that sur-
rounded her. The sun filtered through the draping
moss under which she stood, illuminating the red-
brown bark. She touched the tree as if the feel of it
could clarify the mystery. An explanation eluded her.

In the distance she saw several cottages with bright-
colored wash flapping on clotheslines. Beyond the cot-

tages lay fields of lush cane shimmering emerald in the sun. In front of her a white graveled road wound around a curve and disappeared. More of the massive trees lined the road, their gnarled roots hugging the bank of the creek she had seen from the air. They looked for all the world like a ragged line of soldiers returning, battle scarred, from war. Here and there the blanket of hyacinths was broken by a rugged stump and the black water shown silvery where the sun managed to find a hole in overhanging leafage. It was the first time Jennifer had been so deep into rural America, and the magic of the Acadian swamp had her firmly in tow. Jennifer's ancestor's would have recognized the feeling. It was the deep emotion of one pulled into nature's forces—primitive, earthy, and humbling.

Adrien and Etienne approached, both of them perspiring from the exertion of rolling the plane into its shelter. Etienne hoisted himself into the back of the pickup with the luggage while she and Adrien climbed into the air-conditioned comfort of the cab. The strange feeling that plagued her seemed only to intensify her curiosity about Adrien.

Chapter Eight

"Have you lived all your life on Lafourche?"

"We say Lafoosh," Adrien replied, correcting her pronunciation with a smile. "Yes, I've lived all my life here, except when I was at college. I was born here and I want to die here."

"You don't have to be so morbid," Jennifer told him, frowning. She had in mind beginnings, not endings.

He chuckled under his breath. "I'm not morbid. Here in the swamp life is all around us and its natural progression is death. Everyone ought to have a place to live and a place to die...or so I've been told, and in between a place to call home. For me all three are the same. What about you?" He looked over at her, his little half smile inquisitive, as though this were the most natural sort of conversation two people could attempt.

"I haven't given it much thought. I have enough trouble just getting along day to day." Especially recently, she thought wryly.

"City living does that to you," he said. "Now out here our world is confined to a few square miles of creeks, swamps, and farmland, where most of us do a little fishing, shrimping, and oystering. Others raise a bit of rice, a few acres of cane, and cattle, and some fortunate few combine all three to make it pay.''

"And own a hotel or two in New Orleans?" Jennifer said sweetly.

"An unprofitable venture these past few years, my little friend," he shot back, wondering how the knowledge of his ownership had come to Jennifer. He specifically forbade any top-level executives to reveal this fact. "I inherited the hotel," he added with no attempt at modesty, "but I prefer my life on Lafourche."

Jennifer thought about that for a moment, trying to decide what point he was trying to make or if this was just an attempt to impress her. On to something else, she decided. "Do you live alone?" She wanted confirmation that he had no wife. As she watched his face the truck sped into a forest. Dim and cool, it threw everything into shadow, including Adrien's features.

There was wry amusement in his answer. "Mostly. You're being awfully nosy. Filling up your gossip column for when you get back to the Guilbeaux?"

Jennifer prickled. "No. Do you think you're that interesting?"

He gave a half smile as they emerged into sunlight once again. "Hope so."

"Egomaniac," she stated dryly.

He laughed. "My cousin housekeeps for me—"

"Your cousin? If you have family here, why do you need me?"

Adrien hesitated. Now was the perfect opportunity to tell Jennifer about Berty. As much as he wanted her reaction, Berty's private hell was her own affair and up to her to share with Jennifer or anyone else. "I need a professional for this event," he said smoothly. "You're it. Berty only keeps house for me when she's in the mood for it...which isn't often. She likes her privacy. On top of that, she's independent as hell...."

"That wouldn't be a family trait, would it?"

"It might be. What's yours, tongue sharpeners?"

Jennifer ignored the remark. She was on edge. Why couldn't she stop making all these pithy comebacks and be nice, show him her good side? she admonished herself. At least there was no mention of a wife. Yet the man was an enigma, drenching her with charm one moment, as though he liked her, and in the next acting as though he couldn't make up his mind—about what? she wondered. For one special moment when they had been airborne she had imagined there to be something almost noble about him. *That's your problem up front, Jennifer DeWitt. You do manage to let your imagination carry you away.*

Her eyes shifted here and there, looking everywhere except at Adrien, watching the landscape as they traveled past. The truck slowed, turning onto a shell-paved drive leading to a two-story whitewashed house. Barns and outbuildings were just visible beyond a screen of live oaks and magnolia, but the house drew her immediate attention.

Eight white columns rose from the front veranda supporting a floor of overhanging rooms. Enormous windows were trimmed with dark green shutters and each of the side porches was roofed. Visible through one of the windows was a great bouquet of white roses arranged on a pedestal. Against the eaves, bowed in the middle with roof-high canes, a trellis leaned precariously, laden with more of the roses. Honeysuckle crept in and out among the roses to reach above the roof to chimneys where it seemed content to make its home. The trees on the lawn appeared swathed in gray lace, and they shaded the house, lending its white exterior a luminous green tint.

"It's beautiful," Jennifer said quietly as Adrien

helped her from the truck. Lafourche was every bit as romantic as it sounded. "You should have told me you owned a plantation."

"It's just a plain old simple working farm house," he told her. "Underneath all that whitewash is native timber, moss, and mud." As much as he decried Jennifer's description, he sounded pleased. She stood by the truck while he instructed Etienne to dispose of the luggage, then to meet him in the barns. Jennifer was enthralled. She inhaled the dulcet smell of honeysuckle. "This is marvelous," she said, visualizing idyllic moments and the rest she would enjoy.

"Who, me?" Adrien asked teasingly as he took her arm, guiding her up the flagstoned walk.

She gave him a look of insolent sweetness. "I was talking about the house."

"Just keep in mind I go with it," he said, beginning a wide grin and remembering his dimple only just in time.

"I'll do that." The wondrous urgency she felt began to pick up momentum.

In the drawing room Roberta Merril Brown stood in the shadows, peeking out a window. She was in an unsettled mood; one of half panic at meeting this stranger and half anger at Adrien. He had *ordered*...ordered her, to be on the front veranda when he brought this woman, his first overnight guest in more than two years, home. "You're family, Berty, and I won't let you shrug off this duty. Be there!" He had insisted on the roses, too. In the window they were like a veritable signal, causing the neighbors to drive by, their curiosity aroused, though none had dared call or ask what the occasion.

Fingering the gris-gris that lay under her gray dress for courage, she watched for the last possible moment to make her appearance. The woman was looking at the house with a kind of awe on her face while Etienne unloaded luggage from the back of the truck. She was nothing like Eleanor, Berty noted with relief, and she was dressed sensibly. Eleanor had sneered at the house, called it unmodern, though Adrien wouldn't let her change a thing. And Eleanor had worn spiked heels that sank an inch in the mossy ground everytime she had stepped outdoors—not that she had very often. Now Adrien was taking the woman's arm, crossing the flagstones. No time left, she knew. Berty took a gulp of air, hurried into the hall, pushed open the enormous screen door, and advanced to the top step.

"Ah! Berty," Adrien said and introduced Jennifer to his cousin.

"Allo," she said in that musical accent Jennifer was coming to recognize as unique to Cajuns. "Everyone calls me Berty." Jennifer took the thin outstretched hand in her own and shook it firmly, then bent forward and kissed Berty lightly on her cheek.

"I'm glad to meet you. I hope we'll be friends." Jennifer was smiling, Etienne brushed past, suitcases under each arm, and Berty was riveted to the floor with astonishment. No one had greeted her so warmly, touched her so casually in years. Her eyes lit up and her fear of this stranger began to melt.

"Berty, show Jennifer to her room and the layout of the house. Etienne and I are headed to the barns to check on things there. I'll see you two at dinner."

"Come in...come in," Berty urged Jennifer. "It's too hot to stand around out here, no? We can get better acquainted over something cool—iced tea? Did Adrien tell you I used to work at the Guilbeaux?" Berty chatted nonstop, unable to halt the flood of words. She was like the prisoner held in isolation who had hoarded every thought, every word, saving them for the day of release. Jennifer noticed nothing amiss. She was grateful for the warm welcome into Adrien's home.

Hurrying to the barn, Adrien was enmeshed in thought. From the beginning he had wanted Jennifer, yet he was wary of letting their relationship go too far...too quickly. There was the business of the Ballesta visit. Selling a herd of heifers required concentration, attention to every detail, no matter how minor. The cash would enable him to develop the expensive, yet profitable science of artificial insemination on his breeder cows and the even more costly production of transferring embryos to carrier cows or surrogates. In that way he could maintain a small herd of Limousins, taking care to purchase and brood animals that could produce ten full-blooded offspring a year, provided he could afford the expense of transplanting. It was the newest method, perfected in Canada and proving to be a viable part of the cattle breeding industry, especially with the cost of feed skyrocketing.

He would find time, somewhere, to spend with Jennifer. He had to know more about her, lest he make the same mistake he had with Eleanor—choosing with his heart instead of his mind. Yet, he couldn't shake the strange up feeling that swept through him whenever he was near her...or the excitement mere thought of her generated. Morosely he wondered about her ambitions. Women today wanted careers first, families second. He wanted total commitment from his woman. Every man, he suspected, wanted that quality in a wife. As for himself, he wouldn't settle for less. He turned into the barn. It's warm rich smells brought him back to the immediate present. He noticed approvingly the bales of neatly stacked newly mown hay and, putting all thoughts of Jennifer aside, went to find Ralph. It was time to begin culling newborn calves.

Berty had mentioned the Guilbeaux a dozen times and she was disappointed that Jennifer hadn't picked up on it. She wanted desperately to ask about Henri Augustin. How had the past half dozen years treated him? Was he still happy-go-lucky? Still single? But the opening for casual inquiry just wasn't there, and she didn't dare initiate the questions herself. Sighing, she stopped at the kitchen entrance, beckoning Jennifer ahead, and saw the dismay written on the younger woman's face. Instinctively she knew its cause. The house.

All the doors along the hall were open, and in passing Jennifer had glanced into each. Her heart sank. The idyllic odyssey she had envisioned for the next few days was out of the question. Only the drawiwng room appeared to have seen recent use, and it might not stand close inspection. The dining room was cloaked in dust sheets, and even the drapes were shrouded. She could only wonder what condition the upstairs was in...and she was to have this house in pristine order for company by Sunday, plus arrange an elaborate meal for nine, then keep it in order and plan all the other meals for the few days the Ballestas were to be in residence?

Berty tried to be encouraging. "I know everything isn't what it should be, but since Eleanor left nothing has been the same—" she blurted. Oh! She had done the very thing Adrien had warned her not to. Nervously she rushed past the slip, hoping Jennifer wouldn't catch it. "The house isn't in as bad a shape as it looks. A little dusting, polishing, and airing will work wonders. I'll help," she volunteered.

Since Eleanor left? All thoughts of work, the Ballestas, food service, and housecleaning shot from Jennifer's mind. "Who is Eleanor?" she asked, pretending a pleasant calmness that she didn't feel.

"Uh, that's why the house is in such disorder," Berty said.

"But who exactly is Eleanor?" Jennifer pressed, not to be put off.

Pausing as she filled their glasses with iced tea, Berty's words came slowly, as though she wanted to examine each one of them before she spoke it aloud. "I'm not supposed to be mentioning her name—except Adrien isn't here, so how would he know? She was his wife. He met her one week when he was in Kansas City at an auction, married her the next and brought her here, and, well..." Her voice trailed off. There were some things better left unsaid. Even by her.

Jennifer sat down at the ancient wooden table, every bone in her body feeling like it had turned to water. "And—?" she asked, barely managing to whisper the word.

Berty shrugged. "She didn't like it here."

"She's gone?" Jennifer's heart began to thud unmercifully. "Is he—are they still married?"

"Oh, no. Eleanor made sure of that. More tea, no?" The conversation was running to dangerous ground, like quicksand, Berty guiltily feeling she had said far too much. "Please, don't mention this to Adrien... he's so touchy when it comes to Eleanor."

I'll just bet he is, Jennifer thought. "Of course not. I wouldn't dream of betraying a confidence," she assured Berty.

"It's not that so much. Everybody here knows everyone else's business, we live in such a small community, but—"

Jennifer reached across the table and laid her hand on Berty's. "It's okay. I understand." It was a disillusioning discovery, and she wouldn't feel comfortable about it until Adrien himself told her. "The tea hit the spot, but I'd better get upstairs and unpack now." As they stepped back into the hall Jennifer noticed for the first time a door tucked under the stairwell. "What's in there?" she asked.

"Adrien's study. We don't have to worry with it. He *likes* it messy."

Everything in the bedroom Berty led Jennifer to was sparkling, from the polished four-poster bed with a dotted swiss canopy to the wicker rocking chair padded with a plump inviting pillow. Beside the rocker a low table held a small lamp, while its twin nestled beside the bed, holding a much taller brass lamp. There was an efficient but serviceable bath, complete with tub. Snowy white linen was piled high on openwork shelves. The room was refreshingly cool, and the breeze brushing against her held the scent of flowers and fresh-cut hay. A closet was redolent with sachets of clove and mint.

"Except for the drawing room, we pull up all the carpets in the summer," Berty was saying, "so if you prefer something on the floor, I can have Ralph, our handyman, lay it down."

"Oh, no. This is lovely. If I can get the rest of the house looking like this, we'll be home free," she said.

Berty was pleased with her response. "I wish I'd had time to get the rest of the house like this, but Adrien keeps everything to himself until the last minute, though I thought you ought not have to make up your own bed on your first night here."

"I appreciate it. Thank you." Jennifer began to unpack. Berty cooed over her clothes, especially the dress she had bought only that morning. "You mentioned you worked at the hotel, Berty. Why did you leave?"

Having given up that talk could be guided back to the hotel, Berty was caught off guard. Her thin hand went to her chest, pressing against the gris-gris, the reposi-

tory of all her fears. "My husband...died," she said,
pausing at the small white lie. "I—I wasn't feeling too
well, so I came back to Lafourche. Adrien built me a
cottage right out back."

"I'm sorry," Jennifer said, noticing the melancholy
sweeping across Berty's face.

"He wasn't all that nice," Berty admitted with surprising truthfulness. "Sometimes I think men were just
put on earth to make us miserable, no?"

Jennifer laughed. "I couldn't agree with you more."

After Berty left to prepare supper, Jennifer fresh-
ened her makeup, discarded the scarf she wore around
her neck, and rewound her chignon. The specter of
Adrien's wife loomed large in her mind as she left
her room—former wife, she reminded herself. Absently she walked to the end of the upstairs hall and
peered out the window overlooking the bayou, dis-
covering that honeysuckle vines had edged themselves
about the windowsill. Hummingbirds were busy gathering nectar from the ivory trumpets. It was very
nice, she thought. Too nice. She could grow to love
this place.

And what about its owner? Could she grow to love
him, too? she wondered.

She liked what she had seen thus far, but she would
have to see more, much more, before she could answer
that with an unequivocal yes.

It never occurred to her that her answer might be no.

Impulsively she decided to take a quick look at the
guest rooms. That way she would be able to discuss
with Berty room assignments for Adrien's guests. Each
was musty, closed up, the beds bare of linen, with silvery cobwebs clinging to ceiling fixtures. She raised
windows as she went from room to room, allowing
fresh, flower-scented air to circulate. Dusted, polished,

beds made, supplied with flowers and the delightful clove and mint sachets, the rooms would take on a welcoming, inviting quality.

The master bedroom was the one beyond hers, facing the front lawns. Jennifer walked past, but curiosity drew her back. Just a quick peek, she admonished, convincing herself it was the appropriate thing to do. She opened the door and stepped into the room. Her breath caught in her throat.

A woman of striking beauty gazed out at her from a life-size portrait, hanging on the wall. The artist had used an innovative technique to create a unique lifelike quality in the oil. He had painted the woman arranging a bowl of white roses on a carved pedestal behind a tall French window. The expression on the woman's face suggested a slight sound had distracted her from her task. The scene was so realistically contrived that the viewer felt he was looking into the room captured on the canvas and perhaps it was his footsteps the lovely woman had heard. A few wisps of golden silky hair escaped the crown of braids, softening the barely perceptible frown the artist had painted above wide dark eyes. The eyebrows were arched, the nose was straight, and the full wide mouth was curved in a hesitant smile. Jennifer felt that at any moment the woman would step away from the window and knew, with unerring instinct, that the woman was Eleanor.

Why did Adrien keep her portrait here in his bedroom? And hung in such a manner that Eleanor's gaze seemed to wander over the bed?

The answer that Jennifer formed in her mind caused a thread of chill to knot itself firmly around her heart. Turning her back on the portrait, she walked over to Adrien's bed. It was magnificent; old, and carved with posts that reached toward the ceiling. She drew her fingertips across the pale woven spread, and an intensely disturbing sensation settled in her stomach. It was a bed to live in, to love in, and he had shared it. . . .

With difficulty she reminded herself that she was at Lafourche to work, nothing more.

Downstairs, she stood in the middle of the dining room, which would require the most work. She walked slowly across the floor and pulled the shrouded drapes away from the windows to discover they weren't windows at all, but a series of double doors that led onto a gallery or porch, much like the ones in her own apartment. A tranquil scene lay before her. The sun was beginning to slide under the horizon, and a duck, painted gold by the sun's last rays, waddled over a ridge into her view, followed by a line of fluffy yellow balls, miniatures of their parent.

Jennifer threw open the doors, taking deep satisfying breaths of the sweet April air, seeing the force of nature beginning anew all about her. "That must be my problem," she said aloud. "I'm still in the throes of spring fever." In New York and Washington spring had meant only changing wardrobes, vacations, a slight break in routine. Here it was something more basic, the renewal of life in nature's timetable. Her own feelings gave her a sharp awareness of the timeless cycle.

As she crossed the hall she entered the drawing room. One entire wall was given over to books, and Jennifer couldn't resist running her fingers along the titles. *The Adventures of Huckleberry Finn* was squeezed between Longfellow's *Evangeline* and Shakespeare's sonnets. A thick tome on cattle served as a bookend for masterpieces by Faulkner, Steinbeck, Hemingway, and Saul Bellow. A 1932 edition of *The Good Earth* kept company with a 1939 edition of *Jazzmen*. Above the fireplace were four lithographs, their frames a muted gray to enhance the strong lines of the prints. Two enormous gray velour sofas faced one another across a wide rosewood table that had it been longer could have seated eight for dinner with room to spare. Three Washington wing chairs covered in rich cranberry damask, each with its own footstool, were grouped at the far end of the room where a viewer could watch a built-in television or listen to music, separate from the room, yet a part of the whole. A dozen eighteenth-century miniature Austrian horsemen galloped across a small table, their brightly colored uniforms drawing the eye to the silk carpet covering the floor. The roses on their pedestal gave off a gentle fragrance. The room was unpretentious, exuding an atmosphere of comfort and quiet dignity. Jennifer was enchanted. The strange feeling that had engulfed her when she first arrived swept over her again. She tried to shake it off. Her mood was quiet, introspective, when she joined Berty in the kitchen a few minutes later.

"I heard you puttering around in the drawing room," she told Jennifer. "I'll get Ralph to take down all those dustcovers. They're too heavy for either one of us, anyway, no?"

Smiling, Jennifer agreed. "I won't argue with that. I'll take all the help I can get." For the next few minutes they discussed housework, food, and flower arrangements. Then Jennifer asked the question that lay heavy in her mind.

"When I was going over the upstairs, I accidentally wandered into Adrien's room.... Is the portrait up there of Eleanor?"

"Yes, but—"

The back door squeaked open. "Talking about me?" Adrien's mellow voice sounded directly behind Jennifer. "Again?" he added softly, bending low and putting the words into her ear as he walked on through the kitchen. Jennifer got a brief view of his sweat-soaked shirt. "Fix me a plate, Berty. I'll be back in a minute.

Ralph's on his way, too." He disappeared into the hall. When she could hear his footsteps taking the stairs two at a time, Jennifer turned back to Berty.

"What were you about to say?" Inside she was cold with dread and anxiety. She had to know why Adrien kept the portrait of Eleanor.

"Nothing." Berty's voice was frigid. She turned her attention to ladling ratatouille into a serving dish, and no amount of coaxing could get her back on the subject of Eleanor.

Ralph arrived and was introduced to Jennifer. He doffed his hat just enough for her to get a glimpse of a very large, very pink head, then he adjusted the cap firmly on his head again. He looked incredibly old, as bent and knobby and ancient as cypress stumps that jutted from the swamp. Jennifer half expected moss to sprout behind his ears, which drooped at the sides of his head like faithful retainers. The skin on his face, arms and hands were a continuous map of wrinkles, reflecting the sun and wind that had burnished it into a tough old leather. His eyes were dark and small, yet they darted everywhere, missing nothing, and he had a wide mustache of which he seemed inordinately proud. He stroked it now and then as he waited silently for food to be served.

"Ralph doesn't speak any English," Berty said. "So just tell me if there's anything you want him to do, though you'll have to wave food under his nose to get him into the house. He'd rather be out in the barns with his animals, as you can tell by the smell." Berty wrinkled her nose. "Never met a man so adverse to soap and water in my life." She spoke to him sharply in the Cajun patois. His beady eyes shot a look at Jennifer, then, disgruntled, he got up and washed his hands at the sink.

Adrien returned, bringing with him the fresh car-

bolic scent of Lifebuoy and wearing a clean plaid shirt.
"I suppose Berty has been telling you all our family
secrets," he said, sitting down next to Jennifer. The
plate Berty was putting before him nearly slid from her
fingers.

"No, we were discussing the Ballestas, assigning
rooms, and deciding how to split up the work." Jennifer spoke up and saw relief wash over Berty.

"Is that so?" His voice mocked disbelief.

"Yes, it is so," Jennifer countered. "I've just been
trying to convince her that she shouldn't be serving at
all during the dinner. As family, she should be at the
table—"

"Oh, no!" Berty butted in. "I'm happy the way
things are." She was horrified. "The less you involve
me, the better I like it."

"Even so," Jennifer went on, "there's still going to
be a problem with just you to serve dinner. Henri can
help some, but he'll be tied to the kitchen with his last-
minute sauces and garnishes. There just has to be a
third person to remove dishes between courses, unless
you prefer that I do it." She looked directly at Adrien.

"You can't do it, you're the hostess. It wouldn't be
seemly."

"Seemly? Where do you get your stubborn sense of
etiquette? That's so old-fashioned."

"There are some values that never go out of date,"
he replied firmly. "Berty, can we get Leddy to help?"

"Might," she said hesitantly. "But you know that
she and Etienne aren't getting along all that well, and
she's spending a lot of time at her *maman's.*"

Adrien's fork stopped in midair, a glimmer of surprise on his face. "They aren't getting along already?
They just got married. What's happened?"

Berty shrugged. "Well, I heard from Louisa, who
heard from—"

"Spare me that," he said sharply. "Just what's the problem?"

"Leddy won't accept congress," she answered, "and it's driving Etienne wild."

"Mon Dieu," he murmured thoughtfully as he began to eat again. "Strange, I haven't noticed. His work is okay."

Intrigued, Jennifer spoke up. "You mean this girl Leddy won't accept the Congress of the United States, and they're fighting over politics?"

Adrien laughed. Berty was smiling, too. "No," she said, "sexual congress. Leddy won't allow Etienne into their marriage bed."

"Oh." Jennifer felt herself becoming pink.

Adrien finished his meal, spoke a few words to Ralph, then stood up. "C'mon," he said to Jennifer. "I'll show you around before it gets too dark." It was more of a command than an invitation. Jennifer was willing to go in either instance. Adrien lifted a battered tin plate filled with food scraps from the sink counter. "Is this for the Old Man?"

Berty told him yes. "But set it well away from the back porch. I don't want him prancing and squawking so close to the house," she said.

"Cat?" Jennifer asked, following Adrien out the back door.

"No." He walked several yards away from the stoop, set the tin dish down, and moved back to Jennifer. Suddenly a huge and heavy bird flew down from a cedar and began pecking away at the food in a preemptive manner. Jennifer gasped in delight.

"A peacock! It's beautiful."

"Smart, too. Taught me all I know about women — negatively speaking," he said, taking Jennifer's hand. Walking down a path bordered on one side by lush green cane and on the other by lines of great trees hung

with moss, Jennifer found the landscape harsh and for-
bidding. Perhaps it was just the deep gloom of twilight,
the way the roots of the trees gnarled and dipped into
the blackwater swamp. Adrien talked of rice, cane, the
cattle he hoped to sell, but said nothing of himself, his
personal self. He didn't mention Eleanor. His voice had
a buoyancy, a throaty contentment that hadn't been
prominent in New Orleans. It was as though he had
taken on another personality, or perhaps she was just
seeing another side of him. Yet, there was a harshness
in the lines of his face, expressing a deep-felt bitterness, seemingly put there by experience rather than by
the wind or the weather. There was about him a quality
of ownership, of possessiveness, that, as in truth, he
owned all that he surveyed. Jennifer put questions to
him carefully, as though reluctant to pry, but the intensity of her gaze, of her golden-flecked eyes as she
looked at him, and the way she tilted her head so as not
to miss a word he said gave her away. He told her of
Uncle Jean-Marc, of hunting trips with his father, of
rogue alligators that devoured newborn calves, but
nothing of the present. A dog barked in the distance
and, closer, cows lowed. Frogs in the creek began their
mating songs. Jennifer sighed inwardly as Adrien led
her toward a levee.

She was aware of the sounds in some faraway sense,
but every vibrant nerve in her body was attuned to the
man walking at her side as he swung her hand, clasped
firmly in his. Words no longer seemed necessary as
they walked in companionable silence along the bayou.
Adrien stopped abruptly at a wooden bench nearly hidden from view by trailing branches. He sat down and
unexpectedly drew Jennifer onto his lap.

"Mmm, finally, I have you to myself," he murmured, clamping an arm across her legs to hold her
precisely where he wanted her.

"Turn me loose," Jennifer said, surprised that the words rushed out when she desired exactly the opposite.

"Not a chance," he retorted, "after all the trouble I've gone to to get you here." He nuzzled her earlobe, tickled her neck with his lips in featherlight kisses, while his fingers seemed to be setting their brand to her hip and thigh. Jennifer thought the tingling sensation under her skin would turn it inside out. Her mind emptied of every thought, as there was no room for any but the recording of the deliciousness of the moment.

It was as though her body had been waiting, searching for just such a moment for release from self-imposed restraint, and the throbbing vein where Adrien's lips were pressed dispatched this message of incessant desire and need.

"What trouble?" she whispered, mesmerized, while his hands and lips continued their journey of exploration.

"Lots of trouble," he said from somewhere deep in his throat. "I owe you this one," he murmured, trailing a tantalizing path across her cheek, "for driving me crazy."

"Crazy?" Jennifer said, her lips moving against his, slightly parted to welcome him.

"Straightjacket crazy," he told her, claiming her mouth, and their language became that of lovers: caresses, soft moans, kisses beginning and ending, only to start again. Jennifer was breathless, responding to him with an ardency that both delighted and surprised Adrien. Her nerves skimmed to the very edge of her skin, absorbing sensation after erotic sensation. His skin tasted of soap, and for Jennifer it was like an aphrodisiac concocted to quench a long-standing thirst.

Adrien toyed with the buttons on her jacket and, using trembling fingers, opened it wide, revealing her soft round breasts, perfectly shaped twins of burnished gold in the cool white light of the rising moon.

"You're beautiful," he said softly, cupping her breasts in his hands and kissing the deep cleft between them.

Unable to watch, Jennifer threw her head back, glorying in ecstacy as his lips and tongue began teasing her nipples until they peaked. It was this moment that she had envisioned in her dreams—Adrien's hands moving passionately over her flesh, his mouth tender, forceful, demanding, and seemingly insatiable. She lost herself in the sensual excitement, floating, riding the crest of a celestial storm. It was the prelude to total fulfillment. She raised her lashes fractionally, uncovering eyes smoldering with desire. The house loomed in the background, barely visible through the trees, as stage scenery, and she and Adrien were the actors in a play of incredible passion. The lights came on in the drawing room, and she was looking into the scene on the canvas. The bowl of white roses was clearly illuminated, waiting only for the delicate hands of Eleanor....

His kisses, caresses, and hoarse imprecations of love were made meaningless, and the flaming desire snuffed itself out. Gulping air, she jumped out of his lap, shattering the intensity and shamelessness of their abandonment in one another.

Taken by surprise, Adrien stared at her through bewildered, lust-laden eyes, and when he spoke, though his voice was low, it seemed to thunder across the lawn. "What—? *Mon Dieu!*"

"*Mon Dieu*...yourself," she mimicked precisely, yet hesitantly, her tongue unused to the turn of phrase. "Is this your standard employee—employer relationship?" she quipped to cover the confused maelstrom trembling within her.

Adrien couldn't understand her sudden reversal of feelings. "This has nothing to do with work; it's of the heart. You want this as much as I do. You like me—a man knows these things," he said, certain of himself as his mind cleared.

She stood a few feet away, not trusting herself to be too close, yet reluctant to leave. The air was charged with the musky scent of desire, of their wanting, and she was miserable. She wanted to be made love to, wanted to love back.... Frank Crompton had spurned her for another woman. Now Adrien Merril had had a wife and something of her lingered, else why keep her portrait? Jennifer felt she was batting zero in choosing a man. As she sought composure a night bird fluttered overhead, its wings made silvery by moonlight that tinged her skin with ghostly white. She saw Adrien's gaze drop to her heaving breasts, their silken flesh still tumescent from his touch. She buttoned her jacket. "All men know about are their biological urges," she said, telling herself it was one truth undisputed. "You have a whole wall of books, maybe you should include Margaret Mead. She lists them in detail."

"Margaret Me—" he sputtered, still mystified by her behavior. "I have read Margaret Mead, and at least she had the good sense to live with a man before she began to rout his faults."

"Well, lucky you," Jennifer canted softly. "You only have one—you breathe!"

In the next instant he was standing near her, his muscles rippling with unleashed anger—anger that had been balled up inside of him for two years—his hands crushed into fists, rigid at his side. He couldn't trust them to flail the air. "What's come over you? Is it that you think you're too good...too sophisticated for a Lafourchais?"

"I didn't mean that at all," she said, recoiling at his

attack. His words continued to fly across the small space between them.

"Oh? You prance around here, no?—with your nose in the air, wearing all those fine clothes, expensive perfume..., I know your kind, intimately! As well I should. I was married to—" He stopped his tirade abruptly. The sense of rejection he had felt when Jennifer leaped from his arms reminded him of Eleanor, who had drowned his ego in that bayou flowing past his door for all to see. Adrien heaved a great moan. Jennifer was not to blame for his mistake. He had the ferocious instinct of the hawk: soar high, survive, with no apologies. *Mon Dieu!* he thought. He had stepped off a precipice without a glance at the chasm below. His fury died down as quickly as it had flared.

The twin beams of a car swung across them as it turned into the drive. A car door slammed, and as Adrien looked past her a mask slid over his features, hiding his emotions. "Some friends of mine," he explained. "I've invited them for coffee tonight so you won't feel so among strangers on Sunday night." He took her elbow, his fingers biting into her flesh as a warning. "We'll talk this out later. Come along, I'll introduce you."

Jennifer was too weary, too drained, to do anything except let herself be propelled along in helpless acquiescence.

Barbara Dubois had a perfect body: long legs, a thin waist, full breasts, and silky brown hair that accentuated the oval contours of a creamy complexioned face that was lit with smiling violet eyes. She was petite, with an appearance like that of an exquisite porcelain doll that had somehow in the magic of wonderland grown up. Her eyes flashed with quick intelligence, a sharp wit, and she gave off the exuberance of one who loves life. She also had an uncanny instinct for ferreting out the most sensitive details of one's life.

Her husband, on the other hand, was positively the ugliest man Jennifer had ever laid eyes on. Jean Dubois had a large head, short-cropped hair, which was prematurely graying, a long nose which literally seemed to droop over his thin mouth, and a squat compact body, featuring enormous hands that held one's attention, if only you could get past his Adam's apple, which bobbed incessantly. There were laugh lines about his eyes and mouth in darkly tanned skin that was the texture of unfinished concrete. He spoke to Jennifer in a low, gravelly voice, then took Adrien's arm and whisked him to the group of wing chairs, leaving the women to sprawl on the gray velour sofas. Fascinated, Jennifer couldn't seem to draw her eyes away from Jean. She noticed Barbara watching her and, embarrassed, looked away.

Barbara laughed gently. "Jean always creates a sensation when he meets strangers. He knows he's ugly," she said forthrightly. "His story is that after everyone else on earth was created, God looked around and saw all these extra parts, and not one to waste, He made Jean up of all those leftovers. He's sort of like a short squat Frankenstein who is very kind and marvelously tender," she added softly.

"I'm—sorry I was staring," Jennifer admitted.

"Amazing as it sounds," Barbara said, laughing, "he's proud of his looks and would be disappointed if you hadn't." Barbara glanced around the room approvingly. "Don't you just love this house? Everything is so old—renovated every now and then, but still old. Take those wing chairs, for instance. They're reproductions of the original in the Smithsonian, but a hundred years old themselves. Imagine a copy that's an antique itself!"

Jennifer smiled politely. "Adrien said he invited you

for coffee, so I'd better see about it. Will you excuse me?''

"Oh. I didn't mean to bore you," Barbara said. "You have a sort of drawn look. I thought I would stay away from any touchy subjects. I'll come with you. The men are going to be talking cattle, and I know every blessed thing about cattle that I ever want to know."

Jennifer was taken aback by Barbara's openness and her observation. She was silent as she led the way into the kitchen. Berty had left. The dishes were air-drying on a wooden drain that covered one of the cavernous sinks. Feeling Barbara's eyes following her as she scrounged for coffee, cups, and saucers in the unfamiliar kitchen put her on an emotional edge. The scene with Adrien had left her visibly vulnerable, and Barbara picked up on this vulnerability like a magnet pulling tacks.

She said, "This is the first time I've been here since Eleanor left." At the startled look on Jennifer's face she thought, Aha! Home run. "But you must know all about Eleanor."

"Only that there is—was—that she exists," Jennifer said flatly.

"Hmmm, that's strange. You'd think Adrien would tell you everything, clear the air, so to speak."

"Oh, no," Jennifer denied, suddenly aware of where the conversation was leading. "I was brought here only to take care of the Ballesta visit. I'm catering manager at the Guilbeaux—"

"Adrien's white elephant," Barbara injected.

"He needed a hostess for the upcoming week, and my boss sent me."

"Pooh. Adrien doesn't have to go through all this trouble to impress a cattle buyer—he never has before. It's just an excuse. Frankly, everybody has been buzzing with speculation since you arrived."

Privately, Jennifer was aghast. Aloud, she said smoothly, "There's not a thing to speculate about. I was sent here to do a job, and that's it."

Barbara administered the coup de grace. "What were you two doing out on the lawn when we drove up?"

Jennifer felt the heat sweep up from her breasts and move like a red tide to her cheeks. "Uh, Adrien was showing me the grounds. I've never been in the country before." The coffee was perking, filling the room with its rich sharp aroma. All of Jennifer's senses were alert. She felt like the captain on a sinking ship. She knew she couldn't save it, but she gave it her best try. "I know what you're thinking. But there's nothing between us. I only just met him last month."

Barbara smiled and accepted the lie courteously. "You know, you have a look about you—you could easily be taken for one of us."

"One of you?" Jennifer was puzzled.

"Acadian."

They were on safer ground, for which Jennifer was relieved. She laughed. "There's not a drop of French blood in me. I'm Irish and Lithuanian."

"A volatile combination. I'll bet you have temper tantrums...."

Jennifer smiled. "Like a fishwife lately, it seems."

"I knew it!" Barbara advanced with glee. "We interrupted a lovers' quarrel. I recognized that look on your face when Adrien introduced us. And you were too civilized—covering up. You do like Adrien," she added quietly.

Jennifer went down with the ship. "A little bit, perhaps. But truly, there's no commitment...I mean—"

"Listen," Barbara said in a confidential whisper, "you have to understand these Cajun men. They carry their pride in their back pockets like handkerchiefs, and every time they even suspect someone is going to

sneeze on their precious egos, they yank it out and
wave it like protective armor. The problem with Adrien
is, he misjudged Eleanor and now he doesn't trust
women. You can overcome that—it just takes patience,
and you might as well begin storing it up, because it
takes an ungodly amount of it to survive in these back-
waters. The coffee's ready," she said as an aside. Jennifer began loading up the serving cart that sat against a
far wall. Barbara continued talking.

"Adrien feels certain things about his family. He's
really tuned into his past and the future, especially the
future. I don't know how to explain it, except it's sort
of like a mistress thing. And he's so traditional—
father-son customs mean a lot to him. He was practically destroyed when Eleanor aborted his baby. It was a
hateful thing for her to do."

Jennifer was stunned. "I didn't know. Why? Why
would she do a thing like that?"

Barbara shrugged. "She wasn't what you would call
the mothering type."

And Adrien had accused her of being like Eleanor,
Jennifer thought. She shuddered. It wasn't fair.

With that all-knowing woman's instinct, Barbara said
nothing more of Adrien's former wife. Jennifer could
figure the rest out for herself. Back in the drawing
room, they spent another hour pleasantly discussing
fashions, Cajun customs, and working women. When
the antique clock on the mantel under the lithographs
chimed the hour of nine, she signaled Jean it was time
to leave. To Jennifer, she explained, "It's a school
night, and we've got a baby-sitter to get home."

After the Duboises drove away, Jennifer began to
clear away the used dishware. Cups rattled in their
saucers, clinking and jangling, just like her nerves.
Adrien stood in front of the windows, looking outward, deep in thought. They were alone, his back was

to her, yet there was a sudden tightening of tension between them that hovered in the air.

Jennifer longed to leave the room, but she stayed where she was, too tired to even predict what Adrien would say or do next. He turned to gaze at her, his face etched with concentration. "About this evening... out on the levee. I didn't mean what I said."

What about what you did? Was that a mistake, too? She desperately wanted the answer to this, yet the accusation he had hurled at her bit deeper now in light of what Barbara Dubois had revealed about Eleanor. She couldn't just let him sweep it under the rug. "You could have fooled me," she replied and, turning her back, swept imperiously from the room. She was on the third step, her hand gliding along the cool railing, when he reached her. His hand closed over hers.

"You're behaving like a snob," he said grimly.

She snatched her hand out from under his. "I'm behaving like me. If you don't like it, that's your problem." She negotiated the remaining stairs with his dark eyes boring into her back.

"Perhaps I wasn't wrong," he said softly, savagely. "Women are all alike."

Jennifer heard the muted words and bent over the railing, looking down at him in the dimly lit hall. "If you mean that every female body has twenty square feet of skin and thirteen billion nerve cells that you seem to have a knack for rubbing raw," she said with silky reasonableness, "then, yes, you're right—we are all alike. Good night."

Chapter Nine

On Friday morning Jennifer awoke early, her supple body sore and aching, still taut with the tension she had carried into bed with her last night. She felt guilty. Her own ego had gotten in the way of her accepting his apology last night. If only he hadn't been so stiff-necked about it. Falling in love was too painful. It was wondrous and it hurt. It had never been this way with Frank Crompton. She thought back on those days as her silly youth. It was a measure of Jennifer's determination that she spoke aloud as she climbed from the canopied bed. "I'll make him love me. I'll make him forget all about Eleanor."

But she had no opportunity to put this reckless, impetuous ambition into action. Wearing a white blouse, a comfortable wraparound skirt, with her thick red-brown hair arranged in a single braid, she hurried downstairs, only to discover that Adrien had arisen far earlier and had left the house.

Disappointed, she took coffee and a light breakfast with Berty. They divided the household chores and began work. Adrien didn't come up to the house for lunch. Another disappointment. Jennifer put all her energy into cleaning. By midafternoon the house was taking shape. The upstairs bedrooms were ready and the drawing room and hall had had a thorough going-over. Tired, but satisfied with the progress they were making, Jennifer went into the kitchen for something cool to drink. Berty, Ralph, and Etienne were clustered around the table. Upon seeing Jennifer, Etienne blushed furiously and jumped up, knocking over his chair. Puzzled at Etienne's seeming embarrassment, Jennifer asked, "Am I interrupting something?"

"No, no." Berty smiled, waving the men out of the kitchen. "Etienne, you can pick this up later," she said, indicating the tall pitcher of juice that sat on the old rosewood table.

"They don't have to leave on my account," Jennifer protested, but Etienne was already backing out the door, followed by Ralph, who was grinning slyly. "For heaven's sake! What was that all about?" she asked Berty as the screen door slammed shut behind the men.

"Ah, well...you'll hear about it sooner or later—nothing is sacred on this bayou."

"Hear what?" Jennifer said absently, looking in the refrigerator for a 7-Up or a Coke.

"You remember last night we were talking about Leddy and Etienne? Now he's getting desperate and worrisome. He's asked me for a love potion, a gris-gris."

Jennifer slanted a skeptical glance at the older woman. "Gris-gris? Am I hearing what I think I'm hearing?—in the twentieth century? Don't tell me you believe in that sort of superstitious nonsense. It sounds like what your history books accused Marie Laveau, the voodoo queen, of doing."

"Anybody can make a gris-gris to eat, drink, or wear," Berty insisted shyly, patting the one she wore safely out of sight. "They don't hurt anything, and Etienne believes—that's all that counts."

"Do you believe?" Jennifer asked.

Berty struggled for an answer. She didn't want to get in trouble with God. "It's not as good as prayer, I guess," she said slowly.

Jennifer, the city girl, watched with fascination while Berty sorted herbs, a pinch of this, a leaf of that, stirring them into the pitcher. She picked up the herbs and sniffed. Bay leaf. Crumbled basil. "Berty, I know these herbs, and that"—she pointed to the glass pitcher—"smells and looks like tomato juice to me."

"Tomatoes were once thought to be love apples, no?" Berty countered. "This is a love tonic...one sip and your true love will love you forever."

"Oh, pooh," Jennifer said, smiling, and then because she couldn't help it, she asked, "Does it really work?"

"We'll just have to wait and see, no?" Berty replied, enjoying immensely the attention she was receiving from Jennifer.

"We're going to have drop-ins," Adrien rumbled as he came hurrying into the kitchen, startling both women. They turned to stare as he moved through the room.

"Drop-ins?" Jennifer muttered. "Wait a minute!" she called to Adrien. "Who's dropping in? For what? The Ballestas? Two whole days ahead of schedule?" She fired the questions at him with a sense of growing horror. There was so much yet to do!

Adrien paused on the threshold to the hall. "No, my neighbors. Mrs. Prejean just sent a message to Ralph to escort her. She's over ninety and can't hobble about without help."

"When? What time?" Jennifer followed up anxiously.

"Three o'clock."

Jennifer glanced at her watch. "Good lord! That's only ten minutes from now. You're sure?"

"I'm positive. The English have their tea at four, the Americans their cocktails at five, and we Cajuns break for coffee and visiting at three—"

"Can't you head them off? We're just not prepared," Jennifer pleaded.

"I can't. They know the house is open again and they know you're here. They'd be insulted if I did. They're my neighbors; friends of mine, and my parents before me. It's custom, Jennifer. You better get cracking."

"What does my being here have to do with this?"

"I'll explain later," he said. "We're just wasting time. I've got to clean myself up—"

"How many?" Jennifer asked, dreading his answer.

"About ten, possibly more if they bring their children, which they are bound to do."

Jennifer moaned. "All that work in the drawing room. It'll be a wreck!"

Adrien's eyes narrowed. "You'll just have to clean it up again, won't you?" he muttered sarcastically.

"And to think I was feeling guilty about not accepting your apology last night." She whipped the words out, glaring at him.

"What apology?" he asked, throwing the retort over his shoulder. "I have to clean up."

"Out!" Jennifer hissed at him. "Just get out of here before I throw something!" Adrien stepped back into the kitchen and took her by the arm, pulling her into the privacy of the hall.

"Don't you ever speak to me in my own house like that again," he said, anger making his eyes appear black.

"I don't have to take that from you," she spat, jerking her arm loose.

"You do as long as you're working for me—you will!"

"Who do you think you are? King of the Swamp or something? I quit."

"I don't give a damn what you do after Tuesday," he stormed, "but right now you get in that kitchen and get coffee going—lots of it." As he stalked up the stairs Jennifer stood riveted to the floor, watching him ascend, then, shaking her head in misery, she stepped back into the kitchen. Berty glanced once at Jennifer, then averted her eyes. She began to remove her apron, edging toward the back screen door.

"Are you really going to quit?" she asked.

"No. I say foolish things when I get angry. I'm sorry you had to hear—" Now Berty had her apron off, folded over her arm, her lace cuffs rolled down. Understanding dawned on Jennifer. "Berty! Where are you going? What on earth— Aren't you going to help me?" She latched onto Berty's arm before she could complete her escape.

Swallowing hard, Berty muttered her reluctance. "I can't. Adrien didn't ask me."

"I'm asking," Jennifer pleaded in rising panic. Those people would be on the doorstep any minute now. "I'll never be able to handle so many on short notice like this. Don't run out on me."

"They—they'll be uncomfortable if I'm around," Berty said firmly. "It'll just make things go bad for you, no?"

Jennifer almost laughed in hysteria. "How could anything be worse than it is right this minute?" She took a deep breath. "Now, Berty, be reasonable. You know these people. I don't even speak the language. You can't make anything bad for me. You're acting like you have some horrid social disease. Now, please—"

"I do," Berty admitted fearfully. "Leprosy, and they know it." Berty heard herself saying the word she had promised never to mention again to a living soul and wondered why she felt so compelled to utter these inner secrets to a complete stranger.

Jennifer almost fainted from embarrassment. It had to be the truth. No one would lie about such a thing. She was stumped for words, but at the wretched look on Berty's thin face she knew she had to speak—and quickly. She slid her arm around Berty's shoulders. "I'm so sorry. Please, forgive me. Adrien got me riled up, and I never think before I speak. I didn't mean to hurt your feelings. You've been just wonderful. Look, I understand, I'll manage this somehow. Just show me where more coffeepots are, as I'll need two at least."

Berty hesitated as Jennifer moved toward the pantry. "Jennifer, you mean you're not scared of me? You're not going to run away? You're not afraid to touch me?"

Astounded, Jennifer halted in midstep, then moved quickly back to Berty and took the woman's thin trembling hands in her own. "Berty, I don't know why you have such an idea about me, but no, I'm not going to run away, and I'm certainly not afraid to touch you. You're living in the dark ages. I've never known anyone with leprosy before, but I do know that it's not contagious. So why should I be afraid of you?" She bent and kissed Berty on the cheek.

"Eleanor was," Berty said with deep sadness. "That's why she left Adrien and—and why she wouldn't have his baby."

"Dear God," Jennifer said softly. Berty began to cry, sobbing into the folded apron. Jennifer was pulled in two directions at once: that of comforting Berty, whom she liked, and getting things prepared for Adrien's neighbors, who would appear any minute now. "Berty," she said quietly, "a woman doesn't leave a man she loves because of something like this, nor does she abort his baby. The trouble goes deeper, a dissatisfaction somewhere along the line...something in their marriage that just didn't click. And Adrien...well, he doesn't seem to be a man who's easy to live with."

"He didn't used to be like he is now," Berty said between sobs. She hunted for the pocket in her apron, drew out a handkerchief, and blew her nose.

Jennifer smiled. "Now, Berty, you can't tell me that man hasn't always been stubborn and pigheaded."

Berty gave her a tentative smile. "He is that. I—I guess I've just been feeling sorry for myself all these years. I want to tell you something. My husband isn't dead. I'm not a widow. He left me when I got sick."

"He's an imbecile," said Jennifer, "and you've had a lot of trauma to deal with. That takes courage."

Suddenly Berty felt very brave. "You know what? I'll stay and help you, no? So what if everyone stares at me like I'm a freak!" She felt herself coming alive, backing out of her shell like the blue crabs did when they began to molt and formed new hard skins.

Jennifer sighed.

"Berty, if anybody says anything out of the way or behaves rudely, why—we'll just take them outside and toss them into the creek."

"There's some pound cake I baked before you came and strawberry shortcake in the fridge. What do you think?" Berty said as she found a fresh apron and began to bustle about the kitchen. A car door slammed, and there was the babble of voices as Adrien greeted his neighbors.

"I think you're a lifesaver," Jennifer told her as she began to stack cups, saucers, cream, and sugar on the trolley. She couldn't know how warmly indebted to her Berty felt at that moment.

For the next hour and a half Jennifer performed

skillfully with the finesse she had learned at the Guilbeaux. More than two dozen of Adrien's neighbors showed up. She was stared at, talked to in the patois she didn't understand, whispered about, smiled at, and had her fortune told by old Mrs. Prejean. She didn't understand a word, but the old woman kept nodding her head and smiling at Jennifer so that she felt there had been no dire predictions. Adrien moved among his guests with serene equability. He smiled at the women, talked with the men, and picked up and hugged each of the children, who seemed to adore him, while Jennifer ignored him. Berty was aglow. No one was the least standoffish toward her, and two of the women followed her to and from the kitchen as she perked more coffee, brought in more cake, and found cookies for the children. They filled her ears with gossip so that Jennifer overheard only her exclamations. "No!" "*Mon Dieu!*" "How awful, no?" "She really did?" "What did her husband say?" One pleasant surprise for Jennifer was that Leddy Beauchamp, Etienne's wife, came with her mother, and she promised Jennifer she would arrive early the next morning to help.

As Adrien saw the last of the lot to the front door, Jennifer stood in the middle of the room, surveying the damage. The Austrian horsemen no longer pranced across the table, but lay scattered about where the children had engaged in a game of war. She gathered the miniatures, which were incredibly sticky. A fat strawberry, still coated with whipped cream, lay under the coffee table on the silk carpet. Ashtrays were filled, napkins and dirty dishes and silverware lay everywhere. She began moving about the room, putting it in order.

"Can you leave that a minute, Jennifer?" Adrien asked as he paused at the door. "Come into my study."

She didn't like the prospect but followed him anyway. The study had that pack rat look that reminded her of her mother's studio office. She felt an instant of melancholy. She hadn't seen her parents in almost a year. The feeling was swept away as Adrien cleared a spot for her to sit on the cowhide sofa, then went to sit behind his desk.

"Yes, boss?" she said, filling the words with animosity.

He had the grace to wince. "You—look, can we back-pedal?"

Their eyes met. She saw something flicker in the depth of his gaze that she couldn't put a name to. "On a professional level...or personal?" she asked, taking the plunge.

"Both."

He was making it hard for her. She sat up straighter. "I'd have to think about it."

He pushed some papers around on his desk. "You're a beautiful and stubborn woman." There might have been the tiniest of smiles beginning at the corner of his mouth.

"You're a prideful man, and you know what they say about that—'pride goeth...before a fall.'"

"Comes with the territory," he said. "A terrible burden." His face became serious. "I don't know what you said or did to Berty to—"

"We had a nice talk." Jennifer stood up, smoothing her skirt. "Will that be all?"

"Yes, except that you were a big hit with my friends. They liked you."

"I liked them, too." She was remembering the vow she had made to herself to make him love her as she left the study. She paused and turned back. "We're about even, aren't we?"

"Not in my book," he said derisively. "I'd say I've been routed, thoroughly, no?"

Jennifer smiled. If he had stepped out from behind his desk and taken her into his arms at that very minute, she would have melted. He didn't, and she returned to the tasks at hand.

Adrien leaned back in his chair and closed his eyes. His thoughts drifted. Unbidden, Eleanor came into his mind. He realized with an evanescent sixth sense that she reminded him only of his grief for the loss of his child, and he had grieved long enough. He needed to wash his mind of the past. He knew it as well as he knew the lines around his eyes or the scent he left behind in the swamp when he went hunting.

Recalling Mrs. Prejean's fortune-telling, he smiled. If Jennifer knew the old lady had predicted that he and Jennifer would have a long, happy marriage, five children, and grow wealthy in years to come, Jennifer would not have sat across from him just now so calmly. His thoughts slipped to the previous evening, to the few minutes of ecstacy they had shared on the levee. There was the velvety feel of her skin; soft breasts that responded so willingly to his touch. By and by the little gremlins that pestered him when he least expected it became acutely active, making it impossible for him to sit still any longer. Reluctantly he returned to work among his cattle.

At dinner that night Jennifer and Adrien spoke to each other briefly and then only in the most polite terms, combatants who, having tentatively spoken of truce, now carefully explored alternatives. Ralph ate in silence, but Berty was animated with her success earlier in the day. She put questions to Adrien, translated Cajun French comments for Jennifer, and shot disapproving looks at Ralph, reminding him that his help would be required in the house the following morning.

Adrien was the first to finish dinner. He stood up.

"Henri is driving in tonight after he finishes his shift at the Guilbeaux. Is his room ready?" He directed the question to Jennifer.

"Yes, the one across from me. Okay?"

"Fine. I have work to do, so I'll wait up for him. He should arrive by midnight."

A few hours later on a deep creek on a renovated barge moored to a dry island, Etienne Beauchamp lay on a cot and waited impatiently for the gris-gris to take effect on his bride. In an unheard-of burst of domesticity in a Cajun man he had prepared a dinner of fried catfish and boiled potatoes, serving it up with a spicy tomato juice instead of tea or coffee. Leddy had been pleased and praised his efforts and drank deeply of the juice he urged on her.

Something should have happened by now, he decided. He slipped off the cot and shuffled quietly into the area he had created for their bedroom. Leddy lay curled in a soft heap, her even breathing telling him what he feared the most. She was sound asleep. *Mon Dieu!* He would have to begin again. Something stronger this time, he thought.

A few miles away Roberta Merril Brown sat on the end of the tiny pier in front of her cottage, watching the fireflies flicker and blink while the bayou flowed black beneath her feet. All the while she and Jennifer had been doing supper dishes she had wanted to ask about Henri Augustin, but she could find no casual way to inject his name into their conversation.

Henri Augustin was a flirt. She knew it when she had worked at the Guilbeaux. He hadn't meant a thing by those looks he had slanted her way and which she had pretended to ignore. After all, she had had no choice, for then she had been a married woman.

But now...now— How could he possibly be interested in her? Would he even remember her? she wondered. She had changed, lost weight—and there was no gris-gris in the world powerful enough to undo the disease that tore at her. The medication, the miracle drug she took had halted its progression, but she was still a leper—a fifty-six-year-old love-starved leper. Sad, Berty got up and went into her tiny cottage. She undressed for bed and, naked, stood in front of her mirror.

Do you see anything there, she asked her image silently, that would please a man? She peered closer, noting the lines about her eyes and mouth, her work-worn hands. She didn't even have any makeup any more—she just hadn't been interested. But suppose... just suppose Henri Augustin did remember her? Suppose there had been something in that gleam in his eyes? *Oh, but that was so many years ago, no?... I know, I know,* she told the thin wraith staring back at her, *but all I'm asking is: Just suppose?* Berty slipped into a robe and hurried into the kitchen.

A woman her age ought to take care of herself, especially a sick woman, or end up looking like death warmed over, she realized. She moved around the kitchen with a speed that would have challenged a ten-year-old searching for a well-hidden cookie jar. From a shelf she took down a pot of homemade strawberry jam and pried off its paraffin seal. She washed the wax and set it to melting in a pan over a low flame. As it melted she added a heaping tablespoon of Jergens all-purpose face cream, stirring the concoction until it bubbled and was smooth. She took up a feather baster she had fashioned herself and carried the warm mixture into her bedroom and sat down before the mirror. Working fast before the mixture cooled, she brushed it over her face, her neck, then the top of each hand.

There was still a little bit left in the pan and she eyed it. Oh, who was to know? she thought, and did the most wicked, sinful thing she had ever done in her life. She opened her robe, removed the amulet from around her neck, and brushed the remaining mixture on her breasts.

Standing at the window in her room, dressed in pajamas, Jennifer watched as a John Steinbeck gray flannel fog began to drift in over the bayou, blotting out the moon and the lights in cottages hidden among the pecan groves where cattle grazed beyond the barns. She had padded down to the kitchen twice in the past hour, first to make tea, then to return the cup. Each time the study door had remained closed, though she had deliberately rattled the tea kettle against the stove, coughed when she passed the door. Finally, she had determined to knock—just to say good night—and as she stood there, hand raised, the telephone rang and she heard Adrien's deep voice engage in conversation. She dallied outside the door a moment longer, deciphering that he was talking to his good friend Jean. When it became apparent that he had settled back to talk awhile, she retreated.

Now, in the privacy of her room with time to think, the angry words that had spilled and spat at one another, the cat-and-mouse games, the man versus woman competition in which they had indulged, seemed foolish. She left the window, making her way across the darkened room, and threw herself across the bed. The hunger she felt for Adrien lay bone deep, a creeping urgency that continued to swell within her, condemning her to wakefulness. She considered leaving her door open, a lamp lit, an invitation, but she dared not. She was tired. Suppose she fell asleep? She wouldn't know if the invitation had been accepted—or refused.

There's always tomorrow, she told herself and burrowed under the coverlets, welcoming the visions and dreams of Adrien that burned her skin and made her breathless even in sleep.

Chapter Ten

Jennifer was awakened by someone touching her shoulder. Leddy Beauchamp was smiling over her. "I've brought you coffee." She pointed to a napkin-covered tray on the bedside table. "I'm sorry to wake you, but we've gone as far as we can without instruction in the dining room."

"I asked you here to help with cleaning and serving guests, not to wait on me," Jennifer said, struggling to come fully awake. "What time is it, anyway?"

"Nine thirty," Leddy answered, moving to sit in the old-fashioned rocker.

"Good Lord!" Jennifer sat up and swung her legs off the bed.

Leddy Beauchamp's shadowy dark eyes glimmered with mischief that belied a wisdom beyond her years. She had a pointed, intelligent face and a pert head full of unruly raven-black curls that danced and bobbed as she talked, which was often and animated. Unlike her husband, Etienne, she wasn't at all shy. There was a rhythmic squeak of the rockers on the bare floor that lent a cadence to her soft voice. "There is no need to rush, no? I'll tell you what has been done this morning while you drink, then you can instruct me from there, if you're willing?"

"I'm willing," said Jennifer, smiling. She removed

the napkin from the tray. Lying next to the spoon was a creamy rosebud, its perfect petals just beginning to turn outward, revealing early morning dew. Jennifer frowned. The rose reminded her of the portrait of Eleanor that hung in Adrien's room. She set the rose aside as she stirred cream into her coffee. She looked at Leddy over the rim of her cup and found the young woman staring at her, a serious expression on her face. "Have I done something wrong? Is there some custom with this coffee service I've overlooked?" she asked, puzzled.

"No. No," Leddy answered quickly. "But you don't like the rose, no?"

"It's beautiful. Was it your idea?" Jennifer asked quickly.

"Today, yes, but it is *Tante* Marie's tradition, her custom. A happy welcome. You don't feel welcome to Lafourche?"

"Leddy, of course I do. It's just that— Whoever is *Tante* Marie?"

"Why—Adrien's mother. They're her roses, and the roses of her mother before her and her mother before her.... You don't know? Adrien hasn't told you, no?"

Jennifer gave a weak smile. "No, Adrien hasn't told me. The only thing I know about these roses is that they were painted in the portrait of—"

"Aha! The artist chose them. Clever, yes? But that is not the story of the roses. In the old country of Acadia, which you Americans now call Nova Scotia, *Tante* Marie's great-great-great—perhaps even another great—grandmother was preparing for her wedding when the British came and took away her groom. They took all the men and boys and sent them far away. *Tante* Marie's grandmother had woven the roses into her hair. She followed the men as they were hurled onto ships and she pressed a rose into her lover's hand. Soon the women too were forced from their homes, and the young woman grandmother took with her a cutting of the rose vine, for it had come all the way from the northern province of France, where she had been born. When she finally arrived in Louisiana, she planted the tiny cutting, so that when her lover came for her, he would recognize her house by the roses. It was to be his welcome, the sign of her faith, but he never came. She married later, and when her daughters married, they took cuttings and planted the vine. When company is expected one quickly runs to count the roses, and cuts only the finest, the most perfect. When *Tante* Marie grew old, she was blind and she couldn't see her roses, but if visitors were coming, you could hear her call, 'Quick, quick, go count the roses!' For very important persons there were many roses, like for you... those in the window. We all saw.''

"I think," said Jennifer slowly, "you are making too much of this legend, or story—truthful as it may be," she amended, not wishing to hurt Leddy's feelings.

"Ah! You don't believe. I will convince you! When Adrien brought his Eleanor to Lafourche, it was the dead of winter, and there were no roses, and no one to count them if there had been. It was an ill omen, no?"

"I don't think that marriage failed just because there were no roses." Then Jennifer laughed. "Leddy, is everything on this bayou done up in custom and legend?"

"Ah! The cynicism of the city holds you, but you will learn," Leddy predicted with a smile on her pixie-ish face.

"What I'd better learn right now is what is going on downstairs," Jennifer said, getting off the bed and stretching. Leddy threw up her hands in the old-world gesture of exasperation. "Ralph and Etienne have been working in the dining room since six. The dustcovers are down, the room is clean, the table pulled apart, the leaves inserted and polished, the chairs too, dusted and polished, the windows washed, and this minute the chandelier teardrops are being washed in vinegar. Next I will vacuum and wax the floors, then set the flowers out in the manner you wish."

"My gosh, you managed all that since six? And the flowers arrived already? I told Campeaus to deliver them as late as possible."

"He did. He closes at noon on Saturdays, but they are very nice—freesias and tiny tulips. Also there are chinese lanterns and candles."

"And Berty? What's she been up to this morning? I promised her I'd be down early."

Leddy rolled her eyes heavenward. "*Tante* Berty is useless to us today. She is following that great cook around the kitchen like a newborn kitten snuffles for its *maman's* teat."

"What? What are you talking about? Berty following the cook—you mean Henri?"

"Yes. The Henri Augustin with the blue eyes. He and *Tante* Berty were friends from long ago, no? Now *Tante* Berty no longer acts like the little gray mouse. I think she has been sipping those potions she's been making for Etienne," Leddy said, smiling.

What is going on in this house? Jennifer asked silently. But she should have known. Henri had been at the hotel at least twenty years or more. He and Berty would have known each other when she worked there. Yet Berty had said not a word. Would wonders never cease? Aloud, she asked, "Uh, Leddy, you know about the potions that Berty makes for Etienne?"

Leddy's curls danced as she laughed, a soft tinkling

that sounded remarkably like the musical clock in the drawing room. "Oh, yes, I know, and they won't work without the most needed magic."

"And what is the most needed magic?" Jennifer asked.

"Our men—perhaps all men," Leddy said wisely, "they take so much for granted, no? We women—we cook, have the babies, take care of the house, the men's needs.... When I was sixteen, Etienne said we would marry. Since I love him, I said yes. When I am twenty, we marry, but not once has Etienne said aloud that he loves me. I will not allow him into our marriage bed until he does," she stated firmly.

"Good grief! Leddy! You mean that's all it is? That's the only reason you and Etienne haven't—haven't—"

"It's enough, don't you think? A woman wants to know she's loved, wants to hear it, no?"

Suddenly, Jennifer understood all that Leddy wanted. Most men did take their women for granted. Leddy was holding out—if that was the right word—just making sure that no matter what happened down the road, no matter in what direction her marriage went, that Etienne would never take her for granted. He would never, ever forget these first few weeks of his marriage...a powerful weapon. Jennifer knew she would never have such strength—she didn't have it now.

"Leddy, I admire you. I couldn't do it, but I wish you much happiness and I hope Etienne gets the message."

"Oh, he will, and soon." She laughed again softly. "For I'm not as strong as you think. Now I must get downstairs. Henri Augustin has promised to feed Ralph for me, but only after the dining room is clean, and the old man longs to return to his calves; they must be shampooed and dried for this Senor Ballesta who is so important to Adrien. And Etienne has asked for time off to find the most perfect frog for a more powerful potion, no? One that will perhaps work?" Leddy moved out of the rocking chair to the door. "When you come down, you can show me which linens and silver you wish to use, then I will see to it." She paused at the threshold, overcome with a shyness that was so out of character for her. "It is very nice to have a woman in this house again," she said with careful emphasis. "Especially for Adrien. He is a man of many sorrows. A Cajun man has this powerful feeling for his family. It's a kind of fierce proudness, no?" she said, stating a truth with which she had been born. Never had she spoken of it before, but then few outlanders had ever affected her as Jennifer. She hoped secretly they would become firm friends. "With Eleanor, this proudness in Adrien shriveled up like a grape drying in the sun." With this last pearl of wisdom Leddy smiled and retreated, pulling the door shut behind her.

"I just might learn a few things from Leddy," Jennifer mused aloud as she made her way into the bath—hot, sudsy, and scented with Tatiana. She envied the young French girl her feminine armor, for it was a strength she could never hope to match. If Adrien touched her, she would melt and the word *no* would vanish from her vocabulary forever. Jennifer luxuriated in the tub until the water became cool, and only then did she begin to feel guilty, hurrying. She toweldried, put on a pink teddy, brown slacks, and a tan knit top. She brushed her slightly damp and curling hair and again built a single casual braid.

The garrulous old sous chef, Henri, was chopping vegetables when she entered the kitchen. Berty was nowhere about. "Morning, Henri."

"Ah, *ma petite*," he admonished, a twinkling in his vivid blue eyes. "It takes little for you to learn the ways of the wealthy, eh? It's already past ten."

"I overslept. We've been working our rear ends off," she said, suddenly feeling more at ease than she had in days. Having a familiar face here at Lafourche was a blessing. At least now with a professional cook on hand, she was less worried about something going awry. "So what's been going on at the hotel? Anything new?"

Henri frowned. "Auditors and management consultants running in every department," he said in a low voice. "Old Britz is fluttering around like a plucked chicken. Al Albert, the chief engineer, is in hot water.... He can't account for some expenditures."

"They'll figure it out. He's as honest as the day is long, but not a bookkeeper. What's up with Ellie?"

"She said to tell you not to get lost in the swamp, and that she's covering for you."

"Uh, Henri," Jennifer said casually, "what's with you and Adrien's cousin, Berty?" Henri's knife stopped in midair, and the old man actually blushed, his three chins and cheeks turning a flaming pink.

"Shhh," he said. "I'll not tolerate any of your Irish tricks in this kitchen."

"What Irish tricks?" Jennifer grinned. "Tell or I'll tattle, Henri."

"She's the love of my life," he said simply. "I knew her years ago as Berty Brown, but I lost track of her after she left the Guilbeaux."

"Henri," Jennifer said solemnly, "you're the biggest flirt this side of the Mississippi River, so you'd better keep in mind who she's related to. Adrien Merril owns the hotel, you know."

"Bah!" Henri muttered, turning back to his vegetables. "What do you young pups know about true love?"

Jennifer smiled at his wide back as she poured herself a cup of coffee. She started to ask what the gossip about Eva Wilcox and Milton Richards was these days, but changed her mind. Why spoil a day that was moving along so perfectly? she wondered. She took her coffee and stepped outside. Berty was hurrying up the path from the outbuildings, and she had something cradled in her apron. As she came closer Jennifer noticed her gray dress, its collar and cuffs. All were freshly starched and ironed. Berty's face was radiant, her brown eyes clear with a confidence that had been absent for years.

"Morning, Berty. What's that you have in your apron?"

"Oh, Jennifer. *Allo*," she answered, smiling, opening the apron somewhat so Jennifer could peek in. Two huge white eggs lay cradled in the cotton nest. "Goose eggs. For Etienne." She lowered her voice. "The other didn't work."

"So I heard. But I thought he was after frogs today." Startled, Berty looked up. "He told you?"

"No, Leddy did," Jennifer said, laughing. "So, how does this one work?"

"Oh, it's easy. You make a little hole in one end of the egg, take out the insides and put the frog in, and then you pray over it—hard."

"I see. And then what?"

"Your lover comes to your bed and never leaves."

"Well, I hope it works for Etienne's sake. But you have two eggs," she added innocently. "Are you making more than one, for someone else, perhaps?"

"Uh, no. It's just in case I break it wrong—no?" she stuttered. "I have to go in now. I promised Henri I would help him today. He remembers me from when I used to work at the Guilbeaux."

"I'm sure he does," Jennifer said softly. "You're not an easy person to forget." She stepped aside to let the older woman slip into the kitchen, then she folded herself down on the step and sighed. The sun was slanting through the trees, forming pools of sprinkled gold on the soft earth. Bees droned, a swamp sparrow cried, and there was the soft susurration of the wind as it ruffled leaves in the tops of the trees. *I might,* Jennifer thought, *be on the verge of ordering a love potion for Adrien.* She sipped on the coffee, telling herself she should go inside and help Leddy. And still she sat, enjoying the peace of the morning. Horse's hooves pounding the soil at a fast trot drew her attention a moment before it came into view from around the nearest barn. Adrien was its rider. Spotting Jennifer on the porch, he slowed to a canter, guiding the roan to within a few feet of her before he dismounted. He let the reins trail the ground, effectively hobbling the well-trained horse. Rivulets of sweat trickled down his face from under his hat, his liking for outdoor life showing in his tough muscular frame. Jennifer felt her heart tilt ever so slightly when his mild gaze met hers.

"Got anything cool to drink?" he asked, taking a place next to her on the step.

"I'll see," Jennifer replied and went into the kitchen, returning a moment later with a pitcher of iced tea and a glass filled with ice. "Berty says this will do."

Adrien nodded, taking the glass and tea from her hands. Several long seconds passed while they stared at one another until Jennifer, feeling a flush creep up her neck, turned away, ostensibly to take a sip from the cup of coffee. Her mouth and throat were suddenly dry, and the coffee, now cold and tasteless, did not quell the hot feeling that traveled from her lips to her thigh. Adrien quenched his thirst. Cords of muscles stood out on his neck as he tilted his head back to drain the glass.

"That hit the spot," he said. "Did you sleep well?"

"I slept fine, and late," Jennifer replied. "You should've gotten me up. Leddy's been carrying on since six."

"Oh, I gave it some thought," he said, and let the comment lie between them as he slanted a smile at her, leaving no room for doubt in the meaning of his words. Jennifer began to feel pleasantly warm.

Abruptly he stood up, gathered the reins, and swung onto the horse. He held out his hand toward her. "C'mon up. I'll take you for a ride."

Jennifer scrambled to her feet. "Not me, not on a horse—no!" The animal loomed larger than life to her. "I've never been on a horse in my life."

"There's a first time for everything. Give me your hand," he commanded. Jennifer's hands went behind her back. "You've done wonders with the house—you need a break to get some country air and sunshine."

"I'm getting it right here on the porch," Jennifer asserted, watching him coax the horse nearer the step with his knees. Then, with the swiftness of lightning, his arm shot out and circled her waist, and in the next instant Jennifer was in the saddle in front of him.

"Now, that didn't hurt a bit, did it?" He slid back, giving her room. "Just throw your leg over the saddle horn. We'll ride to the barn, and I'll saddle you up a nice quiet mare." Jennifer was busy refilling her lungs from a soundless, surprised gasp.

"Let me down off this thing," she said, finding her voice. "We're too high off the ground." She gripped the saddle horn with both hands as the roan, Striker, began to trot toward the barn. Sensations were beating against Jennifer's senses: the jolt of Adrien's nearness; intimate; the earthy smell of leather and horse and male sweat; his arm that had not loosened its grip. She leaned forward only to succeed in resting her breasts provocatively on his arm. His grip tightened, and her breasts began to hum with excitement.

"Relax. I want to spend some time with you—alone," he murmured, bending forward to put the words in her ear. "*Mon Dieu,* but you smell lovely," he added, his voice throaty, filling with emotion. Jennifer had an irrational urge to say no, yet this was what she had hoped for, longed for, and the simple word refused to be formed on her lips. She made a feeble protest, one that could be easily overruled.

"They're waiting on me in the house. They won't know where I've gone to—"

"Berty's watching out the kitchen window. No one will think the local loup-garou has carried you off."

And because she didn't want him to think her too eager, too willing, Jennifer applied a trace amount of sarcasm. "Is this supposed to be a part of my employee benefits package? One I haven't signed up for?" Her voice was shaky, and the sarcasm fell flat.

"I won't rise to the bait," he replied. "No fighting today."

"What about this business of all women being alike?" Jennifer cursed her tongue; once animated, it refused to be curbed.

Adrien smiled at the back of her head. "You're different. You smell different, you walk different, you talk—you talk, too much," he insisted as they entered the shadowy interior of the barn. He called for Ralph to saddle a mare named Honey.

"I thought you said you were going to saddle a horse for me," she challenged.

"Changed my mind." His arm moved up her ribs to touch lightly her upraised nipples, and Jennifer caught her breath. "Wanting you is driving me crazy," he said quietly. "If we don't have some time together, I won't have any business sense by the time Laurean Ballesta arrives. I'll end up selling him my herd for twenty cents."

Jennifer's head was swirling. She barely noticed getting down off Striker, being instructed how to mount

Honey, following his advice distractedly. They were in a dusty lane dappled with gray-green shadows before she came out of her trancelike state.

"There's not all that much to riding a horse, really, is there?" she commented as they rode side by side. She wanted to say something powerful, something to make him remember, but her mind kept reverting to a blankness that allowed for only the innate, the ordinary.

They rode past a small stream where a dozen of the enormous rust-colored Limousins stood up to their underbellies in the trough, their wet hides glistening like copper, and the odor of swamp, mud, and cattle droppings rose like steam. Jennifer became aware of the heat, the warmth of the leather between her thighs, the rhythm of her horse beneath her. On a narrow path lined with bald cypress and live oak, her eyes rested on the strong square back of Adrien.

He rode loosely in the saddle, his hat tilted forward, his neck tanned, his green plaid shirt pulled taut across his shoulders, damp and clinging to his spine. Jennifer felt sweat trickle down between her breasts, realizing that the warmth saturating her body was building up from within. Thoughts of the man in front of her were creating a fervor, catching fire, casting a sensuous spell that rained down on her as though the shards of sunlight that shot through the leafy cloister contained one of Berty's love potions. Adrien pulled up and dismounted as they approached a narrow gate. He opened it, motioning her through, openly watching the undulation of her breasts moving in harmonious emphasis to the slow-moving horse. "We can walk the rest of the way," he told her, holding the reins while she too dismounted.

"Rest of the way where?"

"A little creek I keep fenced off from the cattle. I'd like a swim."

"I don't have a swimsuit," she said as his eyes, dark and insistent, met hers.

"Neither do I."

Anticipation created a silence between them as they walked, neither daring to touch the other or speak, lest a thoughtless gesture, a sharp word, or a questioning look caused the other to falter and shatter the spell that assailed them both. The marshy landscape gave way to a small meadow, and a carpet of wild violets in bloom threw their scent, as sweet as syrup, into the air.

A small creek not ten yards wide tumbled through the edge of the meadow. Water willows dipped into the slow-moving stream, its surface glittering black and silver as bars of sunlight cast reflections. Adrien hobbled his horse in a thicket of swamp Cyrilla, then without once glancing at Jennifer, he strode to the creek and began to undress.

Hesitantly, taking more time than she needed, Jennifer wrapped her reins around the branch of the bushy tree. She tried to avoid looking at Adrien but gave it up, drawn like a magnet to watch as he shed his clothes. She stood on tiptoe, watching over the saddle. His whole body was tanned and muscular so that she knew he swam here often and naked. She couldn't tear her eyes away until he stood poised on the sandy bank and dove, disappearing into the black water.

Floundering in a backwash of emotion, Jennifer slowly disrobed, folding each item neatly as she removed it, and set the clothes aside on a lichen-covered stump. Finally, clad only in the pink silk teddy, she walked barefoot through the feathery ferns and violets to the rim of the creek. Treading water lazily, Adrien caught sight of her and stopped.

Jennifer's face was delicately beautiful. Leafy shadows caught hollows in her cheeks, skimming her cheekbones, and lay deep along the sides of her throat.

Her eyes appeared golden and depthless. Her breasts were thrust against the scrap of silk and her legs delighted him—they were shapely and wonderfully long. "Ahhh, Jennifer..." he murmured under his breath. Since the disaster with Eleanor no other woman had broken through the long-lasting pain of that experience, and no woman—ever—had given him this helpless thundering feeling of need that coursed through his veins this moment. Jennifer dove into the water, and when she surfaced, breathless and sputtering with laughter, he moved to meet her. Strands of hair slipped the braid, and she brushed them from her eyes.

"This water is freezing! You should've warned me!"

"An underground spring feeds it near here," he said, smiling, moving closer. "If it didn't, it wouldn't be safe to dip a finger in, what with snakes and 'gators—"

"Snakes!" Jennifer headed for shore.

"Hey!" He grabbed her braid. "We're safe enough. Water's too cool this time of year."

"You're sure?" She swam out of his reach.

"Yes," he answered, lunging for her. His hands slid up her arms, across her shoulders, and down again, lowering the straps of the teddy. "I want to kiss you, make love to you," he whispered. A statement, not a question.

Jennifer's first inclination was to back out of his arms, refuse his kiss, ignore his hands rippling over her body as the silk began to float about her waist. But as his hands slid down her back, kneading bare flesh, the inclination melted from the fiery need. Her arms went around his neck, drawing him closer, and their lips met. After this first lingering kiss, there was no turning back.

The cool water heightened their warmth, their burning desire, their awareness of each others' nakedness. Jennifer's passion divorced her from reality, and when

Adrien lifted her into his arms, she clung to him, eyes
closed, her lips pressed against his neck sending shock-
ing stabs of tremulous need deep into Adrien's groin,
where it joined the gremlins that had wreaked so much
havoc.

They lay on their sides in the ferns and violets near
an uprooted tree, facing one another. The smell of
moist woodsy earth mingled with the musky fragrance
of physical want. To Jennifer there was only the cathe-
drallike silence of the forest broken by the warbling of a
sparrow, the chirping of a katydid whose timing was
off—and Adrien. Her thighs began to meet his muscular contours; her breasts quivered at the first incredibly
gentle touch when flesh met flesh. The hair on his
chest felt like threads of velvet against her skin. She
was intoxicated with the feel of him, the smell of him,
the taste of him. Captivated, she sank into the wondrous irresistible swirl of feelings.

He murmured her name softly, like a caress, and for
long agonizing moments fought against the urge to take
her at once to satisfy his passion. He touched her
gently, skillfully, consummately, exploring with his
hands every tiny crevice in her body. His lips were on
her neck, her shoulders, her breasts, and his tongue
flicked at droplets of water on her stomach—moist
little forays that sent exquisite tremors racing through
her, impelling erotic sensations to parts of her that she
hadn't known existed. As she began to respond to his
touch Adrien paused, absorbing the beauty of her no
longer hidden from him, marveling at her willingness
with all her silken softness.

No longer able to curb the need to experience all of
her, to withhold a passion built to bursting, he moved
into her, slowly, tumescent, transported with pleasure.
It was a coupling of oneness, of incredible emotions, a
lovely depthless frenzy until there was a wild explosion

of feeling that left them both weak and gasping for breath.

Jennifer's legs were caught up in Adrien's, and as she moved to untangle them he gently took her face in his hands and kissed her. His tongue met hers, his lips lingered, and his need once again became a hard and driving thing so that their bodies united, slower, yet no less fervent as they moved toward a magnificent surrender. He whispered her name, love imprecations against her eyelids, her cheeks, the fragrant hollows in her neck, and Jennifer responded utterly. She brought her face up to his, lips slightly parted, trembling, welcoming him in. Her fingers, seeking to learn and know, caressed his body, encouraging, moving sensually, abetting his desire, and the ferns and violets were crushed beneath them.

Shadows grew shorter, foretelling high noon, as they lay in each others' arms, sated, replete. Jennifer, feeling the glare through her eyelids, turned over, propping her chin in her hands before opening her eyes. The earth spun for a moment until she regained a degree of equilibrium. She was exhausted, filled with a warm ebullience. Adrien lay stretched out beside her, dozing lightly, his hands folded behind his head, one leg crossed over the other. His muscles rippled even as he rested. She studied him, aware that he was oblivious of her.

He was not an ordinary man, she thought, but then she had known that the first moment their eyes had met. He was a man in tune with nature, the very essence of life, and he was possessive, independent—a man who held things close to himself. She feared being possessed and wondered if there was a middle road. She loved him and wondered if she could adjust; wondered if she could keep him. She reached out and drew her fingertips down his cheek, stopping at the dimple he seemed to abhor. He smiled and opened his eyes, squinting against the glare of the sun. "What now?" she asked softly.

"A quick swim. We dress and ride back to the house and wait for nightfall." He turned on his side, observing her. "I want you in my bed tonight—all night."

Jennifer frowned. "I couldn't...that portrait of—of Eleanor," she dared. "She seems to be looking right at the bed."

"You've been in my room?"

"Yes, I couldn't help it."

He smiled. "I'll take the portrait down today. Anything else?"

"Is all that in the past, Adrien? Is Eleanor a ghost that's going to come between us?"

His brows drew together in a frown. All the old anger began to seep back into his veins. "What do you want, a confession?" he asked, his voice harsh. "Let's get that swim."

Jennifer watched him as he moved to the edge of the creek and dove in. She followed slowly. She knew the truth now—the unwanted truth. Adrien's bitterness over his failed marriage would lie between them like a bomb, ticking away, loosening its horror when least expected. He couldn't trust—himself or her—and wasn't trust the foundation upon which all lasting relationships grew?

The rest of the day was a blur. Once back at the house, they ate lunch, prepared by Henri Augustin, then Jennifer worked side by side with Leddy in the great dining hall until it met with her satisfaction. True to his word, Adrien had Etienne and Ralph remove Eleanor's portrait and pack it for shipping. Berty watched it go out the back door with raised eyebrows and went to find Jennifer.

"What's happening? Is that the last we'll see or hear of Eleanor?"

Jennifer shrugged. "Can you erase his mind?" she asked, and seeing the look on her face, Berty retreated to the kitchen, shaking her head. *More is going on here than meets the eye, no?* she told herself silently. But Berty had little time to muse about Jennifer and Adrien. Henri Augustin had been flirting with her all morning.

In the dining hall Leddy sat on the floor, putting together the Chinese lanterns, then carefully inserting in each a citronella candle. She watched Jennifer out of the corner of her eye methodically laying out silver: salad fork, dining fork, dessert fork, then the other side of the plate; knife, butter knife, soup spoon, demitasse spoon. When Jennifer was nearer she said, "It's not the happiness that must be erased from Adrien's mind, it is the unhappiness. It plugs him up like a stopped-up sink."

Jennifer gave Leddy a barely perceptible smile. "I know."

"Eleanor was *frisee* and *rougie*. She stayed puffed up all the time. She and Adrien fought like two crabs in a net. Etienne says she got so mad, she made the moon fall."

"What is *frisee* and *rougie*? More superstition?" Jennifer queried.

"Oh, no! A flirt, all dressed up with makeup, *toute gougou*, even in the morning."

"Did you work here often when she was here?"

Leddy was aghast. "No. We came to welcome her as we did you, but she wouldn't come down from her room. She made Adrien lose face among his friends. That's not a Cajun woman's way, no?"

Jennifer was weary of the subject of Eleanor. She moved to something more pleasant. "How are you and

Etienne getting along? Like two crabs in a net?" she teased.

"Ah! Like *deux colombes*!" Leddy grinned, mentioning the traditional two doves happily married Cajuns refer to.

"I noticed this morning that Berty was gathering up the things for a love potion...." Jennifer watched Leddy's curls bob and a contrite grimace take over her pert features.

"Yes. Also, she broke the eggs wrong and let the beautiful frog get away. Now Etienne must begin again, find another frog—"

Jennifer couldn't keep from laughing. "Just tell me, what exactly does this frog do?—after Etienne prays over it?" she added, recalling Berty's description of the love potion.

Leddy finished the last of the lanterns, then lined it against the wall with the others before she answered, eyeing Jennifer with a secret little smile. "No amount of prayer will keep that frog inside the egg, no? When it jumps out into my bed, I think I will be very frightened and ask Etienne to comfort me."

"And if he doesn't say the magic words?"

"He will," Leddy said determinedly. "—Jennifer, *Tante* Berty said probably you wouldn't mind if I asked a favor of you, no?"

"No, I wouldn't mind at all. I owe you one. What is it?"

"The perfume that's on your bathroom shelf—may I use some, tomorrow, before I leave, I mean.... It's heavenly," she said, pleading, "and I need a potion that's much more powerful than Etienne's." The look on Leddy's face was rapt. She was seeing into the future, and Jennifer understood that Etienne didn't stand a chance against this girl...only Leddy was going to let him think everything that would happen was his doing.

If only she had that sort of magic to offer Adrien, she thought wistfully. "Help yourself, but are you sure it—it will be tomorrow night?"

Leddy's eyes lit with humor. "I'm so sure, no? Even if I have to make the potion for Etienne myself!" She retied the sash on her apron, then walked around the table. "It's lovely. Adrien will be very proud and sell all his cattle, too."

"Well, everything is fine except the candles. I want you to take each of them out of their holders and from the bottom cut them down to only six inches, no more, then put them into the crystal candelabras."

"But why?" Leddy asked, puzzled. "The candles, they're brand-new, no?"

"Yes, but a woman looks far more beautiful with flickering candlelight and shadows coming up from below than above her head, and I want everyone, including me, to look beautiful tomorrow night."

"Ah!" Leddy said with total understanding. "More magic, no?"

"No," Jennifer said lightly, "just good sense."

As Leddy went about hanging the lanterns from the rafters on the side porch, she meditated on Jennifer. She liked her new friend immensely, and with a knowledge that had its roots deep in her being, she understood that Jennifer was to become a part of their lives on the bayou. Jennifer fit as Eleanor had not, but Leddy sensed Jennifer wasn't yet aware of this great happening, nor had Jennifer understood the significance of the ivory roses. Every bride in *Tante* Marie's family had been welcomed thus, with the roses in the special brass bowl—that was why Adrien had allowed them to be painted. Leddy yearned to explain to Jennifer the intricacies of the bayou—that the men were supreme beings unto themselves, rulers of the kingdom, and that the women allowed them this facade. Leddy did not think the word *facade,* it wasn't in her vocabulary. She thought of face saving. She could give as an example this business of her marriage bed. When she had refused Etienne admittance, he had gone directly to Father Dumont, who in turn had delicately approached her *maman,* who then had talked to her own friends, but never dared to visit on the subject with Leddy herself, as was proper. And so up and down the bayou people talked, they teased Etienne, but because it was a private thing between them, Leddy herself would never discuss it to give credence to Etienne's humiliation and distress. The men, of course, rooted for Etienne, offered suggestions, but once Etienne lay claim to her marriage bed, there would be no doubt among the women to whom the victory would belong. This was the proper way, and Etienne would not be a joke among his friends, he would be respected, and a woman must see to the respect of her husband. This, Leddy persuaded herself, was what Jennifer must do. Her thinking upon Jennifer and Adrien contrived to bring her own situation forward in her mind. Leddy's breast began to flutter. Tomorrow morning she would moor herself like a boat tied fast to *Tante* Berty until Etienne's potion was fashioned safely—and delivered! Old women who fell in love were among the most helpless, and *Tante* Berty, she had observed, was positively defenseless against the cook, Henri Augustin, which rendered her useless to ordinary cares.

Chapter Eleven

Jennifer prepared herself for bed—with Adrien. She bathed, shampooed her hair, blow-dried it, and let it swing free. She manicured her nails, all twenty of them, and began an argument with herself that she should not go to him—an argument that she lost the instant it formed in her mind. But there was one war that waged internally that she couldn't disregard. She had not realized until she went away to college how possessive her mother had been, and even then the full force of recognition had not seeped into her until she was entirely on her own in New Orleans. In the past months recognition had brought with it a sense of resentment. There had never been any natural course of rebellion against Nell's possessiveness, for her mother had in her loving, selfish way maneuvered Jennifer into thinking that what Nell had wanted was exactly Jennifer's wishes. Now, in maturity, in love, Jennifer found herself fighting for an independence too long delayed, rebelling against what she desired most, doggedly refusing to become submissive. It was a case of the wrong feeling at the wrong time against the very person with whom she wished to spend the rest of her life. Yet, she yielded to Adrien's magnetism like a leaf caught in a slow swirling eddy, circling and circling until it was drawn into the depths.

The house was silent. Outside, the wind fluttered vines against the roof, an owl cried, and then the quietude inside was broken by the golden chimes of the old clock that ticked away the time—centuries of time, Jennifer thought, as she held her breath and peeked around the door. If Henri should appear as she was making her way to Adrien's room, dressed in a revealing nightgown, she would be at a loss for an explanation. But Henri did not appear, and she knocked softly at Adrien's door and slipped inside his room. The great palisander bed with its silken hangings was empty. She called his name. Adrien emerged from his bathroom, a towel wrapped about his midriff, his face lathered, a razor in his hand, and beheld Jennifer.

His heart rate picked up with a curious offbeat, skipping a dozen, he was certain. She wore a cotton batiste gown that ranged down around her calves, and the soft lighting delineated her contours into relief. She smiled hesitantly as she came nearer, the gown giving off slight susurrus, as the diaphanous fabric rustled against her creamy skin. He had not seen her hair loose before and was astonished at its length and thickness. He kissed her lightly, leaving a smear of Old Spice lather. "Your hair is beautiful like that. You should wear it down more often."

She wiped away the soap he had deposited on her lips. "I work around food, remember? Losing a hair in someone's gumbo is the first mortal sin in the restaurant business, ill-preparing a steak is the second."

"I see what you mean," he said, moving back into the bath. "Talk with me while I finish shaving?"

Jennifer leaned against the doorframe, her arms folded, watching his every move. "Well, tomorrow's the big day," she said, just to say something, anything to fill the silence she felt would come between them if she didn't.

"Yes, I'll be glad when they've come and gone, too. To tell the truth, I halfway wish I hadn't invited the Ballestas here. The hotel would have done just as well."

"Then you would've had no—need for me to be here." She almost used the word *excuse,* catching herself only in time.

"There's a need," he answered quietly, realizing that their relationship, begun by himself almost as a lark, had taken on a serious depth and complexity. He sensed too Jennifer's antagonism toward him, and dallied with the notion that he had nourished it, but it was only a vague idea, and the act of shaving took up his concentration. He washed the lather from his face, dried it, carefully replacing the towel, knowing that Jennifer was watching him. No sense letting her see now that he was a man who required picking up after, he realized. He took her hand and led her to bed. "You got a little sun today," he observed. "Does it bother you?"

"Not yet, at least not on my shoulders." Jennifer sighed as she climbed into the bed, helped by Adrien. It felt so right, damn it, to be coming to the end of a full day like this in Adrien's company.

He moved around the room, turning out lights, making sure the door was closed securely, then, discarding the towel draped at his waist, he joined her on the bed. In the filtered moonlight their voices were subdued. Adrien lounged against the pillows with Jennifer cradled in his arms. She sensed a certain caution and reticence in him, and when he began to talk, understood. He wanted to play "what if" games. It had to happen sooner or later. Jennifer was thankful for the darkness.

"If you were married," he said, "what would you do?"

"About what?" she countered. She knew he didn't

want to reveal himself, but be damned if she would let him by with less than precise questions.

"About anything. Work, for instance," he offered resolutely.

"I'd keep on working—at something, anyway—to keep my hand in. Who knows how long one's marriage will last these days?"

Adrien winced. The comment stung. He plowed on. "How could you handle a job and having children? They take a lot of time and care, no half measures...."

Jennifer felt herself faced with the eternal problem of tell all so the male animal could make his decision, and the thought struck that Adrien Merril had not once offered to her even the remotest bit of personal information. He had told her of his long-dead ancestors, quipped about the financial status of the Guilbeaux, generalized about his crops and hunting in the swamp, and always managed to turn the conversation to his infernal cattle. Every personal thing she had learned of him had been from her own observations or others: Ellie, Berty, Leddy; joking remarks by his friends Jean and Barbara Dubois. Irritation began to build. It wasn't fair that he wanted her views—an integral part of her character laid open for his inspection when he refused the same queries! The irritation built up steam like a locomotive puffing up a steep hill. "Listen, Adrien, if you have something to ask me, ask it and take your chances!"

It was a fish-or-cut-bait situation if he had ever heard one. He began to reel in. His silence infuriated Jennifer. She tore herself out of his arms.

"I know what you're trying to do...you're interviewing me for a—a job! And one I might not even be interested in. Consider that, why don't you? I'm sick of the way you're acting. First you blackmail me into having dinner with you, then I don't hear from you for a month, though you say you left a message for me that I never got. Next you get old Britz to order me here to prepare a dinner party for which I work my fingers to the bone to get this mausoleum in shape for guests, and just when I think I might get a break—I've worked two weeks without a day off, by the way—you force me on a horse against my will until my bones ache, you make love to me in the woods, and now you want to sneak around and ask me all sorts of personal questions without—without— Look all I've gotten out of this other than sheer exhaustion is a two-hundred-dollar petty cash voucher for personal expenses that I had to spend for a dress because you want to throw a formal affair to impress some cattle buyer.'' She took a deep breath and scooted off the bed. ''Put your damn picture back up. I'm not sleeping in this bed with you tonight or any other night!''

His hand shot out in the dark, grasping her wrist. ''Damnation! What brought all that on? Get back into this bed.''

''No! That's all you're good for, isn't it? Ordering somebody around. You can forget about ordering me. I've had it.''

He kept his grip firm on her wrist as he swung his legs off the bed and switched on the lamp. ''You're making a hell of a lot of fuss and accusations. I'd like to remind you that yesterday I asked you—nicely—into my study. I wanted to talk, but you'd have none of it—''

''Sure you did...after you saw your neighbors approved of me—or at least that they didn't disapprove.''

''Not fair, Jennifer DeWitt,'' he said with utter calmness. ''You had the opportunity to say no—to everything. I'm glad my neighbors took to you, but I didn't invite them, they just came. I never thought you were a weak-kneed ninny, and I don't think you're one now, and you haven't been coy. If you'd ever once said back off and meant it, I would've. I've been made a fool of once on this bayou, and I don't aim to see it happen again. You want personal, I'll give you personal. I married a woman who thought I was a toy, and when the Christmas season was over, she left. She was carrying my child and she killed it. If I could have gotten my hands on her, I would've killed her! Want to know why? When we impregnate a cow with sperm, we go back five days later to remove a live embryo to implant in a surrogate. Nine months later that carrier cow gives birth to a calf. Eleanor was fifteen weeks pregnant when she left. Do you know what forms first on the human embryo? The face... within two weeks of inception the face that child—that person—will carry through life is formed. It had my face, or the face of my mother, or the face of my father. I keep thinking and I keep remembering, and if I offend you with my questions, well, by damn, I'm not making that mistake again, because I can't live with it." He turned her arm loose, now white where he had tightened his fingers during his diatribe, and lay back on the bed. His dark, brooding gaze did not leave Jennifer's face. "There you have it, the Merril family linen. Satisfied?"

Jennifer squirmed. It was this that she had wanted to hear, but not this way, not in this manner. She wanted confidences exchanged, sympathies revealed, issues laid open for introspection, but not like this! Still, she wouldn't be made the scapegoat. "No. I'm sorry that happened, but I'm not Eleanor, and it seems to me there's a double standard in there somewhere. You worry about a wife being pregnant, but what about me? You're forgetting that we made love. I could be pregnant right this minute—or was that just a trial run to see if I'm capable of producing the dynasty you seem to hunger for?" All the blood drained from Adrien's face, turning it pale beneath his tan. Seeing his reaction, Jennifer knew then that he was just as vulnerable as she, and hurried on before her courage failed her. "I'm not, but did you take any precautions? Did you ask if I had? We both know the answer to that, don't we. You're a man, Adrien, and you only worry after the fact. We women have to worry before and after. But I don't think that's the issue here. You want everything one way—yours. I want some things my way. I believe in marriage. I believe in having children—that's what you wanted to know, isn't it? But I'm not giving up my right to make decisions that concern me and about what I want in life. I've earned that privilege."

There was a maddening, prolonged moment as they glared at one another while each fully absorbed the other's outburst. Adrien's brain was racing, cataloging Jennifer's words, her gestures, the expression that had flitted across her face. There were no differences interposed between them now. He had put into words his innermost feelings—angry words, to be sure, yet he felt no humiliation. Jennifer had not smirked at him, not belittled him. He realized with explosive clarity that he had not expected these two responses from her. He had trusted that—trusted! The word hung in his consciousness as though impaled. He did trust Jennifer, as he had never trusted a woman in his life. He loved. The knowledge lifted him to an unknown height of joyousness, but being the man he was, raised as he had been among long-standing customs, even as Etienne had been, it didn't occur to him to tell Jennifer any of this. He saw in Jennifer his own reaction, and yielded first to the silence that had grown uncomfortable. His voice was tempered with an irony of his own doing. *"Mon Dieu,* I believe you love me."

Jennifer was dumbfounded. The golden flecks in her

clear brown eyes recorded the tempest with which she struggled. What with all that had just passed between them, she thought he had lost his sanity, yet she had an unutterable urge to thrust herself into his arms, tell him yes, tell him that she loved him very much, but the words wouldn't come and the way into his arms at that moment appeared an unnavigable path. He was lying there, stretched out, naked, adopting that cynical little half smile that so infuriated her, his thoughts impenetrable. She waited a half minute longer for more sensible conversation from him. None came.

"Believe what you will," she answered. "I'm going back to my room. I'm in no mood for sexual gymnastics." She turned, walking neither too fast nor too slow, but at a deliberately measured pace, the gown brushing her body at intervals.

Adrien watched her moving toward the door, fighting his basic instinct to take control by bringing her back to his bed. To him, Jennifer appeared cool, though he couldn't know it was her New Yorker cool, that something indefinable that said if you could survive the madness that was New York, you could survive anything, anywhere. Even the bag ladies had it, those wretched creatures who lived in the streets, in alleys, and Grand Central Station. But Adrien had never been to New York, nor had he ever seen a bag lady. He only knew that he had to say something, to leave an emotional bridge upon which they could meet.

"You'll grant that we've cleared the air, no?"

"I'll grant that," said Jennifer, continuing her pace into the hall.

She pulled the door closed, leaving Adrien behind to suffer a hunger in the lingering image of a fresh, clean woman scented with Ivoire. He punched down his pillows, flopped over on his stomach, and began to wrestle with the problem of what Jennifer could be induced to do to occupy herself at Lafourche beyond keeping house and having his babies. For he would not cross her in this. More than ever he was conscious of his limits, the foundation upon which his life was built. A working wife was a radical concept, almost heretical against the precepts he had held all of his life, yet he was an astute man. He recognized that Jennifer's urge to maintain a semblance of independence was to her a personal moat, a buffer zone, a mysterious inner core that appealed to him.

At long last Adrien felt himself emerging completely from the wreckage that had been his life for the past two-plus years. The day that he had emptied Lafourche of Eleanor's things had only been the beginning, sheering away the madness that had bound him. Removing her portrait had cleansed him of the bitterness that had embedded itself in his heart. There only remained the painfully deep rift in his soul to be healed, grief for the loss of his unborn child.

As he drifted into sleep the fragrance of crushed violets and soft ferns came to him, unleashing a savage flood of yearning that sent desire coursing into his groin, a throbbing anguish frantic with need that no dream could satisfy.

The female mosquito engorges on blood before she mates to sustain herself through the trying period of coupling on the wing and the exhausting process of laying thousands of fertile eggs in a waterproof sac. Any warm-blooded mammal will suffice for this ceremonial and necessary meal—cow, dog, chicken, human. At this moment Henri Augustin, sitting next to Berty on the pier in front of her cottage, was the unwilling host to a swarm of the voracious female insects. He was certain he was being sucked dry by the whining pests.

"Berty, my love," he said with some adroitness, "I

don't want to embarrass you, but I hope asking me to come fishing tonight was just a genteel excuse to be in my company, because if you're really serious about catching fish, you'll have to do it without me. I'm being eaten alive.'' He slapped at a mosquito, feeling it squish on his skin. Putting his cane pole aside, he hauled his great bulk to his feet.

Having lived his entire life in the city of New Orleans and having spent the past thirty of his sixty years working at the Guilbeaux, Henri was as cosmopolitan as any easterner. The closest he had ever come to country, cows, rivers, and swamp was on the levee that faced the Mississippi in the French Quarter, and that was as close to the wilds as he ever wanted to be. For the past two hours he had sat on this tiny wharf, his legs hanging over the edge, enduring mosquitos, the horrible screetch of that egotistical peacock who kept trying to steal their bait, and the horrendous bellows of a bull alligator somewhere nearby. Too nearby, he thought with a shudder he made no effort to conceal.

"We can go in the house. I'll make coffee," Berty offered tentatively as she too rose to her feet. She didn't want this evening to end. Henri had been blatantly flirting with her all day: little jokes, winks, calling her my love or my sweet. Of course, she had behaved as though it were all most ordinary, but her heart fluttered and her stomach had disappeared.

"Coffee is nice, but I need something stronger to thicken my blood. It's been considerably thinned these past two hours."

"Rum, then, no?" she offered hopefully.

"An unqualified restorative," agreed Henri. A few minutes later he sat across from Berty in her tiny immaculate kitchen, sipping on a second toddy of rum; the first he had drunk neat, feeling the need strongly. His insides warmed with the drink like a soothing poul-

tice. Berty's furniture was comfortable and held his
great weight with ease. He had to mind things like that
of late. He paid attention to many things, and knew
himself to the point of moroseness, though he never
quarreled with reality. He liked food, deriving an almost sensual pleasure from preparing it and eating it,
and he loved women. He couldn't think of a finer use
God could have made of Adam's rib. Henri had decided long ago that he would give up neither food nor
women. What he lacked in looks he made up with sin-
cere charm. He knew his blue eyes were his finest
physical feature. Though most people his size had to
contend with eyes being lost in folds of puffy fat about
the face, Henri was spared this problem by the province
of God and his triple chins, which he shaved carefully
every day. They weighted his face, keeping it smooth,
even enhancing the wide set of his vivid blue eyes.
They were twinkling now as he looked at Berty.

She fidgeted, averted her face, avoiding looking at
him at all costs. He was amazed that a woman her age
could be so damnably shy. He recalled the first time he
had seen her. She had walked through the kitchen at
the Guilbeaux on her way to the storeroom, and he had
watched her progress out of the corner of his eye.
There had been something in the way she carried herself that spoke of a healthy sensuality, announcing that
here was a woman made for love, a woman filled with
hidden and exciting passions. On her return he had
managed to get into her path, their eyes had met, the
chemistry held, and then he had noticed the gold band
on her finger. And he knew with a certainty that she
was a woman who honored the integrity of all that for
which the thin circle of gold stood. She was thinner
now than before; sad too, if he read the deep melancholy in her eyes right. But happily, for him, she no
longer wore the thin gold band, her passions banked.

The urge to fan those passions into full flame swept through him.

"I've missed you, Berty Brown," he said softly.

Berty's head jerked up, her hand flew to her chest, feeling for the gris-gris, but its comfortable presence wasn't there. It lay on her dresser, where she had left it the night before. She stumbled over these first intimate seconds, the first few words. "I—I missed you too... and everybody at the Guilbeaux," she added, fearful that he would think her brazen.

"You left so abruptly, not telling anyone where you were going—"

"I got sick, there wasn't any time." How much could she tell him, she wondered, before he leaped horrified from his chair and ran from her? She thought about the purple nodules on her arms, but she was clean now. Oh, the miracle of sulfone drugs—clofazimine, rifampin, and dapsone....

"I know," he said, reaching for her hand when he saw panic begin to overtake the melancholy in her eyes.

"How?" she breathed, feeling her mouth go suddenly dry, conscious of his fingers on hers, that he was touching her. She felt bare and vulnerable as her apprehension mounted.

"I knew you left in the middle of a pay period, so I just went up to payroll and told them I owed you some money. Where could I send it? I asked. The address they gave me was the hospital in Carville. I happen to know they only treat one disease there— Berty, don't look at me like that. It doesn't matter. I even went down to see you once, but I wasn't on any visitors' list so I couldn't get in. Then I wrote you a note, but it came back person unknown."

"My husband left me. I used my maiden name— Merril."

"Ah, that explains it, then." A tremor ran through

him at the frailty of the woman who sat across from him. What she must have suffered! His fingers unconsciously tightened about her hand. "Berty"—he paused—"we've been friends a long time, haven't we?" He waited for her nod. "We can say anything we feel to one another, can't we?"

"Yes." She drew out the word in a hushed voice.

His voice dropped an octave, becoming hoarse. "I want to make love to you. I have for a long time...."

Her face constricted with disbelief, wondrous relief. Something in her chest expanded, making it difficult for her to breathe, to talk. She stared at him blankly. "Right now?" she whispered.

Henri chuckled, a laughter that rumbled deep inside his vast chest. "Ah, my love, I could wait maybe five more minutes...."

Chapter Twelve

Gentle rain tapping on windows, a mossy smell of damp country air, the aroma of freshly brewed coffee, and the rattle of cups and saucers entered Jennifer's subconscious before she came fully awake. She began a leisurely, sleepy stretch. Pain shot along her bones, every single one of them, it seemed, making her eyes fly open. A low moan escaped her lips.

"Jennifer," Leddy said in a hushed voice. "I've just brought your coffee. Are you all right?"

"Noooo, noooo." The groan, louder now, accompanied another abortive stretch. "I'm paralyzed. I can't move a thing. It hurts so..." Jennifer's face was ashen in the glow of the bedside lamp Leddy had switched on. Alarmed, Leddy rushed from the room and ran headlong into Adrien. His square solid body absorbed the impact while he reached out a hand to steady Leddy.

"Mon Dieu! Let's have a little decorum in this house," he said sharply. Then he saw the anxiety on Leddy's face. "What's wrong?"

"It's Jennifer—she's sick."

"Sick!" He brushed past Leddy hurriedly, approaching Jennifer's bed in several long strides. To him, Jennifer looked beautiful, not sick. Her red-gold hair was scattered on the pillow and her eyes were closed. The beauty mark by her lip stood out against her lightly tanned face, and her supple body was outlined beneath the light coverlet.

"Jennifer—?"

"Her eyes flew open. "Oh, Adrien, I can't move... maybe I have polio or something—everything hurts."

He sat down on the bed. "Everything? Like where?"

"My legs, my back, my arms, my neck—"

He began to smile. Jennifer saw the smirk. "It's not funny!"

"No...no, but it's not polio. You should've gotten down off that mare when I told you to yesterday. You're just out of shape, my girl."

Skepticism was laced with pain. "Riding a horse for an hour couldn't possibly do this to me."

"Yes," he said positively. "And add that to all the physical work you've been doing—pushing and shoving furniture around, swimming—" Aware that Leddy was still standing in the doorway, he bent closer and whispered, "Also, making love on the ground instead of a nice soft bed..."

"That was your idea—all of it was your idea. Now, do something! I can't lie here all day like a log."

He left her side, gave Leddy a message, sent her on her way, then returned to Jennifer. "Want to drink this coffee before we get started?"

She uttered a low pain-filled groan as Adrien put his hands under her and lifted, plumped her pillows, leaned her back, then put the coffee cup in her hands. "Can you manage that to your mouth?" he asked with an air of solicitude."

She could, just, and held the cup to her lips, constantly aware that the skin across her shoulders felt hot and stretched. The muscles in her stomach and groin ached so badly, she dared not breathe deeply. The coffee was warm and soothing, but it did little more than bring her more fully awake so that her brain recorded the stabs of pain with excruciating clarity. With Adrien sitting next to her on the bed she felt like she was under siege. "Quit staring at me."

"I was just thinking how beautiful you look in the morning."

"Oh, I'm just gorgeous in the morning," she replied sarcastically. "It's the only time I have my picture taken."

He refilled her cup from the coffee service. "Drink a little more, it might lessen your irritability. Are you always this hostile in the morning?"

"You don't give up, do you? You're still interviewing me."

"I merely asked you a question, a civilized device to pass the time." His tone was conciliatory, but both were reminded of their harsh words of the night before and that the evening had ended in a manner that pleased neither.

Leddy came hurrying into the room, carrying a wooden jar. "*Tante* Berty says this should do it," she said, handing the jar to Adrien. "You want me to stay and help, no?"

"No, I can manage this alone. And, Leddy, close the door on your way out, please." When she was gone, Adrien set the jar aside and began rolling up his sleeves. Jennifer watched him with misgivings. "Now, we can get started. I'll have you on your feet in no time." He took the coffee cup from Jennifer's fingers, rolled down the bedclothes, and began to remove her gown.

"Hey! What are doing? Stop that," she protested, startled. He ignored her objections, and she was incapable of defending herself. The gown lay in a pile on the floor. Lying there naked, Jennifer felt inescapably vulnerable, yet Adrien had an innate sense of the fitness of things. He was all business.

"First, we'll get you onto your stomach. I'll start with your feet and ankles and work up." Gently, but swiftly he turned her over, ignoring again her plaintive moans and unladylike expletives ground out through clenched teeth. For a tenth of a second he admired the shape of her back, the curve of her hips, the wonderfully long legs. Then he began stroking on the evil-smelling salve. He worked it up over her buttocks, her back, her shoulders, returning to her ankles and calves, manipulating her skin with firm, measured strokes that left Jennifer breathless with suffering.

"Oh, please, stop, I can't stand it," she moaned.

Adrien could not help but chuckle. "You'll have to. It'll feel better in a few minutes, I promise," he told her and moved to her thighs. Jennifer sucked in air.

"Watch where you put your hands!"

"I am, don't worry," he said, laughing outright as his fingers slid to her inner thighs. Jennifer gasped with pain and decided to die.

Ten minutes later and still alive, having been smothered with the horrible salve back and front, she looked at Adrien from beneath lowered lashes that hid eyes seething with fury and humiliation. With magnificent decorum he avoided looking at her as he pulled the sheet up to her neck.

"Better, no?" he said, and met her stare.

"Much, thank you." Her voice was icy.

"Tell you what," he said softly. "I'll let you get revenge. After our guests leave on Tuesday, you can give me a massage."

"You'd love it!" she sputtered.

"I'll pretend otherwise," he replied dryly. "Now, do you want help into the tub or—"

"No!" She was adamant.

"All right." He was grinning "I'll send Leddy up with some chamomile tea. You drink it while you're soaking, and I guarantee you'll be like new." He went into the bath, washed his hands, emerging a few moments later, rolling the sleeves down on his shirt. Jennifer still lay huddled under the sanctuary of the bedcovers. He sat on the bed, his irregular features growing serious.

"About last night . . ." he began cautiously.

"I don't want to talk about last night."

"I do. You know you're a classic study of a stubborn woman, but it must intrigue me, because I think we have something special." He watched her face go carefully blank, sensing that she was retreating behind the stiff vertical walls she had built to protect her independent spirit. He continued, speaking his innermost thoughts aloud. There was something agonizingly pleasant about it. "You know what I want—a wife and children. Day before yesterday, I would have decided for both of us. I know you love me, but I realized last night that you don't know it, or that you do and won't accept it. Whichever, it's up to you now."

Jennifer was breathing hard as though undergoing some strain. Her pulse was racing, her head swimming. "Up to me how? What do you want me to do, lay myself at your feet, say okay, and let you swallow me up?"

"Is that what you're afraid of? Losing your identity, your individuality? Haven't I made myself clear? I want a partner, an equal."

She drew her hand over her eyes as though she could erase her confused emotions. "Adrien, no one is equal to you."

"Ah, my first compliment from you. I'll cherish it always, but as usual, you're skirting the issue." He bent and kissed her lightly on the lips. "You take it easy this morning, read the paper, get Berty and Leddy to do any last-minute chores. I have work piled up in the barns. Are you listening?"

"Yes, yes, I'm listening. Take it easy, read the paper..." She repeated the words mechanically.

"Give some thought to what I've said," he added, giving her a little half smile.

"Another order?" asked Jennifer, unwilling to acknowledge that he had been deferring to her.

"A mere wish," he said and left.

There was a languorous feeling of sweet relief as Jennifer lay back in the tub of bone-softening hot water scented with Tatiana. She dampened her hair, lathered it, and piled the shampoo-laden mass on top of her head to soak. Hanging loose during Adrien's ministrations, it had accumulated its share of the evil-smelling salve. Her thoughts moved slowly from the previous night to this morning. Had Adrien proposed marriage? No, but he was laying the groundwork. She should be ecstatic. She wanted him more than anything on earth, so why this uneasy stab of fear that clutched at her whenever he got close to her, inside her personal boundaries? She closed her eyes, longing for the familiar: her cozy apartment, the everyday ritual of getting up, dressing, and going to work.

Leddy knocked on the bathroom door, then bustled in, carrying a tray with cup and teapot. Jennifer sighed. Would she not be allowed even a modicum of modesty today?

"Chamomile tea," Leddy announced. "I've put in honey. It makes it go down easier, no?" She smiled, her curls bouncing, her dark eyes alive with questions "You feel better?"

"Yes, thank you. I was just stiff from horseback riding yesterday," she said, and took the cup from Leddy

The young girl hesitated nervously, then said, "You haven't forgotten that you said I could borrow some perfume, no?"

Jennifer smiled. "Of course not. Take what you want

now, and good luck. By the way, how's the love potion coming?"

"Oh, made and delivered," Leddy answered. "*Tante* Berty, though, is full of excitement, different from yesterday. The cook, Henri Augustin, spent the night with her."

"What!"

Leddy looked up from her inspection of bottles and creams and held up the Tatiana. "This one I think, okay?"

"Yes, yes," Jennifer said. "But what's this about Berty and Henri?"

"Just two old people in love," Leddy answered simply.

"But they can't be!"

Leddy was puzzled. "Why not? Old Mrs. Prejean is ninety. She's outlived three husbands and is looking for a fourth. She would take Ralph, but complains he smells of the barns."

"Good grief!" Jennifer said aloud, but hoping silently that this turn of events wouldn't complicate an already complicated situation. Yet, there was nothing, absolutely nothing, she could do, beyond accept it.

Leddy tucked the perfume into her apron pocket. "Adrien says I'm to look after you this morning. So, you must not stay in this water much longer, or your skin will be like crepe paper, no?"

Jennifer laughed. "No, I'm getting out, just as soon as you leave. So, scoot!"

Etienne had just finished hanging the last of the Chinese lanterns from the rafters of the *garconniere* under Jennifer's watchful supervision when Leddy came rushing through the dining room.

"They're here," she announced, speaking of the Ballestas. "Adrien says to come quickly."

"Thy master calls," Jennifer muttered under her breath. "That's fine, Etienne. Just remember as soon as it begins to get dark to light them up, okay?" He nodded, smiled shyly past her to Leddy, then folded up the ladder and disappeared around the house.

Jennifer stood for a moment, gathering resolve to carry her through the rest of the evening. The rain had stopped at noon, and for that she was thankful, but now stringy threads of fog began to lift from the bayou. Well, it would just make everything more cozy, she thought, and turned to follow Leddy, who had been impatiently waiting in the entrance hall.

Adrien was already on the front veranda greeting his guests, and he drew Jennifer into introductions. Laurean Ballesta was thin, tall, with graying hair cut short, and an aristocratic bearing.

"Call me Laurean," he suggested to Jennifer with a personable smile. His eyes swept briefly over the ikat print frock with it's low becoming neckline. "You're a lovely young woman," he added courteously.

"Thank you," she murmured, aware that Adrien was beaming with approval, and turned her attention to Laurean's wife.

Francesca Ballesta was birdlike, small, and spare with silver-streaked hair that flared away from her face, accentuating finely boned features. There was a drawn look about her eyes and mouth, as though she were very tired or suffering from an illness. She touched Jennifer's hand with trembling fingers. "I'm Francesca." Her voice, like her husband's, held a musical lilt. Jennifer felt an immediate, if silent, rapport with the older woman.

Venida Ballesta watched from the backseat of the limousine, waiting for the rush and confusion of introductions to end. She looked at Adrien with hungry eyes, then shifted her gaze to the woman greeting her mother. Her lips curled in contempt. Then she checked her makeup in a compact, ran her fingers through her hair to give it a calculated look of dishabille, and when she judged the moment was right, she emerged from the car. Smoothing the white silk over her hips, she unhurriedly walked up the steps and intercepted Adrien as he was about to follow her parents into the house.

Ignoring Jennifer standing beside Adrien, she carefully put her arms around his neck, looked into his eyes briefly, and kissed him. "Adrien, darling... have you forgotten about me?" She let her hands slide down his chest. "I've missed you."

Jennifer felt a fever in her stomach. She didn't like this, not one tiny bit. When she caught sight of Venida's moist pink tongue dart out to touch Adrien's mouth, she brushed past them. Adrien's hand shot out and gripped her arm even as he disengaged himself from Venida.

He said smoothly, "It's good to see you again too, Venida. Let me introduce you to Jennifer DeWitt, your hostess. She'll see you to your room so you can freshen up."

Venida sized Jennifer up with a look of aloof hauteur. "How kind of you to introduce me to your servants, Adrien," she cooed, taking his arm. "But I'm quite refreshed for now. Perhaps a drink?"

Jennifer smiled her coldest. "Excuse me, I'll just see to Laurean and Francesca."

Laurean opted for a drink with Adrien and his daughter, but Francesca, sitting stiffly on the edge of one of the sofas, nodded to Jennifer. "I would like to go to my room to rest before dinner, if it wouldn't be an imposition."

"Of course not." Jennifer led the way and found Ralph in the hall with Leddy, hauling suitcases. "Which are yours and Laurean's, Francesca? Ralph can bring them up now."

She pointed them out and followed Jennifer upstairs. "Oh, this is lovely," she said. "But Laurean and I don't share bedrooms," she told Jennifer as Ralph deposited the luggage inside the door.

"Oh, I'm sorry, I didn't know," Jennifer answered, wondering what she was to do. Damn! she thought. "Ralph, take Senor Ballesta's luggage into Henri's room. Leddy, you pack Henri's things and take them down to the kitchen," she said when Leddy came trailing in with cosmetic cases.

"I hate to put you out like this," Francesca apologized.

"It's no problem, really. There are cottages on the ranch. We can bunk Henri—he's our chef—elsewhere." And Jennifer was beginning to realize exactly where he would be most welcome—with Berty.

"What time is dinner, then?"

"At eight, but we're having cocktails in the drawing room at seven thirty."

"I wonder," Francesca said softly, "if I might have a bottle of whiskey, perhaps bourbon, here in my room?"

Alarm bells started going off in Jennifer's head. She saw the evening turning into a disaster. First the daughter, now the wife. She hoped Adrien would at least sell his cattle. "Of course," she answered.

"Miss DeWitt," Francesca called as Jennifer was leaving.

She turned. "Jennifer."

"Jennifer, then. I—I won't embarrass you, if that's what you're thinking. Laurean wouldn't tolerate it. He'd go into a rage."

Jennifer hardly knew what to say. "I'm sure you won't, Francesca, but do try to get some rest before dinner. Our chef is from the Guilbeaux Hotel in New

Orleans, and he's preparing a masterful dinner for you."

"I'll thank him personally, and ask for recipes," Francesca assured her with a dry polite smile.

In the kitchen, Henri was staring at his battered old suitcase Leddy had just deposited in a corner of the kitchen. He looked up at Jennifer. "What's going on? Am I fired?"

"No, but the senior Ballestas don't share bedrooms. I've had to put Laurean in yours."

"I have a spare bedroom," Berty piped. "Henri can stay with me if he likes, no?" She glanced sideways at Henri, caught his eye, and blushed. Jennifer hid her smile.

"Berty, you're a lifesaver. Okay by you, Henri?"

He cleared his throat. "I can sleep anywhere. A bed's a bed," he said gruffly. "Now, everybody outta my kitchen, or I'm going to serve up raw fish and uncooked vegetables." He turned back to the stove, but not before he gave Berty a broad wink that Jennifer pretended not to see.

"Berty, we have another slight problem. Find a decanter, a small decanter," she emphasized, "fill it about three quarters full of bourbon, and have Leddy take it up to Mrs. Ballesta."

"Uh-oh," Berty said, catching Jennifer's drift.

"My sentiments exactly," said Jennifer. She could almost use a drink herself, or a cigarette, and she didn't even smoke.

"Where've you been?" Adrien hissed at her as she emerged into the hall.

"Trying to sort out your guests. What now? This place is getting almost as hectic as the hotel."

"Where are the hors d'oeuvres? The boiled shrimp and cheese and crackers?"

"Oh! In the dining room on the serving cart. I'll bring them right in. Anything else?"

"Just come into the drawing room, have a drink with us, and calm down."

"Adrien, I don't know how long I can promise to stay calm watching that—that she-cat work on you."

"You're jealous?" His good rich voice sounded mock incredulity.

"It's one of my finer traits," she replied with just the right amount of self-deprecation. Truly, it was the first time in her life she had ever experienced such an emotion. It was dreadful. "Just don't let it go to your head."

An eyebrow lifted. "Naturally not. And I expect you not to blow that little scene on the veranda all out of proportion."

She eyed him from head to toe, taking in the fitted white cotton shirt, the beltless fawn-colored slacks, the dark brown hair curling about his ears. "I wouldn't dream of it."

For the next hour and a half Jennifer suffered. Sitting on the periphery of the group she might as well have been invisible. Laurean and Adrien were engrossed in conversation, bending forward in the wing-backed chairs, talking cattle, feed conversion, the price of bulls, and crossbreeding. Venida sat on the arm of Adrien's chair. Whenever the men desired a refill, she leaped up to fix it. Whenever she wanted a drink, she dangled the glass under Jennifer's nose disdainfully, and Jennifer had no choice but to comply, politely on the outside, raging on the inside. Occasionally Venida would take a shrimp from the serving cart and feed it to Adrien. Absently he took it into his mouth and swallowed.

More than once Jennifer felt like jumping up and storming from the room, but intuition told her this

was exactly the response for which Venida hoped.
Striking an introspective pose, as though she were
busy with her own thoughts, she casually studied Venida. The woman was full breasted, slim hipped, and
her black hair was in deliberate disarray. She made
heavy use of cosmetics, especially about her dark eyes
and pouty lips, though they were exquisitely applied.
She was, Jennifer thought unhappily, sexy to the
bone.

The Latin beauty's attractions were so obviously
transparent, Jennifer couldn't comprehend why Adrien
didn't seem to notice. Slowly she became aware of a
phenomenon that she would learn to recognize instantly in the future: Adrien, when discussing cattle,
especially the exotic Limousin breed of which he was
so enamored, or its crossbreeding to Brahmas, was
oblivious of what was going on about him. He was absorbed by the subject, like a thirsty sponge soaking up
water, his concentration total. He was no more conscious of Venida crowding his elbow than he was of the
air he was breathing, or even Jennifer, for that matter.
That was the reason she felt invisible. He had shut her
out along with everything else.

Poor Venida, Jennifer thought. Sitting there, feeding
Adrien delicate tidbits from the serving cart, stroking
his neck, leaning into him, inhaling that gorgeous male
scent of his, and getting all quivery inside—all to no
avail! How lovely. She smiled when there was a lull in
the conversation and spoke over the silence.

"If all of you will excuse me, I'll go check on diner,
then go up to change. The Bakers and Duboises will be
arriving in less than an hour for cocktails," she said,
reminding Adrien of the time.

His mind was still on cattle, and he looked at her
blankly for a moment, then stood up, nearly unseating
Venida. That brought him into the present. "Oh,

sorry." He looked to Jennifer. "Less than an hour, you say?" She nodded. "Well, then, Laurean, we can still make a quick trip to the barns, where I've singled out some one- and two-year-old heifers for you to look over."

"I'd like that," he acquiesced, and with courteous nods to Jennifer and Venida, they hurried off.

Turning to Venida and wearing a genuine smile, Jennifer asked, "Would you like to see your room now?"

"Yes," she answered, and had to catch herself before she added an automatic thank you.

"Where's my mother's room?" Venida asked once they were in the upstairs hall.

"There." Jennifer pointed. "The second door on your left."

"And my father's?"

Again Jennifer pointed, indicating the room across from her own.

"And where is Adrien's room?" Venida asked slyly.

"That first room, facing the lawns, and here's yours." She opened the door. Venida held back. Jennifer could practically see the wheels turning in the other woman's head.

"Move my things," Venida ordered. "I want the room next to Adrien's."

Ah! If she wants to bivouac under Adrien's nose, she'll have to do it without help from me, Jennifer thought. "Oh, I couldn't do that," she said sweetly. "You see, that room is already occupied."

"By whom?" Venida asked acidly.

"Me," replied Jennifer softly, and grinned as Venida flounced into her room, slamming the door. The sharp sound echoed in the house.

Leddy emerged from Francesca's room. "Shhh," she whispered, her finger to her lips. "Mrs. Ballesta is sleeping."

"Wonder of wonders," Jennifer advanced under her breath. "How much of that whiskey did she drink?"

"Very little," Leddy answered, smiling. "We talked. She is a woman of many sorrows, no?" Leddy smiled impishly. "One of which is a daughter who is *frisee* and *rougie*, yes?"

"Very *frisee* and *rougie*," Jennifer agreed with a tight smile. "I've got to dress for dinner, Leddy. Why don't you go find Etienne, and you two grab something to eat before everyone arrives?"

At the mention of Etienne, Leddy's face took on a radiance, a faraway look, as though she were looking into the future. As it happened she was, the very immediate future. "Jennifer," she began slowly, "would it be all right if I left right after dessert is served? Etienne will be waiting..." She fingered the small bottle of Tatiana in her apron pocket.

Smiling, Jennifer agreed. "I hope everything goes well for you tonight, Leddy."

"It has to," she replied. There was the sound of steely determination in her voice, which Jennifer envied. *I wish I had some of her Cajun backbone,* Jennifer thought as she turned into her room. A small inner voice asked, *So, what's wrong with your own backbone, kiddo?*

For a moment after she entered her room Jennifer gazed vacantly at the rocking chair, the bed, out the window, and then with indefinable resolve she began to get ready for dinner. Purposefully she bathed, creamed her skin until it glowed translucent, and applied cosmetics while she stood naked at the sink. She contoured her face with foundation, blended it, brushed on pink to highlight the shimmering of tan, and applied mascara and a smoky line of shadow highlighted with ivory until her eyes took on a golden cast.

She drew on hose, silk panties, and a lacy camisole,

then stepped into the magnificent beige dress, luxuriating in the feel of its cool silk lining against her flesh. Each tiny pearl button from hem to neck had to be coaxed into a tiny loop. Exasperated with this tedious operation, she left a half dozen undone below her knee. The stand-up mandarin collar trimmed with vignettes of Chantilly lace circled her neck as though its delicacy were all that was required to support the slender column of her neck and her regal head. A single glance in the mirror at her image, and Jennifer knew that a chignon would not do. Hand-stitched seams under her breasts and the sedate drape of gossamer fabric over her hips gave her such a look of Victorian innocence, she almost laughed aloud. But there was too a depthless shadow in her eyes that camouflaged the heated passion of a woman in love. She brushed her hair until it gleamed coppery and swirled it on top of her head, locking it in place with pins and combs. A strand here and there escaped a pin and clung to her neck. She wore a single ivory pearl in each delicate ear, then dabbed Ivoire behind them, at her wrists beneath the lace, behind her knees, then sprayed a minute amount on the hem of her dress. Gazing at her image once again, she knew the gown was exactly right, and strangely she felt that she was a part of Lafourche, almost as if she were bayou born and swamp raised. It was a feeling she couldn't shake, reminding her of the peculiar sensation she'd felt when she first emerged from the aircraft upon arriving on the bayou.

The mood stayed with her as she began to descend the stairs. Midway down a slight sound caught her attention and she looked up. Adrien was leaning over the banister. He appeared mesmerized, making no move to greet her beyond silently forming her name on his lips. Her eyes met his and there was that electrifying jolt of chemistry arcing between them. It was a golden and beautiful moment, barren of words, but none were needed. The front door opened just then, bringing in the Duboises and the Bakers, and the splendor of the moment was gone but held forever in the recesses of memory.

"I'll be down in a few minutes," Adrien said. "Laurean and Venida are already in the drawing room. Will you take care of introductions?"

"Yes." She nodded and went to greet them. She met the Bakers, an older couple of German ancestry but Cajuns none-the-less. The chatter and laughter in the hall as the women admired one another's gowns brought Venida from the drawing room. Jennifer coolly introduced her.

Jean Dubois's eyes widened at the sight of Venida in her clinging purple. "Oooohee," he muttered under his breath. "Does that ever look like a million dollars...."

Barbara gave her husband a dry, caustic look and said, "Oh, would that be in loose change?" Properly chastised, he looked contrite and turned to Laurean Ballesta.

Adrien joined them, wearing a navy suede jacket with leather inserts at the elbow, a light blue silk shirt tucked into navy slacks, soft leather boots, and no tie, as usual. His one touch of elegance was the ebony links in French cuffs. Masterfully he took over his duties as host, speaking to all the women, but soon he and the men gravitated to one corner. Venida clung to him, Jennifer noticed, but she went about her duties skillfully and serenely. The men, after all, were discussing cattle.

Chapter Thirteen

The dinner was a great success and almost anticlimactic. Henri outdid himself cooking, serving, engaging in riposte with Adrien, and speaking kindly and flirtatiously with Francesca, who came to table just as they were all taking seats. Her eyes were clear, her hands firm, and she positively glowed under the mantle of Cajun hospitality. Laurean seemed newly entranced with his wife of thirty years.

Berty kept to the background as she was prone to do, but made sure each course followed the next with precision. They ate *escargot de bourguignon,* fried zucchini, cheese in tagiatelle, *filet mignon au poivre, poisson*-stuffed crab, and washed it down with excellent wines. Leddy kept the table cleared, the glasses filled, and disappeared immediately she placed the last crystal bowl of tantalizing tangerine zabaglione in front of Jennifer.

The men took their brandied coffee and smokes under the glowing lanterns on the *garconniere.* In a brief repreive from her hostess duties, in which she had been as skillful and busy as a marionettist controlling the strings of puppets, Jennifer found time to speak to Barbara Dubois.

"How do you think everything is going?" she asked.

"You've done a magnificent job," Barbara told her. "This old house has come alive. Dinner was superb. I have the feeling I'll never be able to throw a bowl of gumbo on the table and satisfy Jean again. He embarrassed me, asking for double helpings.''

"Henri loved him for it." Jennifer laughed.

"What's with the swamp siren?" Barbara asked, nodding toward Venida, who was hovering about Adrien. "Doesn't it bother you, the way she's hanging on him?"

Jennifer glanced Venida's way, then shrugged noncommittally.

"Boy, I wish I had your confidence," said Barbara with a trace of envy.

"Is that how I seem to you, confident?" Jennifer asked, surprised.

"Cool, calm, and serene," Barbara answered. "Why, are you fooling me tonight?" *Cajun hospitality has its price,* she thought silently.

"Fooling myself most likely," Jennifer muttered, and left Barbara mulling over that while she answered a summons from Mrs. Baker. Out the corner of her eye she watched Venida excuse herself and follow her mother upstairs. Their leaving seemed to be the signal to end the evening. In a flurry of good-byes and compliments the guests left, and Jennifer found herself standing on the front veranda, alone with Adrien. There was no moon, only the lamps in the drawing room cast fingers of light in the fog-shrouded darkness.

They weren't touching, yet his nearness made her short of breath, kept her heart pounding erratically. He had his hands in his pockets, his head tilted, waiting for his eyes to adjust to the darkness so he could see her expression.

"You're a marvelous woman, Jennifer."

The compliment made her go warm all over. "How so?"

"The way you handled everything today. I'd say

there was potential for a half dozen disasters, especially with Francesca's problem. Laurean was pleased to see her so—so happy and animated at dinner. I have a feeling these kind of evenings are few and far between for him."

"That wasn't my doing, it was Leddy's. She talked with Francesca. Somehow Leddy has a way of making you look inside yourself."

"Rumor has it you've loaned Leddy a bit of magic?" His voice was teasing.

Jennifer smiled into the shadows. "Some perfume."

"If it does for Etienne what it does for me, he'll be docile as a lamb in the morning."

"You're docile?"

He laughed softly at her skepticism. "Another thing. I've been trying to thank you. You worked a miracle with Berty—"

"Henri can take the credit for that—"

"No. If it hadn't been for you, she wouldn't have gone within ten feet of him. Believe me, I know. She's almost like her old self." He sighed heavily. "I should have done more for her, but I've been living in my own hell these past two years."

"I know," she said softly.

"This land, as much as anything else, can get to a man sometimes. It makes him harsh, hard around the edges. Plant a crop and the weather doesn't come on right, a man gets frustrated—he feels helpless." Then he added, "That's how I feel about you—helpless."

Surprised at the turn of his conversation, Jennifer tried to make out his features in the shadows. "What do you mean by that?"

"I can't seem to get inside that wall you've built. There doesn't seem to be any opening. You're holding me back. I can sense it. Why?"

There was a long pause while Jennifer's mind raced. Finally, she said, "I was engaged once."

Adrien went very still. "What happened?"

"Not much. He left me for someone else. He said I was going in too many directions at once, that it was too hard to keep up with me."

"That's all?"

"No." She was beginning to feel trapped. "I don't want to talk about it." Suddenly, Jennifer was consumed with unreasoning fears. Make love, be loved, give love, she thought. Every step she took in the direction of Adrien carried her away from the life she had created for herself.

"You have to choose," he said.

Jennifer was startled. It was as if her mind had just been read.

Now was not the time to push for revelations, Adrien decided. "Laurean is waiting for me in my study." He watched her face as she brushed past him into the softly lit hall. "Come to my bed tonight?" he asked in a low voice.

"You're sure?" she queried.

"I think you're the one who needs to answer that, no?"

An hour later Adrien left his study. He was ebullient, almost in a daze with his good fortune. He and Laurean had concluded the cattle deal—a far better one for him than he had envisioned. Not only was Laurean desirous of two small herds of thirty head each, one shipped as soon as possible and the other to be shipped next spring, but he had purchased a bull, too. Not a prize-winner, but certainly choice—thirty thousand dollars worth of choice! *"Mon Dieu!"* he exclaimed happily to himself. If there ever was a situation where he could eat his cake and have it too... Before he shipped that bull he'd get the vet to milk it of sperm, and for the next year he'd have the use of that bull while it grazed and performed its duties in the Colombian mountains for Laurean. The old clock in the drawing room chimed half past midnight. His mind went to Jennifer. He hoped she was awake and waiting for him. At the top of the stairs he paused and, looking toward his door, discovered Jennifer backing out of his room. Had she tired of waiting, or become impatient?

"I didn't mean to be so long." His whisper carried down the length of the hall. Jennifer pivoted. Her eyes were filled with anger and her expression would have done justice to a man who found himself sentenced to hang.

"You failed to mention that I should take a number," she hissed. "Or is this just another of your experimental breeding programs?" Her voice was acid. Adrien stepped into her path as she attempted to sidestep him and enter her room. His fingers bit into her shoulders.

"What the hell are you talking about?"

She jerked her head toward his bedroom. "Venida is in your bed, looking very satisfied and sound asleep," she said with cutting invective. "Now, turn me loose. You're hurting me." She walked into her room, and Adrien followed.

Rage took hold of Adrien, his happiness of a moment before withered. "She's not there by my invitation," he said savagely. "She took it upon herself to crawl into my bed. Do you think I'm so stupid that I'd engage in an affair with a woman so like Eleanor? Carnal? Surface? Selfish? Rude? In love with only herself?" His eyes narrowed to slits, his voice sounding an ominous warning. "Have you learned nothing about me, Jennifer? Is this as far as we've come?"

She took a step back, alarmed at the high fury that

seeped into his words. His body appeared to tremble, and the vein in his jaw pulsated with every rapid beat of his heart. She hugged the white batiste gown about her—useless protection—while her own heart maintained a frenzy of activity. "I don't make it my life's work to go around analyzing people. All I know is, she's in your bed...." Her lower lip began to tremble, her eyes felt hot, close to tears.

"Good Christ! Don't cry," he said, his anger dissolving as rapidly as it had arisen. He took a tentative step toward her.

"I'm not crying. I never cry." Despite this announcement, her eyes began to water. She retreated to the canopied safety of the bed, leaning far back into the drapery's shadows, muffling sniffles.

Sighing heavily, Adrien sat down in the rocking chair. "No, I don't suppose you do. I suspect you liberated women would cut your throat rather than show some human emotion." He bent forward, removed his shoes and socks, then took the links from his cuffs and tossed them onto the table near the rocker. They pinged when they hit the base of the lamp.

"That's not fair," Jennifer told him.

"Whoever said life's fair?" He gave a snort of disgust, stood up, and removed his shirt.

Watching, her confusion mounting, Jennifer asked, "What are you doing?"

"I should think it's obvious. I'm getting undressed, ready for bed."

"You expect to sleep here? In my bed?"

"Give the lady a gold star," he said caustically. "She got it right on the first try."

"No, no, you're not. Go—go sleep on a sofa downstairs, or in your study."

He muttered an inelegant word under his breath, strode over to the bed, where she lay, and brushed back the drapes, flooding her corner of privacy with light. "Let's get one thing straight. I don't sleep on sofas, and I don't camp out in my study—not when there are perfectly good beds available." He sauntered back to the rocker, scooped up his shoes, tossed his shirt over his shoulder, pocketed the gleaming cuff links, then directed his steps toward the hall. He did not glance at Jennifer when he said good night.

"Where are you going to sleep?" she heard herself asking with impotent trepidation.

"In my own bed." There was an imperturbably civil air about his answer that caught Jennifer off guard. She drew oxygen into her lungs as though it were the very last pound available for survival.

"Wait!"

He turned to look at her, a slight curve to his lips, his entire demeanor one of expectation. "Well," he drawled gravelly, "how does it feel to get shoved between a rock and a hard place?"

Reality was always richer than language or dialogue, Jennifer knew. She got off the bed, turned down the covers, switched out the lamp, and crawled back in.

"You're on my side of the bed," he said.

She moved.

Adrien's lovemaking at first had been gentle, but then he became almost brutal, like a madman in his determination to imbue Jennifer with the very essence of himself. He sought with his hands, his lips, every thrust of his powerful body, to invade those little pockets of self that Jennifer held so secret. He refused to accept mere reaction. He insisted she share, give, abet, encourage, until she was helpless with need, dependent upon him for consummation. Then as she conquered her hesitation, her fears, he unleashed his own furious needs, and she learned interdependency. He wanted a commitment from her, and it was the only way he knew.

Finally, exhausted, she lay curled in his arms, drowsy, her silken flesh melded with his, and Adrien knew too the bounds of his possessiveness.

"You awake?" he asked softly.

"Just barely," she murmured, snuggling closer.

"Tell me about this man you almost married." For a long while she didn't speak, but she didn't move from him either. Adrien thought it was a good sign.

"There's not much to tell you, Adrien. He used me to get to my father. He wanted to go into radio." Then, surprisingly, she chuckled softly. "I suppose I used him, too. I was older than my classmates, and he made me feel like I fit in with the crowd.

Listening to her and the manner of her voice, Adrien understood that there was something more, something deeper that made her protect and coddle and savor the competence she had discovered in herself.

"How old was older?" he asked, searching for a clue.

"His twenty-two to my twenty-four. My mother has a drama studio. After I was graduated from high school, I helped her in the office, with schedules, grants, things like that. I thought it was what I wanted to do. But after I got to college, I realized how much I'd been missing. Then, when I moved to New Orleans, I realized that it had been what my mother had wanted for me. I'm an only child and she's... well—manipulative. I mean, I love her and all that, but I've built up a sort of resentment that she held me back." She raised her head up off his shoulder. "Am I making sense?"

"Yes," and he thought, *Far more than you'll ever know.* There was a comfortable silence between them until Adrien thought she had fallen asleep, but she stirred and pulled the sheet over their air-cooled bodies.

"May I ask you a question?" she said. "What did you do with Eleanor's portrait?"

"I sent it to the Guilbeaux along with a note to her attorney telling him it's there if she wants it. If she doesn't, I'll return it to the artist. I don't want it, but I think the workmanship is too fine to destroy. It wouldn't be fair to the talent that created it." Her breath was warm on his neck, the bewitching fragrance of her filled his nostrils, and the last thing in the world he wanted to do this minute was sleep, but he felt her relax completely against him, so he gave up the thoughts that were lurking in his mind.

"That's nice of you," she said, her voice throaty with sleep. "You're so noble."

He drifted into sleep, smiling, thinking that there was nothing so grand as the wicked and wonderful human spirit.

Leddy was late to work. Concerned, Jennifer stood on the back porch, sipping on a cup of midmorning coffee, eyeing the footbridge beyond Berty's cabin. With each minute's passing she expected to see Leddy emerge from the stand of cypress across the bayou and skip across the bridge. After a few more minutes, she gave up her vigil and went to join Francesca in the drawing room. Venida, sullen and dour, remained in her room. As Jennifer emerged into the wide hall from the back, Leddy came flying in the front door.

"Sorry I'm late," she said, hurrying up to Jennifer. "I had to stop by my *maman's* this morning." There was a happy catch in Leddy's voice that made Jennifer take a closer look at Leddy's face. The young bride was positively glowing, her eyes lit with secret knowledge. Even her cap of dark curls seemed to have more bounce. With a woman's intuition Jennifer knew their marriage had been consummated. She smiled at the radiant happiness that emanated from Leddy and felt a pang of bittersweet envy. Her feminine curiosity rose to the fore.

"And what did you have to discuss with your mother that was so important it made you late?"

A flush rose up Leddy's neck and spread across her cheeks, embarrassing her far more than Jennifer's question. For she was a complete woman now with the knowledge to discuss these things candidly, just like her *maman* with the neighbor-women gathered for afternoon coffee. From this day forward she would be among them. She pulled Jennifer into the privacy of the deserted dining room. "Etienne prayed exactly right over the love potion," she said, eyes glittering. "The frog didn't like his new home, no? He was a wonderfully high jumper and landed right here." She touched her hand to her breasts. "I was so terribly frightened," she continued, eyes wide with innocence, "that I called out. Etienne came running from the couch. I showed him where the monster had bitten me but there was nothing there, and then I thought perhaps on my neck—"

Jennifer laughed. "Leddy! You just said it landed on your chest."

"I know, but your perfume—my magic—was behind my ears and on my neck."

"Oh. And what happened then?"

"I thought the monster might be caught up in the folds of my nightgown—possible, no?—so I took it off and Etienne inspected every inch."

"Did he?" Jennifer uttered dryly.

"Oh, yes. And it was so warm last night, I didn't feel the need to cover my nakedness." She shot Jennifer a sideways look from beneath her lashes. "Did you notice how warm it was last night?"

"A hundred degrees, at least," Jennifer admitted,

recalling the heat she and Adrien had generated in the course of their own lovemaking.

"Anyway, Etienne couldn't find it—the monster.... Well...I was too frightened to sleep by myself, no?" Leddy smiled happily, then remembering her duties, said quickly, "Oh, but I must hurry. I promised Mrs. Ballesta I would brush her hair and tell her something of our Acadian history."

Jennifer put her arm out. "Wait a second, Leddy. Did Etienne say he loved you?"

"One thousand times, at least!" she answered, glowing with pride.

"What happened to the monster?"

"Ah! Disappeared without a trace, no? Except I thought I saw Etienne's pant's pocket bulge peculiarly this morning, and after we crossed the bayou, it was flat again."

Smiling, Jennifer said, "Well, if you tell this story to Francesca, she will be totally enthralled."

Leddy was appalled. "Oh, I couldn't. She's an outsider."

"Why, Leddy, so am I."

"No, you're one of us," Leddy answered simply. Then she hesitated, overcome with a shyness so foreign to her nature. "When the baby comes, we want you to stand as godmother. Etienne and I have already discussed it."

Jennifer was astounded. "Me? A godmother? I don't know the first thing about being a godmother."

Leddy frowned. "You go to church, don't you?"

"Well...I—I went Easter Sunday."

"Good!" she stated, as though that were all there was to it, and turned to go.

"Wait a minute, Leddy. How do you know you're pregnant? I mean you just—you know, last night."

The young Cajun smiled with the superiority of her

newly discovered womanhood. "A woman knows these things," she answered with absolute logic.

As she stared after Leddy, her mouth agape, something snapped inside Jennifer. She was unaware of it at the time, but Leddy's words *you're one of us,* snuggled under a flap in her brain and made themselves at home, so that Jennifer ever after would never feel comfortable away from Lafourche for extended periods of time.

Chapter Fourteen

After Lafourche, the Guilbeaux Hotel seemed cold and alien to Jennifer. There was a subdued atmosphere about the staff, and she noticed an unconscious tension in the air, but she shrugged this feeling off as she hurried through the lobby to the coffee shop. In her mind she was still on the veranda at Lafourche, saying good-bye to Leddy, Berty, and Adrien—especially Adrien. On the face of it, they had said very proper good-byes, but privately, though nothing was actually settled between them, there was an unspoken promise—of what exactly and how far it carried into the future, Jennifer wasn't sure. She knew only that the boundries of the stringent independent life-style she had created for herself had been breached. She had begun to feel terribly lonely the moment she and Henri had driven away from Lafourche and its owner.

In the coffee shop Ellie was cashiering—taking checks, counting change, murmuring thank-you's by rote as each customer departed without glancing upward. Jennifer got in line. When it came her turn, she said, "Can the hotel still afford a free cup of coffee these days?"

Ellie's head shot up. "My gosh!" she said breathlessly. "Jennifer DeWitt—manna from heaven. When did you get back?"

"Last night. I drove in with Henri."

"Boy, am I glad to see you. Just a minute. Let me get Ruth to take over for me, and we'll have that coffee" She smiled dourly. "Can't tell nowadays how long coffee will remain one of our free perks. We'd better get it while the getting is good."

"For heaven's sakes, Ellie, what's been going on?" Jennifer asked as she stirred cream into her coffee They sat in a back booth, Ellie chain-smoking nervously, far more agitated than Jennifer had ever seen her.

"This place has been positively awful this past week. Surprise auditors all over the place, management consultants snooping into everything...and I mean everything. If old Britz wasn't bald, he'd have yanked his hair out by now, and"—Ellie lowered her voice— "Milton Richards and Eva Wilcox—well, you'll just have to see them in action. She drools, he passes her a love napkin now and then. One of Mrs. Stacy's housekeepers walked in on them in six-twelve. Wilcox told her she'd have the maid fired if it got back to Britz. So everybody in the hotel knows but the old man himself Richards has been putting on a grand act for the management consultants. Regular staff has been cut to a thirty-five hour work week to decrease payroll, and guess who has to take up the slack? Management—as if we didn't already have enough to do. I've been pulling twelve- and sixteen-hour days." Ellie leaned back and sighed, pulling on the cigarette butt for one last puff

"Are the auditors still here?" Jennifer asked. "How did my department measure up?"

"I don't know, they haven't said, but you can believe no one is going to come up smelling like roses. Al Albert has been fired—a discrepancy in a petty cash voucher. You know how mulish he is...you could hear him bellowing all over the lobby. Richards called the cops to have him removed from the premises! I don't know what's going on—Al may be mulish and bull-headed, but he's honest."

Shock registered in Jennifer's eyes. "Fired! But he's been here for years...." Her voice trailed off. Ellie shrugged wearily.

"Yeah. No telling who's going to be the next to go. Let's talk about something pleasant. How was your mini vacation? Successful? You have a look about you, sort of satisfied—like a cat who just dined on a whipped-cream topped mouse."

"Oh, everything went fine. Adrien Merril sold his cattle, his guests seemed happy when they left, I made some new friends...even got invited to be a god-mother," she said, smiling impishly. "What do you think about that?"

"Sounds like you got your bottom glued in place in the Louisiana swampland. I'm surprised you even came home. What about the original wolf? He's de-mure and wearing sheep's skin, I suppose?"

"We had a few rough spots, but in the end we got along rather well."

Ellie studied Jennifer for a long moment. "You sound just a bit too smug, young lady. You by any chance fall in love or something?"

"Don't be so nosy, Ellie."

"Humph! That's a yes if I ever heard one." Ellie's features became serious. "Everyone is talking about quitting, so if you can get yourself married and out of this rat race, you'll be ahead of the game."

Jennifer was alarmed. "Ellie! You're not thinking of quitting, are you? I mean, it may be rough right now, but these things always blow over, don't they?"

"Maybe so," Ellie replied, sounding unconvinced. "I guess I'd better get back to work. You, too. There's a mountain of inquiries on your desk, and sales, bless their little hearts, have booked us about eight thousand dollars worth of food sales next week. You're welcome to the paperwork."

Jennifer plunged into work, waded through the stack of inquiries, brought the banquet book up to date, revised menus, costed out selections for sales reps who needed the information for their clients, and answered queries with sample menus, price lists, and room arrangements. She too put in sixteen-hour days and went home so weary, it was all she could do to bathe and fall into bed. She dreamed of Adrien, ached for him, expected him to call anytime, but during the day thoughts of him were only fleeting, as she had no time to daydream at the hotel. Milton Richards prowled the premises like a panther looking for prey. When he found an employee standing idle or two engaged in chitchat, more jobs were cut, budgets slashed on the premise that if employees had time to gossip and stand idle, there wasn't enough work to keep them busy.

Tension grew, and everyone kept looking over their shoulders. The staff was strained, and there seemed to be more clashes with guests. Courtesies were abrupt, and the slow, easy charm that so appealed to the regulars disappeared. Customers grumbled.

Organization became a priority, and Jennifer and Ellie devised a plan to keep their staff occupied at all times. Their employees, loyal all, went along, knowing their jobs were on the line. When Jennifer's setup and banquet servers weren't busy, she loaned them to Ellie to bus tables in the coffee shop, the dining room, or the Cove. It was a mark of the strain everyone was under that even Vinnie, when pressed into service to deliver room service orders, acquiesced with nary a word.

An executive staff meeting was called, Al Alberts was conspicuous by his absence, and everyone avoided looking at his vacant chair. No one wanted to be the next to go. Britz announced with ominous significance that every department would be thoroughly evaluated once he received the reports from the auditors and management consultant teams. Milton Richards eyed everyone about the table menacingly.

When Harry, the doorman, spotted Saul Rosenberg, the chief auditor, entering the hotel, the news traveled like lightning and the hotel crackled with electric apprehension.

Jennifer and Ellie were in their office together, an unusual occurrence these days, when they got the news.

"Well, I guess heads are going to roll now," Ellie stated dolefully.

"Not ours, surely," Jennifer said, trying to cheer up her co-worker. "You know, what I don't understand is, the hotel is running smoother in some ways, but couldn't the same results have been achieved with more positive attitudes?"

"Sure it could have," Ellie answered. "But that takes longer. What I don't understand is how old Britz let Milton Richards bamboozle him into this. I've worked for him for twelve years, and I've never known him let loose the reins, no matter what. Richards," she added grimly, "must be one smooth operator."

"He has Eva Wilcox in his pocket, too," Jennifer stated.

Ellie snorted with indignation. "In his bed, you meant to say," she rattled sarcastically. They both looked up as Wayne Ferassini, the front desk manager, entered the tiny office.

"Wayne! What brings you to our hole-in-the-wall?" Ellie asked, surprised.

Ferassini was a thin man: thin hair, thin mustache, thin voice. His bones protruded every which way through his dark front office uniform. He was nervous, which was making his voice reedy. "Mr. Britz told me to come for Jennifer, here." He nodded toward Jennifer, letting his eyes slide to the floor. "I'm to escort her to the executive office."

Jennifer paled. "Escort me? What for?"

"I don't know," he said miserably. "Look, Jennifer, will you just come?" He almost said peaceably. Jennifer looked over to Ellie, her dark eyes wide, the golden barbs buried in alarm.

"Think!" Ellie exclaimed. "Have you done anything? Anything at all that the auditors would question?"

"No." Jennifer was certain. "Ellie, I don't handle money, and catering's books reconcile down to the penny. You know that." She was beginning to tremble. Ferassini cleared his throat.

"Could we go now? Mr. Britz is waiting."

On the mezzanine Eva Wilcox leered triumphantly at Jennifer and guided her into the executive office. Mr. Britz sat behind his huge desk, and Milton Richards stood behind him, looking out the window. Eva Wilcox took a chair against the wall. Saul Rosenberg had left, but the files and folders he had marked as urgent were open on Britz's desk.

"Sit down, Miss DeWitt," Britz said firmly.

Jennifer looked from one to the other in the room. She sat in the horrible chair, her heart thudding, knowing she was no longer among the elite. Britz addressed her formally. Did that mean, too, that she was no longer in favor with Adrien? Oh, why, she wondered, hadn't he called in these past two weeks? All thoughts of Adrien were swept from her mind with Britz's next words.

"I have here a petty cash voucher, Miss DeWitt, that has been altered."

"Altered?" Her mind raced, and she had a cold feeling in her stomach. "Not by me, Mr. Britz," she stated with rigid firmness. "You know I don't use petty cash vouchers. We have no need for them in my department."

There was a long silence. Richards stared at her, an eyebrow raised, and Britz shuffled papers. The sound of Wilcox's pen as she took notes intruded on Jennifer's concentration. She took the petty cash voucher from Britz's outstretched hand. The small slip of paper was smudged with fingerprints from much handling. Jennifer glanced at it and gasped. It was the voucher authorized by Adrien Merril for her trip to Lafourche. An extra digit had been added to the figure. It no longer read two hundred dollars, but twelve-hundred. What was going on here?

"I recognize this, Mr. Britz. It's the voucher you gave me for expenses, but I only received two hundred dollars, not twelve hundred. There's been a mistake."

Milton Richards shot his cuffs, his face impassive. "I'm sorry to dispute your word, Miss DeWitt, but I gave you twelve hundred dollars and didn't question it, as you will recall, since it had both Mr. Britz's signature and that of the hotel's owner."

Jennifer shook her head. This was incredible! Milton Richards was lying. All the blood in her head seemed to pool somewhere down around her feet. She leaped up. "Mr. Richards, that's not true. You didn't give me that money!" She turned to face Eva Wilcox and saw the malevolent gleam in her eyes, the tight little smile on her lips. "*You* took that voucher, Eva, *you* got the money from Richards. You insisted, and I waited in your office."

Wilcox cocked an eyebrow. "I don't recall that," she denied smoothly.

Jennifer swallowed the panic that was forming like a lump of lead in her throat. "Mr. Britz! This is a conspiracy, don't you see that? Eva Wilcox is lying. She's never liked me. She's done this and somehow gotten Richards to go along." The moment the words were out Jennifer knew they sounded petty, ignoble, but it was the truth. Her legs felt rubbery, threatening to collapse, and she sat down heavily in the slanted-forward chair. "Please, listen to me, Mr. Britz. I don't steal. I didn't take the money. I only received two hundred dollars. Call Ad— Call Mr. Merril, he'll vouch for me."

Britz stiffened. "I run this hotel," he said sternly. "Mr. Merril doesn't interfere."

"You just think you run this hotel!" she shot back, gathering anger. It bunched up, making her chest expand, her shoulders square. "Wilcox and Richards have you snowed. They got caught in the surprise audit, and now they're looking for scapegoats! *I did not take that money.*" She spoke this last through clenched teeth.

Britz sighed. He hated scenes like this. "Miss De-Witt, vituperation on your part isn't seemly, nor does it change the situation. The facts speak for themselves. We will not press charges, but you must leave the hotel immediately, and when your conscience starts to bother you, and I hope that it does, we'll accept restitution." He had a grim look on his face as he handed her an envelope. "Your severance and vacation pay." Jennifer accepted it. She had earned it, by damn!

Glaring at Britz, Richards, and Wilcox in turn, she said, "You haven't heard the last of this, I promise you."

Wilcox returned her stare with contempt, Richards shot his cuffs, seemingly unconcerned, and Britz shook his head, a sad expression on his face, as though ashamed of Jennifer's outburst. "Eva will take you to your office to get your things and walk you to the entrance. You understand, obviously, you won't be welcome here, even as a guest."

Jennifer eyed Milton Richards. "You did this to Al Alberts too, didn't you?" Wilcox's fingers were on Jennifer's arm, leading her out of the executive office.

"Take your hand off me," she uttered coldly.

"Really, Jennifer," Wilcox said maliciously, "you should've known better than to try a stunt like that."

"You may think you've won, Eva, but it's only your word against mine. I'll see the truth is known, somehow—"

The executive secretary sneered.

Jennifer became aware of other employees watching as they glided by, and feeling the depth of her humiliation and the injustice of it all, she became silent, saying not another word to anyone as she removed her few personal items under Wilcox's watchful eyes, then made her way to the front entrance. She looked back once and saw Ellie, a horrified expression on her face, standing in the coffee shop. Jennifer attempted an encouraging smile, but it fell flat.

Outside the hotel the sun was shining; one of those glorious late spring days God creates to remind lesser beings of their humble origins. Jennifer glanced at Harry, who stepped back as though she were poison. Well, she couldn't blame him. She had been fired, terminated, labeled a thief. He had his own job to look out for.

While walking home she tried to put a positive face on things, but nothing helped. Her whole life was falling apart. She thought of calling Adrien, appealing to him, but somehow that didn't sit too well. Couldn't she handle this herself? Wasn't she on her own? She didn't need a man to run to, a man to cry to, a man to solve her problems, she realized.

Once home, she did call Al Alberts. Much the same

thing had happened to him. Britz wouldn't listen, accepting evidence presented at face value. He had, he said, consulted an attorney who told Al to be thankful he hadn't been charged with theft. Al could take Britz, Richards, and Wilcox to court—civil court—for slander, but the expense was monumental. His department had been four thousand dollars out of balance.

"Oh, Al, what can we do?" Jennifer pleaded.

"I'm doing nothing," he replied, a trace of sadness in his voice. "You can't fight city hall, Jennifer. No matter what, you can't win. By the time Britz catches onto Richards, they'll have forgotten all about us. Sweep the whole thing under the rug—that's how these corporations operate. I'm just going to draw my social security and go fishing. Why don't you come with me? I haven't had a young'un like you about the house since my daughter ran off and got married."

Jennifer declined. "No. I've got to do something! I'm not old enough to draw social security like you, friend. I'll keep in touch, though."

Later that night she called Ellie at home. "Jennifer! My God! It's all over the hotel, and no one believes it. But everybody is so scared for their own jobs. It's unreal. What are you going to do now?"

"Find another job, to start, but Ellie, I want you to do me a favor. See if you can get into personnel and find out where Richards worked before he came to the Guilbeaux. Get a copy of his résumé if you can."

Ellie's breathlessness came through the wire. "Why? What good will that do? And Jennifer, I can tell you right now, I'll never be able to get my hands on them. Executive records are kept by Eva Wilcox, not personnel."

Clearing her name at the hotel seemed hopeless for the time being, so Jennifer, functioning on adrenaline pumped into her system by deep anger, began job hunting. She filled out applications at dozens of hotels in the area and was close to despair when finally she was called for an interview.

She arrived on time for the appointment and gave her name to the receptionist.

"Oh," the elegantly clad young woman said, "Jennifer DeWitt. I'm sorry, but your interview has been canceled."

"Canceled?" Jennifer repeated, puzzled. "But why? Your personnel director called me himself yesterday afternoon."

"That was yesterday," the receptionist said with an ineffable twitch of her nose. "Your references don't check out. That's all I'm allowed to say."

Jennifer was stunned. She had worked hard at the Guilbeaux. It was her only hotel experience, and she had put it down on her applications.

"What do you mean, my references don't check out?"

The woman sniffed. "Just what I said. Now, if you'll excuse me..."

"Just answer me this," Jennifer said, a sinking sensation in her stomach. "Who checked my references?"

"I did," the receptionist replied and had the grace to avert her eyes from Jennifer's.

"And who did you talk to?"

The woman hesitated, but seeing Jennifer's determination, she yielded. "A Mrs. Wilcox." Then she looked at Jennifer for a moment. She saw a young woman, exquisitely groomed, and nothing about her suggested the character of the person that had been described to her by the woman Wilcox. "Look, Miss DeWitt," she said cautiously, "I shouldn't be telling you this—we have all kinds of privacy rules—but if you want to work in New Orleans, I suggest you stop using the Guilbeaux as a reference."

The well-intentioned advice came far too late. Jennifer had, naively, included it on every application she had filled out.

That night the reality of her situation set in, and despair and depression became a second self. Still, she wouldn't give up and kept looking for work. She found none. She came home each day weary, mentally fatigued, her self-confidence battered, and finally, her resources were demolished.

She called Adrien.

There was no answer. She let the telephone ring ten times, twenty times. She called every hour on the hour. She called at midnight, 4:00 A.M., 6:00 A.M., for days on end, to no avail. It was as if Adrien Merril had disappeared from the face of the earth.

An insidious sense of helplessness overtook her. She was listless, she didn't eat, couldn't sleep, didn't dress. Her apartment was no longer a haven, a sanctuary, but a prison. She felt abandoned by her friends, by Adrien. No one loved her, no one came to her rescue—no one would. She was shamed, disgraced. She couldn't go home. She was a failure. Curling up in her bed, she willed herself to die and when she didn't, she found a bottle of brandy in the cupboard and sat on the sofa, trying to sip herself into oblivion.

Chapter Fifteen

It was long after midnight by the time Adrien had checked himself through customs at the New Orleans airport, called the Guilbeaux to tell them to expect him, and hailed a taxi.

The happenings over the past two weeks seemed unreal. He was still dazed. For the thousandth time he chastised himself for not having called Jennifer. He didn't know how, but it seemed when he got embroiled with cattle, all else slipped from his mind. Tunnel vision, he knew. He would watch that in the future—if he had a future. Jennifer might have given up on him by now. The thought gave him more anxiety than he could handle at that moment.

He shifted his lean square body in his seat as the cab sped along Veteran's Boulevard, and caught a glimpse of his face in the rearview mirror. He was conscious that he had lost weight, because he'd had to move his belt over an extra notch, but the bony, hollowed—out look to his face surprised him. As if to give substance to the sequel of events that had been forced upon him, he closed his eyes, reviewing each incident.

The contract he signed with Laurean Ballesta had been uppermost in his mind. Though he agreed to pay the exorbitant cost of shipping, Laurean had shrewdly inserted a clause that it would fall to Adrien to see that the thirty head of cattle arrived safely at the quarantine sheds in the small village of Turbo on the Gulf of Urabá on the Colombian coast. Adrien did two things. He insured the cattle and decided he would accompany them on their voyage. A second herder was necessary Ralph was far too old, and Etienne flatly refused to be separated from his marriage bed. Adrien was forced to borrow a hand, Christian Dupré, from Jean Dubois. Only fair, he thought, since Jean had started the entire matter in the first place. So, together with the cattle and the bull, he and Dupré boarded the old cargo ship, chosen because the second deck where the cattle pens were located was open to fresh air. Adrien drove him self to distraction worrying that the cattle would be come seasick.

Unfortunately, having lived his entire thirty-four years near and upon water. he never gave the same thought to himself. On the second morning out as they emerged into a stormy Caribbean from the Atlantic. he fell ill. He was so weak by the time they docked in Turbo that he was taken from the ship on a stretcher and flown to a hospital farther up the coast in Barranquilla. Barely conscious, unable to protest, he was mor tified and embarrassed. He had never had a sick day in his life, not even a cold. And as if this weren't already the worst luck, as he began to recover he succumbed to an intestinal virus. Eight days later he was on his feet. but had to wait for a government doctor to ascertain that he was not carrying some exotic disease. Only this morning had they put their stamp of approval on him and allowed him to fly to New Orleans.

And while he had been carted off the ship on a stretcher, the cattle had sashayed down the gangplank as though a five-day voyage were an everyday occurrence. Christian Dupré, he had learned by telegram. had delivered the herd into Laurean's representative's hands safely and returned to Lafourche. Adrien was left with a fourteen-day chunk of his life filled with a happenstance that he prayed fervently would never be repeated.

At the Guilbeaux he was greeted warmly by Ferassini, the front desk manager. Handing Adrien his key, he said with an air of sober efficiency, "Your wife arrived earlier, Mr. Merril. I put her in your usual suite."

Adrien reeled as though he had been struck. "Wife? What wife? I have no wife—" he sputtered hoarsely.

The desk manager paled. "I'm sorry, I must've made a mistake," then quickly tried to prove that he hadn't. He pulled a folio from the registration file and slid it across the marble counter. "She said she was your wife, Mr. Merril. She registered as Eleanor Merril, then a few minutes later you called—I—"

Adrien wasn't listening, he was running for the elevator, which opened miraculously as he approached. He stabbed the button for the eighth floor with impatience. His mind raced, his vision blurred, and he put his hands to his head to stop the thundering. Eleanor! After two years! he thought. Now he would have the opportunity to say to her all those things he had kept packed down tight inside. The elevator came to a halt with a soft swish. Adrien sped toward his suite, his hands trembling so that he could barely twist the key in the lock. In the bedroom he snapped on the light and there she lay, her blond hair strewed out upon the pillow, her figure outlined beneath the thin sheet. As he stood next to the bed, breathing hard, her eyes fluttered open. She sat up, smiled, and let the sheet fall from her shoulders.

"Adrien, what a pleasant surprise. How nice of you to stop by."

He was in no mood for social amenities. "What are you doing here, Eleanor? Slumming?"

"Now, Adrien," she cooed, using the voice that had so entranced him when they first met. It grated on his ears. "Can't we let bygones be bygones? Don't go into one of your rages. I just came to pick up my portrait My attorney—"

"You had no right to use my name. You're no Merril." His voice was utterly low, menacing. Eleanor, aware that she didn't control the situation, pulled the sheet up to cover her breasts.

"This is your hotel. I just thought it would be the thing to do," she said slyly, watching his face. It was going dark with anger, his eyes narrowing to slits.

The dam that held back the flood of hate and frustration in Adrien burst. "The thing to do?" he raged. "Is that what you thought when you ran out on me? Is that what you thought when you aborted my child?"

Eleanor felt a sense of fearful apprehension. It lit up her eyes, and there was something else, excitement that she had provoked his anger, a sensual excitement. "I didn't abort your child," she trilled, laughing. "I never said I was pregnant with your baby. You assumed it was yours, and, of course, that suited me—at the time." She saw his face go blank, uncomprehending. "Why did you think I agreed to marry you so quickly? I was dating a married man, he had been appointed to the president's council, and his wife was threatening to make a scene. She wouldn't accept that I was out of the picture unless I was married. You were handy. He didn't get Senate approval and called me when he got back to Kansas City. I debated a long time whether to go back to him or not, Adrien, truly I did, but I just couldn't stand being pregnant and away from the city I was so bored— Oh, not with you darling...."

He took a step back, feeling weak, feeling like he had just stepped from his sickbed. He couldn't get enough air into his lungs. Then he lunged for her, took her by her shoulders and began shaking her.

"What are you saying?" He ground the words out, saying them over and over, until suddenly he flung himself away from her, afraid that his hands were too willing to slide up from her shoulders to her neck. He was mad enough to kill. Then he looked away from her in disgust. "You left your conscience in the cradle, Eleanor. I'm well rid of you." He thought about the hurt she had done to Berty, to himself, the pain of rejection, the grief over the loss of his child—only now to learn none of it had mattered to her, and the child he wanted so badly, not even his. The realization that his firstborn had yet to be conceived dawned on him slowly. The black hole where his soul should have been filled explosively. His first child—a son, a daughter—not dead. His being seemed to become all warm, joyous. That experience he could share now with the woman whom he loved more than anything on earth—more than himself. He had to get to Jennifer! he thought. He glanced once more at Eleanor. She was flushed, smiling at him.

"I want you out of this hotel in the morning, Eleanor, by seven. If you aren't, I'll throw you out myself."

Her tongue flicked out to moisten her lips. "Stay with me tonight, Adrien—for old time's sake?"

He looked at her, appalled at her suggestion, then broke into laughter. "Making love to you is like making love to a limp fish. Good-bye, Eleanor."

Once outside the suite, he leaned against the door. He felt full, alive, yet there was a lingering sadness for the unborn child he had believed was his. And like Berty had done months ago, he offered up a prayer to God for its soul and put the matter from his mind.

At the front desk he arranged for another room from a very subdued desk manager. It was two o'clock in the morning. Tempted though he was to call Jennifer, he decided against it. Tomorrow would do. He saw himself surprising her as he had on that first day, standing just inside her office. He visualized the sun streaming through the window, casting copper into her red-brown hair. He saw the beauty mark above her lip, her heart-shaped face, and her breasts thrust against the yellow silk. The visions began to set up an inflammation in certain parts of his body that needed action to allay. *Mon Dieu!* he thought. He hoped she would be early to work.

There was no sun streaming through Jennifer's office windows, because the day was overcast, threatening a downpour. Only Ellie occupied the office. Adrien cursed under his breath. He was too early.

"Ellie, what time will Jennifer be here?" he asked, startling her as he had hoped to startle Jennifer.

"Oh, Mr. Merril, I didn't hear you come in." She didn't smile, and the immaculate look Adrien had come to know as Ellie's trademark was absent. Her hair and makeup did not have their usual polished neatness, her nails were chipped, and her clothes were rumpled. Only the overflowing ashtray seemed normal. Jennifer's desk was piled high with work. Ellie flung a hand toward it. "Jennifer's been fired."

"What!" His mouth gaped. Not in a million years had he foreseen such a happening. "Ellie, what the hell is going on here?"

She told him. No longer in awe of her job, of the glamour that kept her spellbound and breathless, she poured out the story while Adrien paced the tiny office like a caged, impatient animal looking for an escape route.

She finished the telling with the same comment she had used to Jennifer. "I don't know what has gotten into Britz. He never used to turn loose the reins. For all his fluttering around here, you know, he had his finger on the pulse of the hotel." Then she added, "We may not have made you a lot of money, Mr. Merril, but nobody here deserves what Milton Richards is dishing out."

"Where is Jennifer now?"

Ellie shrugged. "At home, I guess. I haven't talked to her for days."

Hurrying away from the hotel five minutes later, Adrien felt like kicking himself. He had forgotten all about Saul Rosenberg and the audit. He too was puzzled by Britz's behavior. He'd get an explanation from the man, but first it was Jennifer he wanted to see. He was certain of one thing: She was no thief.

He paid the cabdriver off at the top of the cul-de-sac, and bending his head against the rain, for the bottom had dropped out of the sky, he ran up the path to her corner apartment. He stopped on the threshold, shaking rain from his head, and peered into the dim interior. The doors were propped open and had been for some time. He could tell because dry leaves had blown in and scattered across the floor. Nearer the entrance they were wet where the driving rain had puddled. A twinge of fear grabbed hold of his gut. If something had happened to Jennifer...

He found her sprawled on the sofa, lifeless, the cat, Fred, curled on her stomach. A low moan escaped his lips as he grabbed her up, dislodging the cat. Jennifer's head fell back. That's when the sour smell hit him. Whiskey! Good Christ! She was drunk, he realized. Passed out. If he hadn't already had her cradled in his arms, he would have been happy to throttle her for scaring him half to death.

He moved her to the bed and went to make coffee. While it was perking he went to the old-fashioned bath for a cloth. When she woke, she'd have a head on her

that would require a cold compress. In the linen cabinet
he discovered a half dozen bars of Lifebuoy soap, un-
wrapped, and a nearly empty flacon of Kouros. Another puzzle.

It was many hours later when Jennifer began to stir.
An awful feeling of nausea intruded on her stupor. Her
head was filled with a clutch of horrible little men who
were pounding away on the inside of her skull with
sledgehammers. She had a bizzare dream that she
wasn't alone, that she smelled Adrien, heard his voice.
She wanted to sink down into the comfort of that
dream again, but the pounding behind her eyes forbade
it. Then she smelled coffee, and the nausea became
urgent. She opened her eyes. Adrien was no dream, but
real, standing over her.

"I'm going to be sick," she said, and thrusting her
head over the side of the bed, she was.

Adrien held her hair out of the way, wiped her
mouth and face, and crooned, "That's it, get it all
out."

Jennifer was crying and trying to apologize, and
Adrien was smiling and being sympathetic. He carried
her protesting into the bath, stripped her of her clothes,
and deposited her in the tub and turned on the water.

"Now, you bathe while I clean up that mess, then
we'll have coffee, lots of coffee, and lots of talk."

Jennifer looked up at him, her eyes wide, perplexed.
"Do you know I got fired from the Guilbeaux?"

"Yes, and we'll talk about that, too." He bent down
and kissed her on her nose. "I'm sorry I wasn't here
when you needed me, now, bathe!" He stood back and
eyed the gargantuan tub. "On second thought, that
thing looks big enough for the both of us. I think I'll
wash your back."

"You have a one-track mind," she told him, looking
a shade less doleful.

A half hour later she emerged, wearing a thick terry robe, her freshly shampooed hair woven into a shiny plait. Adrien was setting out cups on the table. He poured fresh coffee.

"I didn't realize you were so domestic, Adrien." She was still embarrassed about having been sick in front of him.

"There's a lot about each other that we don't know," he returned, studying her face. "We could spend a lifetime learning, though." His hands trembled as he placed the percolator back on the stove, and he wondered if Jennifer would always have this effect on him.

"You're talking about marriage?" Good grief! How had that come out so calmly? Her insides were shaking so, they threatened to come loose and get all mixed up. "You'd be marrying a failure." A lump began to form in her throat, and for a fearful minute she thought she was going to be sick again.

He sat down across from her, his eyes flashing. "I'd be marrying a woman of independent means...not too independent," he hastened to add, and thought, *But enough to keep you occupied as long as you felt it necessary.*

Jennifer's curiosity was aroused. "What means?"

"I thought as a wedding gift I'd give you the Guilbeaux. Keep it in the family, but get it off my back."

Jennifer gasped. "Give it to me, you mean just plain out..."

"For one dollar and other considerations. You do have a dollar?"

"Just about."

"Would you like to call your parents, invite them to the wedding?"

Jennifer thought about it for a long moment. "No. My mother has this way about her.... She'd insist we wait, have a big church wedding. Unless you don't mind waiting six months. But she'll make you think it was all your own idea—"

He exploded. "Six months! Good Christ. I want to get married tomorrow."

Opening her eyes, Jennifer found Adrien standing next to the great palisander bed, balancing a tray laden with coffee, bacon, scrambled eggs, and toast. A perfect ivory rose, dewy-wet, lay next to the silver. She smiled up at him. He hadn't yet shaved and his strong features were blurred by beard stubble. "They gave us a marvelous shivaree, don't you think?" she said, stretching luxuriously.

"There's probably not a pot or a pan fit for cooking within ten miles of this ranch." His ears were still ringing from clatter that had continued until two o'clock that morning.

As she pulled herself up against the carved headboard, the lace-trimmed coverlets slipped, exposing breasts tender and still swollen from their lovemaking. Adeptly Adrien set the tray down over her knees, bent his head, and pressed his lips to her warm soft flesh. Inhaling the womanly scent of her, he traced delicious patterns on rosy tips that quivered and thrust against his mouth.

"I love you," he murmured over and over, while Jennifer ran her fingers through his hair, pressing him even closer, savoring the erotic pulses that thundered through her veins and set up a powerful throbbing in her taut loins. She drew his head away from her breasts and up to her lips and kissed him on the nose. Golden barbs danced mischievously in her clear brown eyes.

"It's a good thing you know how to pronounce those three little words," she said with gentle laughter.

"Really, why?"

"They seemed to clog in Etienne's throat, and he spent a very lonely first month of marriage sleeping on a couch."

He absorbed this information. "Etienne is too damn shy."

"A charge one certainly couldn't make against you," said Jennifer, grinning, and pushing his hand away from secret places he had managed to locate under the coverlets. "Now, go shave, while I eat my breakfast. Your beard grows out like sticks."

Adrien complied, stepping out of the bathroom every now and then to see what Jennifer was up to, or to hear more clearly some comment she had made. He loved it when she talked to him while he shaved, or massaged his neck as he bent over accounts in his study. This was the best part of marriage—well, almost. He especially liked stepping into their closet, where the perfume of her body lingered on her clothes and hung in the air. He enjoyed watching her sit in front of the mirror, clad only in a flimsy robe, brushing her hair or applying cosmetics. The truth was, he was lovesick and want of her surged up in him. He prayed silently that no matter how comfortable they became as a married couple, these feelings would always stay with him.

Adjusting the breakfast tray more conveniently above her knees, Jennifer absently took up the rose and sniffed it appreciatively. For the first time she faced what it was like to be dependent on another person: the acceptance; getting out from under one's own ego; forgoing selfishness, alienation, loneliness. She and Adrien fit together, halves making up a whole. That's what she was: half of Adrien, half a marriage, and, strangely, it made her whole as she had never been. She reached for the napkin under the silver, but it wasn't a napkin. There under the silver lay a thick white stack of papers. She pulled it out, unfolded it, and squealed with delight. "Oh, Adrien, the deed to the hotel! Why didn't you tell me it came?"

Grinning through the lather, he said, "First things first. You still owe me a dollar."

She leaped from the bed, nearly upsetting the tray, went to her purse, removed a crisp one-dollar bill, and poked it into the waistband of his trousers as he stood at the sink.

"Thank you." He eyed her nakedness pleasurably: the smooth skin, slender curved hips tapering into the wonderfully long legs he adored having thrown over his at night. "When may I collect those other considerations?" he asked pointedly.

"Tonight," she answered, looking at him from beneath thick dark lashes. "Tonight and every night for the rest of my life, if that suits you."

"A well-struck bargain no respectable Cajun would argue—except a little on account this morning wouldn't go amiss," he teased. Then serious, he added, "What do you want to do now, about the hotel?"

During this past week of bliss the events at the hotel had receded, seeming only to be a filthy dream, but now, with the deed to ownership in her hand, she faced stark reality. She made her plans.

"I want to get this done today. Adrien, you must do something for me. Call Britz and tell him the hotel is changing hands at two o'clock, just don't say to whom." *That ought to give him one whale of a shock,* she thought, though she had a few more in store for him. "Did the reports from Saul Rosenberg come, too? I need to look them over."

"They're on my desk. But, Jennifer, are you sure— today? Your parents will be here tomorrow. Don't you think that's cutting it a bit close?"

Jennifer had been nervous when she called Hank and Nell DeWitt to tell them she was married, and afterward had expressed some hesitant remarks about her mother.

"No," she said with fierce determination. "I have accounts to settle—the sooner the better—and besides, I have to protect my investment."

Adrien glanced at her face. "Just how much Irish blood is there in you, anyhow?"

She grinned. "A fair amount, I'd say. It's only been diluted once by Lithuanian, and that can't hurt."

And Adrien, knowing that Jennifer had stopped using birth control the day they married, pondered aloud, "What will our children be like I wonder?"

"Oh, they wouldn't dare be like anything except their father," she said soothingly. A few minutes later she sat at the dresser, arranging a perfect chignon, deciding upon her wardrobe for the day. The white silk suit with the yellow blouse that she had worn for her first interview at the Guilbeaux. A fitting outfit. Lucky too for beginnings. In the mirror she caught Adrien's eyes on her. In their intimacy she had learned to look beyond the cynical expression, the curved lip tilting at the corner of his mouth. "Adrien, I know you're worried about how I feel about my mother. I just want you to know that, strangely, now that we're married, I can understand her motives. She loves me, wanted to protect me, and she just went overboard. I feel the same way about you."

"You want to protect me?" he uttered, totally astonished.

"I want to keep you mine. I don't want to share you with anyone or anything. The difference between my mother and myself is that I'm just more practical. I mean, I know you're going to fiddle with your cattle. I accept that."

"Fiddle, eh? You've neatly reduced me to a moron."

"Could anyone ever get away with calling you a moron?" she asked with saintly innocence.

He gave her a look of mock sternness. "Get dressed. I'll bring the car around. I suppose you want me along when you do in the executive staff of the Guilbeaux?"

"No. But you can wait for me in the Cove, or go shopping. This is something I have to do alone. And, Adrien, ask Berty if she'd like to drive there with us. She's been moping around, missing Henri."

When they were nearing New Orleans, Jennifer insisted Adrien pull up near a public telephone. She called the hotel and asked for Ellie Broussard.

"Jennifer! For heaven's sake. I've been wondering where you got off to. Did you go back to New York?"

"No, I'll explain things to you later, Ellie. Really, I have some terrific news. Right now I need a favor. I want you to meet me just outside the fence at the hotel under that big old oak by the corner at one fifty-five. Will you do it?" There was a very long silence.

"I—the hotel is changing hands today at two o'clock. The whole place is in an uproar. Couldn't I meet you later, or earlier?"

Jennifer smiled into the receiver. "No, it's important. One fifty-five, precisely, Ellie."

"You're planning something, aren't you?" Ellie's quizzical breathlessness came through the wire. Jennifer remained silent. A coup required tight planning, and she wasn't about to give up the element of surprise. She needed Ellie at her side, just to get past the doorman, and later as a witness, just in case Eva Wilcox— Well, who knew what Wilcox would do? she thought. "Oh, all right," Ellie said finally. "What's a job between friends? None of us may have one after two o'clock, anyway."

Adrien stopped the car at the corner Jennifer had

designated. "Good luck," he said softly. "I'll park this thing and be in the Cove if you need me."

"I'll manage just fine. You and Berty wait ten minutes, please, before you go in." Then she spotted Ellie emerging from the hotel, and stepped away from the car. It would be months before Jennifer learned what it cost Adrien to drive away from the corner and wait the afternoon away in the Cove. He hid his worry beneath years of self-control.

She and Ellie hugged one another briefly. "It's so good to see you," Ellie breathed. "You look ravishing. Maybe I ought to try getting fired. If it does for me what it's done for you—"

Jennifer laughed. "Ellie, you don't know the half of it, and I don't have time to explain now. I need to get to the executive office. I know Harry has orders not to let me in. Could you help me get past him?"

"My God! Jennifer, *No.* I can't. Britz is in a stew, everybody is. Merril sold the hotel—"

Jennifer glanced at her watch. It was time. "Come on," she said and took a reluctant Ellie's hand. They walked onto the shaded courtyard, past the outdoor café, and were nearly up the steps before Harry caught sight of Jennifer.

"Miss DeWitt!" he said, alarmed. "Wait—I'm not supposed to let you in—" Ellie stepped between Harry and Jennifer, who brushed past rapidly. Ellie trailed at her heels as she hurried across the marble lobby and up the stairs to the mezzanine. Wilcox looked up from her desk, the smile about to sweep across her face disintegrating.

"You're not allowed in here," she hurled at Jennifer. To Ellie, she said, "Go back to your office!"

"Stay with me," Jennifer cautioned Ellie quietly, and made for Britz's office.

"You're not going in there," Wilcox said, rushing

around from behind her desk. "If you don't leave, I'm calling the police."

Jennifer stopped dead in her tracks and faced Wilcox. She smiled.

"Do, Eva. And make sure you get the correct department. That would be detective squad—fraud division."

There was something in Jennifer's tone that made Wilcox hesitate. Something in the way she held her head, the body language of one who is in total control and knows it. Wilcox faltered, and in that moment Jennifer moved past her into Britz's office without knocking. Recovering, Wilcox followed, and Ellie trailed in behind her.

"I couldn't stop her, Mr. Britz, she just plowed through," Wilcox said as a startled Britz glanced up at the trio.

"That's not exactly true, Ethan," Jennifer said. "Eva suggested she'd have to call the police, and when I told her exactly whom to call, she changed her mind."

He stood up, his bald head glistening, his anger making his face a mottled red. "What's the meaning of this, Miss DeWitt?"

Softly, very softly, Jennifer said, "You were expecting the new owner at two o'clock, weren't you, Ethan?" Then with deliberate motions she took the legal deed from the brown envelope tucked under her arm and unfolded it, placing it on his desk. He glanced down and paled.

There were gasps from Ellie and Eva, but Jennifer ignored them.

"I—I don't know what to say," Britz stuttered.

"That's all right. I do. Now, if you will please move from behind that desk?" He did with alacrity. "Have Wilcox bring in another chair," she told him, "and get Milton Richards up here. Ellie, you stick to Eva. Don't let her say anything. We don't want to alarm Mr. Richards, now, do we?"

"You won't get away with this," Wilcox sneered.

"Do as the lady says, Eva," Britz ordered.

While they waited for Richards, Jennifer took another paper from the brown envelope and placed it before her on the desk. Britz stood next to the window, watching her. Ellie stood against a bookcase, and Eva took a position next to the door. When Richards strode in, she tried to give him a signal, but he had eyes only for Jennifer, stunned to see her behind Britz's desk. He looked around, then back at Jennifer. *Now he's going to shoot his cuffs,* she thought, and smiled when he did.

"What's this all about?"

Oh, you're cool, she thought, and warmed to her task. "Ethan, why don't you introduce me properly to Mr. Richards," she said.

"Uh, Milton, Miss DeWitt—I mean Mrs. Merril—is the new owner of the Guilbeaux."

Jennifer was pleased to note that the suave exterior of Milton Richards cracked somewhat. He sat down hard in the chair in front of Britz's desk.

"Now, what this is all about...Ethan, perhaps you'd like to repeat the accusation you made to me three weeks ago."

He shook his head. "I only presented the facts as they were presented to me," he said, fishtailing.

"And those facts? Mr. Richards?"

"They were brought to my attention by Eva Wilcox."

"As I recall, you said you gave me twelve hundred dollars on a voucher that originally called for only two hundred."

"Well, I may have been mistaken on that. I might have given it to Eva." Jennifer managed not to look toward the secretary.

"And what became of the extra one thousand dollars?"

Richards shrugged elegantly. "Well, if you didn't receive it, I suppose Eva Wilcox must have it."

Wilcox flew across the room, her face crumbled. "Liar! You can't pin all this on me!" Suddenly, she stopped and looked at Milton Richards. "You said you loved me, that we were going away together...." Eva felt all that she'd worked for, all that she'd never had that had been within her grasp, slipping away. She began to cry. "He made me do it," she sobbed. "He got the money, all of it. He only took me out to dinner He said he was saving it up for us."

"Shut up, you fool!" Richards snarled.

Jennifer turned to Britz. "Are these two bonded?" He nodded yes. "Then call in the bonding company to go over Saul Rosenberg's reports. And we will press charges against Milton Richards. If Eva Wilcox will testify against him, I'll withhold charges against her." Richards was so stunned, he failed to remember to shoot his cuffs. Jennifer nodded to him and Wilcox. "Get out of this office. Wait in the lobby. Ellie, get me Al Alberts on the phone, will you?" Ellie was leaning against the wall now, her mouth agape. "Ellie?"

"Yes. Yes. Dear me," she said, and stumbled from the office.

"Well, that leaves you, Ethan," Jennifer said.

"I owe you an apology," he said sincerely. "And Al Alberts too, if that phone call means what I think it does."

"I'd like to ask a question that both Adrien and Ellie have raised. Why have—why did you turn so much of the hotel's business over to Richards and Wilcox?"

He swallowed nervously, his Adam's apple working. "I worked my way up in the hotel business. Started as a dishwasher, then busser, then bellman, and moved to the front desk. From there it wasn't too much of a jump, with hard work, to assistant manager. Merril hired me—the old man, not Adrien—as manager. And...well, I'm going on fifty-five, and I'd never had any formal training. I thought with all the youngsters coming on, I'd better get some formal training, before they pushed me out. So I've been taking a course in management by objective. It teaches you to delegate authority, leaving yourself free for making decisions—" He shrugged, too embarrassed to smile or to frown. "One of the rules is: Management always backs up its executives so their authority isn't underminded."

Appalled, Jennifer said, "You mean you've been running this hotel by something you read in a book?"

"Well, only since I started the course. That was about five months ago."

"I'm not sure I like you, Ethan, but fortunately, the injustices done here have been corrected. I wonder if you'd give up school and go back to running this hotel? I can put up with your fidgets, providing you don't let anybody steal from us. And I like people to have a chance to speak up for themselves. I don't believe in standing behind someone who's obviously wrong."

"No. I can see your point."

The intercom buzzed. Jennifer snatched it up. "Al? Yes, this is Jennifer. How's the fishing?"

"Lousy."

"Would you be interested in having your old job back at the Guilbeaux?"

"Sure," he said, his voice eloquent with sarcasm. "What've you in mind—waving a magic wand?"

"Something like that. Hold on." She handed the receiver to Britz. "I'll leave you to get everything and everyone in order. Oh, and, Ethan," she said with casual emphasis, "get rid of that chair."

Chapter Sixteen

"Will he nurse?" Jennifer asked, still slightly shaken from the birthing she had just witnessed.

"As soon as he gets his legs," Adrien answered, his attention fully occupied by the newborn calf as he wiped it down with rags. Ralph too was in the stall, coaxing the mother to eat a ration of specially prepared feed. "You take it from here," Adrien told the gnarled old man. He rinsed his hands in a bucket outside the stall, dried them on his shirttail, and beckoned to Jennifer. "Let's get some fresh air."

"You should have told me you were expecting to deliver a calf today, Adrien. I could have put off going into New Orleans."

"Ralph could've handled it if we hadn't gotten back in time. Today was important to you."

When she had marched back into the Cove and said to him "Let's go home," he thought those were the loveliest words he had ever heard. He had feared she would fire the top executives and want to run the Guilbeaux herself. And where would that have left him? But Britz, it seemed, had made a rapid recovery from a midlife crisis. Adrien smiled inwardly. Faced with Jennifer, the old manager's recovery was probably nothing less than miraculous.

They emerged hand in hand from the barn into late

dusk. It was the time of evening when the sky was between sun and moon, when day creatures were settling down and night creatures had yet to begin stirring. Strings of mist wafted up from the bayou, obscuring cypress stumps that had held their places stubbornly for two centuries.

"Want to walk along the levee?" he asked, and when Jennifer agreed, he pulled her into the circle of his arm. They passed Berty's cottage, dark now, because she had elected to stay in New Orleans for a few days—her first tentative step back into the world she had had to leave so suddenly when she fell ill.

They walked at a comfortable pace. Jennifer moved closer to Adrien. He smelled of newmown hay that had been scattered on the floor of the birthing stall. There was a row of cottages across the bayou, each with its own little pier, and there were shadowy movements on the porches. Muted conversation floated across the water.

"All these people," Jennifer spoke suddenly. "They're my neighbors now."

"Yes, you'll have to call on them."

"I will. I'm looking forward to it." A light came on in the tiny house nearest the footbridge just beyond Berty's cottage. "Who lives there, Adrien?"

"Old Mrs. Prejeans," he told her absently, his mind closing in on the woman at his side.

"Ah, our resident fortune-teller, who predicts I'll have great wealth and five children."

"An old woman's fanciful talk," he said, wondering who had translated for her. Leddy, most likely.

"Fanciful talk?" Jennifer whispered, stopping and putting her arms about Adrien's neck. "I was hoping for truth. I wouldn't mind great wealth—"

"And five children?" He buried his face in the fragrant hollows of her neck and velvety skin, pressed her to him so he could feel every curve, the beating of her heart. His voice betrayed the eagerness with which he asked the question.

Jennifer laughed softly and took his face in her hands. She drew a finger tantalizingly down his cheek He didn't seem to mind the dimple so much these days. "Yes, five children, Adrien, but not all at once "

"My love, my heart, my wife," he murmured against her lips. "I think that's a pleasure we can spread out over the years." He kissed her slowly and tenderly, and in his mind's eye he adjusted his vision, his dream.

The success of the hunt, his sons following him safely, exactly, coming home wet and muddy, legs tired, backs aching from carrying a man's share of game, too proud to complain. And there would be Jennifer, lifting the weight off his sons' shoulders, putting mugs of steaming milk-filled coffee before them on the worn rosewood table. *My wife. My sons.*

"Oh, Adrien, I love you so," Jennifer murmured, feeling his passion, feeling his love, the strength in his arms, his warm solid body. He lifted her into his arms and carried her into the house.

While the lovers lay entwined in each others' arms. the moon rose high into the night sky, sending a golden beam into the drawing room, illuminating a bowl of delicate white roses that sat upon a carved pedestal— the foundations of the past.

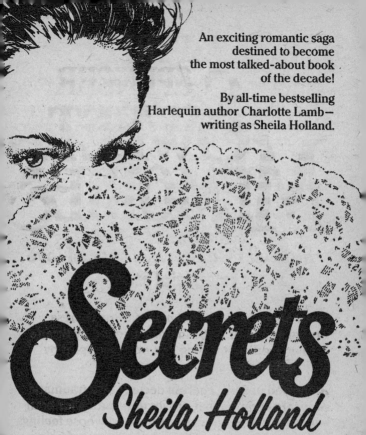

An exciting romantic saga
destined to become
the most talked-about book
of the decade!

By all-time bestselling
Harlequin author Charlotte Lamb—
writing as Sheila Holland.

Secrets
Sheila Holland

Sophia was torn between the love of two men—two
brothers who were part of a great and noble family. As
different as fire and ice, they were rivals whose hatred
for each other was powerful and destructive. Their
legacy to Sophia was a life of passion and regret, and
secrets that must never be told...

Available in April wherever paperback books are sold, or send your
name, address and zip code, along with a check or money order for
$4.25 (includes 75¢ postage and handling) payable to Harlequin
Reader Service, to: Harlequin Reader Service
  P.O. Box 52040
  Phoenix, AZ 85072-2040

SEC-2   *NOT AVAILABLE IN CANADA